3 4028 09184 6080
HARRIS COUNTY PUBLIC LIBRARY

YA Hansen
Hansen, Heather
The breaking light

$9.99
ocn958460087

# BREAKING
# LIGHT

# THE
# BREAKING
# LIGHT

## HEATHER HANSEN

SKYSCAPE

**SKYSCAPE**

This is a work of fiction. Names, characters, organizations, places, events, and incidents are either products of the author's imagination or are used fictitiously. Any resemblance to actual persons, living or dead, or actual events is purely coincidental.

Text copyright © 2017 by Heather Hansen
All rights reserved.

No part of this book may be reproduced, or stored in a retrieval system, or transmitted in any form or by any means, electronic, mechanical, photocopying, recording, or otherwise, without express written permission of the publisher.

Published by Skyscape, New York

www.apub.com

Amazon, the Amazon logo, and Skyscape are trademarks of Amazon.com, Inc., or its affiliates.

ISBN-13: 9781503942684
ISBN-10: 1503942686

Cover design by Mike Heath | Magnus Creative

Printed in the United States of America

*For my mother, who has walked every step of this journey with me. I couldn't have done it without your unfailing support and encouragement.*

*And for my father, who taught me to dream big and then to work hard until it becomes a reality.*

# CHAPTER ONE

Arden ignored the knife pressed to the fragile skin of her neck. She could feel its bite and the wet slickness of blood pooling in the hollow of her throat. Whenever she shifted, the cool metal tightened with the promise of death. Yet she also felt hesitation from the boy holding it, and that more than anything made her curious enough to remain still.

He faced her. His right hand grasped the knife, while his left gripped her hair. He exhaled in fast pants, gulps of air pitting his lungs. He acted like he knew how to use the knife, yet the stress lines grooved in his forehead made her question whether he'd ever taken a life. The boy was missing the hardness that came with life-altering decisions.

She made these observations in a detached way, while unconsciously focusing on his lips. Not that she would ever admit that to her closest friends—the embarrassment would be too much. Yet his mouth enthralled her. How his lips moved slightly with each breath he took. How he tried to catch himself from showing indecision and when he did, his lips pressed shut, only to fall open a second later. Now they were molded into a frown, but they'd transfixed her when they'd been relaxed and achingly kissable.

She could see his features well enough in the dreary light that filtered through the static cloud as it mixed with the glare of the city. It created a diffused glow that made the boy appear even more mysterious. And she liked that, the hint of delicious danger.

Something shadowed the boy's expression, his chocolate-brown eyes full of unanswered questions. She looked straight into them, wanting to understand why she found him so fascinating. He was certainly handsome. Long blond hair dipped over his forehead. His face still held a bit of youth, though hardened angles had taken prominence. He was striking in a way she might have feared if she were a different sort of girl.

The boy swallowed.

She watched his throat work, finding herself drawn to his sun-kissed skin, dusted brown from real sun, not from regulated time in a sun booth. She wanted to press her hand against it to see whether it felt as warm as it looked. Very few people could claim to have seen the sun, for there wasn't direct sunlight to be had, unless you lived in the sky.

She felt as if she were alone with him in this moment even though they stood at the edge of a busy street. Enclosed in a private cocoon of interest and curiosity, and a little bit of lust. Because who wouldn't look at this boy and wonder who he was?

Arden had waited until he moved to the edge of the street before she'd made her move. Beyond them, the city rattled with people, bustling as it always was. But she let the chaos fall away as she focused on him. It wasn't difficult. He held her attention simply by being so different.

"You tried to rob me," the boy said. His voice was measured, yet confident. It sent warmth coiling through her.

She had, in fact, been at that very task, when for some reason he'd felt his pocket being picked. She must be slipping. She hadn't been after his money, though. It had started off as a mercy mission: to help a lone sky boy who was wandering the streets without protection. It was laughable. She'd meant to scare him enough that he'd take better care next time.

Her duty meant she should have murdered him, to honor the blood feud between their families. He was lucky she didn't care for taking lives. But that didn't mean she could let it go if she were placed in a situation where she couldn't ignore him. If she'd been with companions today, she would have been forced to kill him.

Arden frowned, feeling a twinge of sadness. Taking his life seemed wasteful.

Not wanting to tip him off and make the situation into something worse, she blanked her expression and softened her body to appear nonthreatening. His body was larger than hers by two spans. It was not often she felt tiny, as she was tall for a girl. Arden found she liked the illusion of being delicate far more than she should. The image of an innocent girl who conveyed a graceful feminine charm was wholly unrealistic to that of any girl she'd ever known.

"I didn't try to rob you," she said while maintaining eye contact to cement the lie.

His brow arched. "I imagined your hand in my pocket?"

"Perhaps."

The boy made a face as though he'd eaten something sour.

She wanted to laugh at his offended expression. It was adorable. Arden lowered her face to hide her eyes behind half-raised lids.

His fingers subtly relaxed against her head, perhaps due to confusion, or maybe lapsed concentration. Either way, it meant that it would be easy enough to break his hold when she wanted to leave. But right now, she settled in to dig for information. He could know something useful. Though truthfully, she was having a lot of fun teasing him.

As she spoke with him, she made mental notes of each of his features. Of anything that would set him apart and could be later referenced, especially the black tattoo on the left side of his neck just behind his ear. A design she knew without close inspection: a simple black sun, its center a perfect dark circle. Eight spokes surrounded the nucleus at equal intervals, the four points of the compass longer than the others. These spokes did not touch the center, leaving a rim of tanned flesh to break up the design.

It was a label that said he was off-limits. That he was set apart from those not rich enough to flaunt the laws. People like her still broke them, but with consequences. The tattoo was a visible sign that the Solizen wore to warn others not to mess with them. Though often, especially to her gang, it did the opposite. What it did now was help to remind her that this boy was not for her and to focus her wandering thoughts.

His gaze dropped away from hers. His lip pulled up at one corner as his eyes narrowed. "You have a blackout band?"

Even as she was caught up in studying him, apparently he had been doing the same. His attention now focused on the two-inch-wide dull black metal band circling her left wrist. He looked intrigued, his lips now moving into a full smile that flashed straight, even teeth.

Arden's eyes widened with surprise as she flicked the cuff of her cloak over the item in question. The band was designed to cover the implanted data sensor the govies said they used for identification and banking. In reality, they used it to track every citizen's movement, logging the collected information into a database. Breaking the signal was necessary to remain undetected and, needless to say, completely illegal.

She considered how to deny what he had obviously seen, or even whether she should bother doing so. Her response was cut off when he twisted his own wrist, exposing the edge of a matching band.

Shock hit her a second time. Why would he make a point of showing her his band when he could have easily kept it hidden? Exposing vulnerable secrets was not a negotiation tactic she was familiar with. This wasn't typical Solizen behavior. Perhaps he was more devious than she'd given him credit for.

This was yet another reason she allowed herself to remain pressed against the wall. Puzzles were difficult for her to walk away from. Unfortunately, it had gotten rather late, and she had another appointment, one she couldn't miss. She swallowed back irrational disappointment that they'd have to part ways.

"Where's your nursemaid?" she taunted, knowing that the question would cause him to react.

The boy frowned. "Guard."

"What?"

"He's my guard, not nursemaid."

"Call it whatever you want, love," Arden said.

His brows scrunched. Then he had the audacity to remain calm, her words seeming to slide over him like a cool breeze. Worse, he chuckled as if he found her particularly amusing. "What's your name?"

"What's yours?" she countered, annoyed.

"My name is Dade," he said. His eye contact never wavered.

Arden swallowed.

*Dade.* Why did his name sound familiar?

"Which family do you belong to?" she asked. Identifying which of the three Solizen families he was from would go a long way toward choosing how to finish this conversation. It would also help her figure out the reason for the warning that itched in the back of her mind.

His body tensed. "It doesn't matter."

Right. As if that didn't speak volumes. She pushed. "You know you want to tell me, or you wouldn't have asked my name."

"You have a point, but I still want to know who you are." The grin, the constant shining smile, never wavered. Was he always this happy? What an odd thing to be.

"What makes you think I won't lie?"

His eyes widened. "Because I'll be able to tell."

"I doubt that." And for some inexplicable reason, she gave him her real name. "Arden."

"Arden," he repeated, his eyes sliding shut as if he wanted to savor the word on his tongue. When they opened, he looked at her with a new intensity. "Your name is as pretty as you are."

She rolled her eyes, letting out a half huff, half laugh. She wouldn't allow herself to be taken in by his charm.

Then it clicked: the reason he looked familiar. He was a fixture on the visicast. The gossip cams loved him. He was not just a random member of the powerful families, a cousin or kinsman, someone with little power and a big name. He was the prize, the only son of Hernim Croix, the head of the most powerful Solizen family.

She felt a flood of anger, mostly toward herself, at how she'd stepped into this position without foresight. Decisions like this led to disappointment and death. Because in the few minutes she'd spoken to him, she found herself more charmed than she'd ever been. Yet she knew she could never have another intimate moment with him. The realization came with a sadness that was silly, really.

And she'd told him her name. Arden let out a soft exhale, beating herself up with self-recrimination. She looked behind him to strategize her exit. The time had come to go, whether she wanted to or not.

They stood at the edge of the market on Level One, Above. There were no skywalks—open-air pedestrian walkways—on this Level. The ground stretched from one side to the other. She'd made sure when she confronted him to do so in an area where she could minimize attention. That turned out to be a good thing when he'd managed to gain the upper hand.

Flashing lights from neon signs were bright in the fog, beckoning customers to peruse carnal delights, and the sounds of the streets were a familiar riot of calls. It was a busy day as usual. The streets rushed with people. The sky above was perpetually dark with static smog, making anything below it freeze from the constant chill.

It seemed much colder here than where she lived because of the stiff wind that rattled through the empty space of the skyway, where the hovercars and speeders zoomed past. The city soared upward. He was from the highest of the high above the clouds where he could see the purple sky and blood-orange sun. She was from the dregs far below. They couldn't have been farther apart if they had tried.

"As much as I want to continue this, I'm afraid I have to go," Arden said.

"You're not leaving." He pressed the knife closer to her throat as if to emphasize his point. "I may not ever let you go."

In spite of her heart lurching at the possessive heat in his voice, she replied dryly, "You think you can stop me?"

She didn't consider using her weapons on him. There was no need. She wanted to prove a point, not escalate the confrontation. With a fluid movement, she shoved the butt of her hand into his sternum, and then slipped her foot between his parted legs, catching the back side of his heel with a quick turn. At the same time, she pulled forward, shifting him off balance.

Dade gasped for breath, stepping back to right himself before tumbling to the street, while Arden easily stepped out of his hold. People stopped to stare, forming circles around them to give Arden and Dade a wide berth. They didn't have enough self-preservation to scatter. Instead, the pointing started.

She took Dade's free hand, twisting it behind his back, and with her other hand, gripped the wrist holding the knife, her fingers digging into his pressure point. She cocked his wrist until the knife slipped free. When it fell, she caught it, flipping it in the air so that it pointed forward. Then she shoved him around so that his back slammed against the wall in the same spot where she had just been.

Arden held the knife to his neck, in a perfect mirror of their former positions.

They stared at each other. The moment seemed much longer than the mere second it really was. Arden calm, hands steady. Dade, his chest moving up and down, his eyes slightly too wide, and a faint blush staining his cheeks. She waited to let him go until his expression changed from surprise and embarrassment to wariness. It was the reaction she wanted to see. Yet it felt harsh and cruel, and she hated herself for it.

Her feet danced back, separating her from the growing connection between them. She hoped to sever it like she did the press of their bodies.

Dade pushed himself off the wall. He absently rubbed at his wrist as he watched her with narrowed eyes. His shoulders squared, and his body tightened aggressively.

Arden didn't like his new attitude, even though it was one she'd purposely manipulated. It felt antithetical to his natural state. She hardened her thoughts while she flipped the knife in her hand. Up it twisted, spinning, the metal forming a whirligig as it tilted end over end, the pommel landing smoothly back in her palm. She launched it once more. "The takeaway here is that you should never underestimate your opponent."

"I didn't think I had."

"There is a reason your family insists you have protection. You know you shouldn't walk the Levels without your guard. Especially with that." She pointed the tip of the dagger at his tattoo. She wasn't the one walking around with a sign asking for trouble, a sign that served no other purpose whatsoever. "There are too many people who would take advantage of you. Some might kidnap you for ransom—that is, if you're lucky. Others are far more likely to gut you." She hardened her voice, hoping to get beyond his anger to make him feel fear, or at least get him to consider making better choices. "I should kill you and leave your body on the streets for the animals to eat. That is what happens to Solizen who don't stay in their ivory towers."

Unfortunately, he didn't seem cowed. If anything, he grinned with delight, and his eyes sparkled with mirth. Any hardness he'd momentarily displayed slipped away as if it had never been. This day and this boy were very odd, indeed.

Plus, how could she criticize him when she doubted her own threat even as the words left her mouth? Could she really kill him now that she'd spoken with him? Found out that he was *more*? Made him real

8

in her mind? Her stomach clenched, but she swallowed back the sour taste, pointedly keeping her aggressive stance.

"I can take care of myself," he said, showing none of the weakness she'd expected now that their situation had reversed. He looked as comfortable as she'd been.

Arden acknowledged that he was probably right. He did have skill, though it was evident he'd never fought anyone outside of a training room. The way he hesitated showed he really didn't want to hit her. Yet that wasn't the point. She did not want to see him in this position again. Did not want to be forced to kill him. He needed to promise to stay off her streets.

"The real world is a lot different than your Tower," she said. "People on the streets don't play by gentlemen's rules."

His eyes blazed as his fire came back, and his hands tightened into fists at his side. "I'm not a siskin," he said, using the derogatory slang for a Solizen. His voice lowered to a growl. "Next time you won't be able to get away from me so easily."

Arden sighed. Fine then, if he wouldn't listen, there was nothing more she could do. This boy was of no consequence, she reminded herself sternly. He was a cog in a family whose members crushed others beneath their feet. Dade could not be separated from them, just as she could not be separated from her family.

That truth resonated deep inside her, letting her know she was doing the right thing.

With a swift series of moves, Arden kicked out, catching Dade in the stomach. She was careful not to kick hard enough to cause internal damage, merely enough to double him over. Strength could be demonstrated in how much she held back, not only in how thoroughly she could beat people to a bloody pulp. Overt aggression was unnecessary for instilling fear.

Before she left, she slipped his knife back into the sheath at his side. She wanted to add a warning that he should never draw a blade unless he meant to kill. Instead, she leaned in close and said into his ear, "Lead with the phaser instead of the knife next time. Never allow your opponent close contact. Don't hesitate to shoot, and for sun's sake, keep your pretty head on your shoulders."

Then she straightened, turned, and walked away.

Each step felt agonizing. No matter what she did, she couldn't shake the feeling that she was leaving something important behind. Arden drew her hood over her face, blending in with the crowd as she turned her thoughts to her upcoming meeting, the one where she would be planning to crush Dade's family.

# CHAPTER TWO

Colin met her at the subtrain station in the heart of Undercity, originally a mining town when the planet was first terraformed and colonized. The mining carts had been relocated when mineral stripping had been outlawed within the city limits. While the energy fields had been left in place and repurposed, the tracks now used sleek, bullet-shaped cars.

He slouched against a crumbling wall with his arms crossed and a booted heel hooked into the crack in the brick. The hood of his cloak had been pushed down to rest on his shoulders, showing his translucent skin and spiky, pale-blond hair. Hidden under the cloak was the body of an assassin, lithe and whip strong, with a phaser at his hip and knives strapped for easy access.

The city was layered vertically: Undercity, then the Levels, and finally the Sky Towers. At ground level, Undercity was fully encased to support Above, the area comprising the Levels and the Sky Towers. Residents of Undercity couldn't travel to and from the rest of the Levels. They'd been locked in. Arden wasn't sure why, she only knew that it sucked. Undercity and its people functioned as the backbone of the three-tiered city.

Of course, it didn't stop her or her gang from moving as they pleased.

Colin cocked his head when he saw her, his narrowed eyes all-knowing. "You're late."

Arden avoided meeting her cousin's gaze. "I had things to do." Her breath left her mouth in cloudy puffs. The air here tasted rich with thick humidity. The minerals salted her tongue. She pulled her cloak tight about her. Coming home was always depressing. She liked leaving to travel up into the Levels. It might not be much warmer there, but at least it didn't have the constant wet of below.

She shouldn't complain. Arden was used to the cold even if she didn't like it. It had numbed bits of her that never seemed to thaw. Often she wondered if they ever might.

"You're never late."

Arden grunted, the sound both acknowledging the truth of his statement and letting him know that she didn't want to continue this line of questioning.

Unfortunately, as usual Colin had other ideas. "Niall asked why you hadn't replied to your pings. Your comm has been off all afternoon."

She made a show of checking her pockets. "I don't have my datapad on me."

His raised eyebrow nearly reached his hairline. "That's odd."

"It's been an off day." That was the understatement of the year. Arden fought not to fidget, because then he'd know she wasn't telling him everything. Her mind went back over her conversation with Dade. Thinking about him made her feel awkward, an emotion she'd not experienced in forever. It had her walking off, confused, and leaving Colin to catch up.

Not that her lack of explanation could put off Colin. If anything, it would only serve to make him more curious. By the time she reached the pay meters, he stood directly behind her, his face pinched. She refused to meet his penetrating gaze.

They scanned in, then made their way onto the train platform. It was already congested with midday commuters on their way home from their assigned work zones. She'd gotten here later than she realized. They'd be lucky to squeeze into the next train. No wonder Colin was upset.

"You're lying to me," Colin said after they'd navigated through the press of commuters to the edge of the platform. "Me, the one person who always has your back no matter what. I had to take heat from Niall today because you couldn't be bothered to do your job, so I really don't appreciate your taking me for a fool."

He was right that she had lied. She'd turned off her datapad before she'd intercepted Dade and had forgotten to turn it back on. But if she admitted that, it would open the door to a million other questions. The least of which was why she had let Dade go. Instead, she deflected. "I'm not lying."

"Really?" Colin reached into his cloak to pull a handkerchief from one of his many secret pockets. "Let's look at the evidence, shall we? We'll start with the blood."

"The what?"

Colin pointedly lowered his gaze to her throat. He lingered over the vowels. "The blood."

She fingered her neck where the knife had pressed. It felt wet, and when she pulled her hand away, her fingertips were stained. Arden sighed. She should have realized. How badly had meeting Dade thrown her off? She snagged the handkerchief from him and blotted. "It's just a scratch."

Colin took hold of her chin, turning her face to get a better look. "It's not deep. It won't even need a med kit."

He released his fingers, but his gaze never left her.

She turned away from the intensity of his stare. There was nowhere to go on the crowded platform, no way to change the subject or distance herself while she thought up an excuse. The commuters at her back felt like a living thing as they pushed her forward.

It didn't help that Colin looked at her with suspicion and distrust, something she couldn't recall him ever doing. Her shoulders deflated.

"Niall's gonna freak." He smirked as if the thought of her brother losing it amused him, yet the distrust in his gaze didn't lessen.

"I doubt he'll notice."

Colin's lips pressed together, and he raised an eyebrow. Okay, yes, she didn't believe that either. No matter how drugged up Niall was, he'd notice. The anticipation of that discussion started a churning in her stomach.

"What happened? And this time I'd like the truth." The steel in his voice let Arden know that she hadn't been forgiven yet.

She blew out a breath. "Seriously, it was nothing. I had some face time with a Solizen. No biggie."

"No one should have gotten close enough to cut you, especially a siskin. Unless you wanted him in your space." He paused, as if waiting for his words to register. Then his head tilted, and he looked at her shrewdly. "There can be only one explanation."

"What's that?"

Colin paused again dramatically. Then he leaned in close, as if sharing a secret. His voice was low and conspiratorial when he asked, "How gorgeous is he?"

Arden glared, wanting to kick him. Hating that he could read her so easily. Dade had been breathtaking.

Colin laughed loud and hard, nearly doubling over. "We're talking about a war wound, he had to be devastatingly handsome. Did you think I wouldn't figure it out? I know you better than that."

Her frown quirked into a rueful smile, she was unable to stay irritated. At least he was teasing her. That was progress.

"You would have found him attractive," she admitted with a shrug.

He laughed harder. *The jerk.*

"Shut up." She lightly pushed at him with mock anger.

"How'd he get so close to your neck, hmm? You must be into some kinky stuff," Colin said between heaving laughs. "If he was that amazing, I hope you gave him my number."

Arden rolled her eyes. "You wish."

Colin cleared his throat a few times, getting himself back under control. He then let out a long-suffering sigh that she knew was 100 percent fake. "Keep your secrets, if you must. But please be aware that when you fail to show when you're supposed to, my mind begins to run through every disastrous scenario." His tone fell flat, as had his expression.

The guilt felt suffocating. She swallowed against it. "I'm sorry."

He acknowledged her apology with a dismissive wave. "What's done is done. Please don't do it again."

"Agreed." Arden nodded, happy to let it go.

The train arrived, and a ding sounded before the doors dissolved. Disembarking passengers pushed through the waiting crowd. By the time Arden and Colin made it on board, all the seats were taken. She waved her hand over the sensor next to the door frame. Above them, the roof split along both sides, and hand straps dropped down. Arden grabbed one near the back.

Colin stepped close as the train pulled away from the platform. "Are you happy with your life?"

The randomness of the question confused Arden. Colin was all action, fun, and snarky humor. He never failed to take her to task. But he was not introspective in any way. He'd never asked any philosophical questions before, which left her at a loss as to how to answer him now.

"Are you?" he pressed.

"Who's happy, really? We live, we survive." There wasn't much else to life, everyone knew that. Arden hadn't been born to change the world. She wouldn't want that responsibility anyway. There was a comfort in consistency, and she was okay if her life always remained the same.

"Don't you want more?"

"More what?" she asked, genuinely curious. They had food, a place to sleep, and their gang allowed them some autonomy. What more was there?

"More everything."

Arden scrunched her face. If she had a frame of reference for why he was being so weird, perhaps she'd be able to give him the response he wanted. She shook her head, lost.

He seemed to realize that she didn't understand, because he paused a moment, considering, before asking, "I'm curious whether you find your life satisfying. Does it make you feel accomplished?"

"I don't know, maybe?" She'd never thought about it. The fact that he posed the question made her worry. That ache in her gut that was good at signaling disaster started to twist. "Why are you asking this?"

"It's always the same stuff over and over, you know? How much do we gotta see of overdoses and death, knowing we caused them, before it's too much?"

Arden gave a noncommittal grunt. He spoke the truth. One she agonized over a lot. Sometimes the weight of her guilt felt crushing, but what was she supposed to do?

The train pulled in to their stop. Arden and Colin pushed their way out, avoiding the unmanned robots that periodically stopped passengers to check for contraband. They flowed with the crowd out of the station and onto the street, using the moving sidewalks to get them out of the hub faster.

There were no hovercars or speeders in Undercity. It was far too crowded and the streets too narrow for that. They had their own transportation not used in the Levels. Most commuters had a hoverboard or a speedpack that just sort of skimmed along the ground. Arden wasn't opposed to using either option, but she preferred walking. It was easier to get through the tight, crowded spots, and it attracted less attention.

Their destination was a run-down urban neighborhood that had sprung up in what once had been the financial district of Undercity. Once there had been industry, as well as trade between Undercity and Above. People had moved freely into the Levels and back. That had ended, so there was no longer a need for these relics of commerce.

Banking institutions had been gutted, and the ground level had been converted into shops and bars. On the upper floors, hundreds of apartments were squeezed into the space. Rickety stairways had been erected alongside the buildings to create separate entrances.

"Taking over Lasair is the last thing you need," Colin said.

"Who said I'm doing that?" She didn't want Niall's position as gang leader. It came with far too much responsibility. And she wasn't in the gang because she believed in its principles or liked dealing drugs. It was simply a way to survive, and she'd taken it. There weren't any other choices. It wasn't ideal, but it had been her best option, plain and simple. She felt regret about a lot of things. She refused to add anything else to her list. "I have no intention of taking over. Please don't start rumors."

"People are already talking about it."

"Why would they do that?"

Colin looked at her, his expression incredulous. "Because you're in Niall's face all the time. Publicly questioning his every move. Undermining his every idea."

"I'm helping him, not plotting a coup." Even though Niall was her brother, if he heard a rumor that she was scheming to take over, he'd end her life, quickly and efficiently. Nothing got in the way of his leadership. "If I'm going to die, I prefer it to be on my terms."

"I'm telling you to watch yourself. Stop stating your opinions so vocally."

That would be a problem, and they both knew it.

Colin kicked several pieces of trash out of the walkway and into the collected piles that lined the street, before stepping over a puddle of water. "You could go back to school."

Arden laughed.

"I'm serious," he said.

She shook her head. "That didn't work out so well the first time."

"No one made you drop out."

Arden pressed her lips together, refusing to think about that time in her life. In a lot of ways, high school was worse than the streets. "It doesn't matter. My life is good enough."

"It's not the one you should have."

Arden tried to shake off her frustration, convinced he was being deliberately annoying. No one had any choices. Not in this city, at least not in Undercity or the Levels. Maybe the Solizen could do as they pleased.

"What do you think I'm owed?" she asked, knowing the aggression she used to keep others from getting too close had hardened her question. "It's not like we're afforded any opportunities. It's not like I was lucky enough to be born a Solizen, or even a citizen of Above."

The Solizen were the descendants of the original investors and privateers. They'd financially supported the company that'd colonized this city. They'd reaped the benefits of their status with dictatorship-like rule. Even though they'd established city government to "help the people," the Solizen had been in control so long that the balance had never been restored. Arden and Colin's ancestors had been members of the mining crew. Even after all these centuries, after breaking from the Old Planet and setting up sovereign territories on this world, they couldn't shake their fate.

She stopped to face him, hands on her hips. "Get to the point."

"I worry about the gang and the whispers. I worry that Niall is acting illogically and that you're going to get swept up in the blowout. I get your loyalty to your brother, and it's admirable, but the gang is a sinking ship."

"You're loyal to my brother too." At least she thought he was. Now she wasn't so sure.

"I'm loyal to you."

The thought warmed her. "You're saying that if I get out, you'd come with me?"

"No, I'm saying the gang is going in a direction that concerns me. Niall is unstable and getting worse. It's not your job to save him."

Was that what she was doing? Sometimes she seemed to be playing a long game, but she had never been sure of exactly what she wanted.

No family was perfect—hers was certainly questionable. She could admit that. And maybe her family members didn't deserve her loyalty. But they were her *family*. And family supported each other no matter what.

"If he's pressuring you . . ." Colin left the rest of the thought unsaid.

Arden sighed. "I can handle it."

He put his hand on her arm and gave a little squeeze. "All I'm saying is that today is a good example of you slipping. Instead of focusing on staying alive, you show up late and with your neck cut. Am I not supposed to be concerned?"

"I'll be fine," she said, and willed herself to believe it.

# CHAPTER THREE

By the time Dade caught his breath, Arden was gone.

He'd never met a girl so enchanting. The way she'd effortlessly taken his knife had been a shock. He wasn't dumb. He knew his life had been at risk the moment he'd felt her hand slip into his pocket. Still, he'd been foolish enough to think of her as a girl and not as a potential threat. Which made the cat-and-mouse game she'd played all the more stimulating. He'd even felt as if he had been in control at certain points, and now he realized that was what she'd intended.

It was a mistake he wouldn't make again.

She'd practically glowed with confidence, like a star so bright that he couldn't draw his gaze from her. Everything about her enchanted him, from the adorable freckles that bridged her nose to the curls wildly escaping the intricate knot of long golden-brown hair. When she'd smiled, his entire world had tilted on its axis.

Dade sighed and forced himself to focus on what he was supposed to be doing. His confrontation with Arden had eaten more time than he'd realized. He had to be at the meet point within the hour, and he still had another errand to complete.

The stink of rotting garbage and the stench of unwashed bodies mixed unpleasantly with the sulfur-smelling mist cast off from the static cloud as he slipped down the street, weaving through the crowd. He traveled into the Levels more often than his family knew. Each section of the city was built on top of another, expanding upward. At the base of the planet was Undercity, where he suspected Arden was from. He'd always been curious to explore Undercity but had yet to figure out a way in. Obviously, if she'd managed to make it into the Levels, there were ways around the sealed barriers just as he'd suspected.

On top of Undercity, there was a sealed dome on which the Levels, part of the region called Above, had been built. Most of Above's population lived in the Levels, crammed into tiny rooms. Though the farther up the Levels one traveled, the higher the numbers, and the nicer the area became. Poverty and crime were abundant at the lowest Levels.

He lived above the static cloud. He wasn't particularly proud of that. It was a quirk of birth. While he was grateful for it, it made him ashamed, which was why he was constantly here in the Levels trying to make things better.

He crossed the street, walking on the thick glass that had at one time offered a view into Undercity. Pedestrians walked across it now and never once looked down. Not that much could be seen, the glass, now milky white with age, blocking the view into the city below.

He caught the public quadralift to reach the transport grid on Level Four. He waited in line only minutes before the platform hoverdisk docked at the station, then was herded along with a group into the round tube. The light door engaged, the edges of the round pad glowed with a blue light as it rose into the air. The walls' metallic sheeting was scratched with graffiti. Most of the symbols had no meaning to Dade. Except one. His gaze fell on a small outlined sun.

He smiled with satisfaction.

When the light doors opened, he crossed to the nearest station and caught the skytram to U Street. Then he used the stairs to descend to Level Three. Hovercars nearly parked on top of one another in the congested traffic. Speeders wove between them. Some would drive up the side of the open skyway, using the space between traffic and the skywalk as a passing lane. A speeder zoomed by too close, nearly taking Dade out with the backdraft.

Before he reached the dispensary, Dade ducked into an alley. There he slipped a red mask over the upper portion of his face and pulled the hood of his cloak over his head. The mask was made from a synthetic material with nanotech that molded to the face, fitting like a second skin, and wouldn't come off unless he removed it, as the nanotech was coded to his prints.

He withdrew several packages from the carry pouch around his waist. Dade didn't usually make deliveries during the day. It was far too risky. He just hoped that no one would look too hard at him and that the visit wouldn't take long. In seconds he'd be back on the street.

A sign posted in the window of the dispensary announced they'd run out of VitD meds. That hadn't stopped a line from forming outside the door. Ravaged bodies shivered beneath swaddled blankets, decaying from Violet Death. They looked like lumpy piles of garbage rather than people. VitD provided the vitamins essential for humans that normally came from the sun. Regular injections were vital to their health. They would die without it.

No one looked up as Dade passed. He knocked on the dispensary door, impatient to complete his task. A face appeared briefly behind the blinds before the door clicked open. Dade didn't utter a greeting. His face might be covered, but the neighborhood comms could still record his voice. He handed over the packages to the harried-looking man wearing scrubs.

"Bless you, sir," the man said.

Dade nodded before he melted back into the street, where he was swallowed by the crowd. He slipped off his mask and pocketed it before he moved around the corner.

Time ticked like a metronome. Dade was always aware of how quick he needed to be and where his presence was required at any moment. Right now, Saben would already be waiting for him. And while he wouldn't immediately send out a search party, he would worry. Dade wasted no time making his way back to Level One. His destination was marked by a pink neon sign reading "Breck's Gym." It flickered over the doorway of the boxing club. Dade bought tickets from a skinny hawker working the front.

"Thirty credits," the boy said. Dirt streaked his face, and he had the hollow appearance of too little food, no sun booth allotment, and almost no VitD injections.

Dade offered his forearm, keeping the sleeve of his cloak pulled down to cover his blackout band.

The boy used a thin black wand-scanner over the area. A blue light tracked the sleeve as it swept the chip in the band instead of the one imbedded in Dade's arm, collecting the account information Dade kept under an assumed name. The scanner beeped as it accepted the credits.

"Them's fighting it out for the titleship next week," the boy said.

Dade grunted in acknowledgment as the boy pushed a clear orangey-red card Dade's way.

"Go on." The boy waved to the entrance behind him, a narrow walkway that had once been an alley and now served as a covered entrance to the club. Above the walkway, rooms had been built in the narrow space.

Inside the gym, the ticket man sat on a high bar stool. He was burly, dressed in a muscle tee and tight grappling shorts. His attention was focused on a loud match in the ring rather than on the customers coming through the door. Dade handed over his card when he reached the head of the line.

Dade wove his way through the crowd as they pushed to the center of the room while yelling their bets. The stench was a concentrated mixture of heat, sweat, and dirt. Breck's wasn't one of the finer boxing clubs. It was more like a bunch of street thugs beating one another bloody for sport. If the boxers were any good, they could make a name for themselves and move up to a club where the money really flowed.

It wasn't difficult to locate Saben. The man was a mountain and stood out anywhere. His arms were crossed over the brown skin of his shirtless chest. Leather strips rounded his shoulders and crossed his torso in an X. The leather held an assortment of knives and other small weapons, as well as two phasers strapped to his waist. Over this he wore a long black cloak, in deference to the cold.

Seemingly relaxed and interested, he watched the match. Only Dade would notice the slight frown that touched the middle of his forehead.

"You're late," Saben said as Dade stopped next to him. He didn't turn his head, or otherwise acknowledge Dade, keeping his focus on the fight. "Anything I should know about?"

Dade shrugged. He didn't want to talk about Arden. Not yet. Instead, he asked about Saben's errand. "Did you get it?"

Saben nodded once.

Dade exhaled in relief. Good. At least that had gone well. He loved when a plan worked out.

Two new boxers stepped into the ring. Those in the crowd went wild calling out their bets. Hands were held in the air so that scanners could move over wrist sensors, collecting their money.

"Do you miss boxing?" Dade asked. He could see how the adrenaline could become addicting. Though he didn't think he'd particularly enjoy the broken bones.

Saben shrugged. "That was a long time ago."

Dade pointed to the score leader. He was a big guy, heavily muscled, and wearing a pair of synth-silk gym shorts. The man's hair dripped with sweat. He batted it to the side as he taunted his opponent. "Do you think you could take him?"

"Of course." There wasn't any arrogance in Saben's response, just simple truth. He smiled, showing his teeth. That they were still in his mouth spoke to how successful he'd been in the ring despite the scars littering his skin.

Dade laughed.

"Why are you so interested in fighting?" Saben asked. "Planning an alternate career?"

"No." Dade snickered. He watched the match for another few minutes before he asked, "Do you think what we do makes a difference?"

"You're doing the best you can in an impossible situation." Saben shrugged. "Besides, you're the only one willing to try. That counts for something."

"It's not enough."

Dade let the last few seconds of the bout draw his attention. The opponent was clearly tired. He made a valiant effort, but the leader took him out with his next punch, an uppercut to the jaw.

When it was over, the loser's body lay on the floor.

# Chapter Four

Arden followed Colin to the back of Lasair's meeting room. There wasn't much free space available in Undercity to acquire by either legitimate or illegitimate means, so the room wasn't that big and always seemed to be overcrowded with people.

Since this was only the biweekly Lasair meeting where they got their new assignments, it wasn't too bad. These meets tended to include only the higher echelon, who would then delegate the tasks later to other members. Arden didn't manage a group, but she worked directly with Niall, so it was mandatory for her to be here.

She hated this room. It wasn't comfortable and had a musky odor of decay from the furniture they'd rescued from the dump. The Lasair gang was wealthy enough to buy new things. It just chose to spend its profit on tactical gear and new phasers. Comfort wasn't deemed important. Arden had hoped for at least one couch that hadn't been taped to keep its insides from spilling out when Niall had taken over. Yet nothing had changed in the year he'd been in charge. Niall was too focused on world domination and not enough on the gang's well-being.

Uri was already in their usual spot, saving seats and smirking when he saw them. He reached up to brush at the dyed black hair that constantly flopped into his eyes. "You barely made it. Niall is pissed you weren't here an hour ago."

Colin slid into the empty seat next to Uri. "Not my fault. The princess was doing princess things."

Arden grunted as she flopped down next to Colin. She fist-bumped Uri and then slouched into her chair, stretching her legs out and folding her arms.

At the front of the room, Niall called the meeting to order. He looked more like her twin than her older brother. He was attractive, or would have been if his extensive drug use hadn't started to show. The light-caramel color of his hair that he wore long and knotted to his head now had a dull shine. Purple bruises lined his eyes and the area under his nose. The tacky white of his skin had started to turn a shade of yellowish green.

She hadn't spoken with him in days. He looked even worse than the last time she'd seen him. She wondered if he'd been on a bender and if that was how she'd successfully avoided him. Honestly, she didn't want to talk to him, but she knew he'd corner her today. Especially with that pointed look he sent her.

Niall stood behind a podium. Behind him, several maps of the Levels above were displayed in 3-D. Green dots indicated where they thought current shipments of VitD were most likely to be vulnerable. Various escape routes were sketched out. "Shut up," he shouted when they didn't quiet fast enough.

Low coughing trickled through the room, punctuated by a few throats clearing before it fell silent.

"First order of business." Niall looked into the audience much like a prince surveying his kingdom. "We need to deal with the douchebag who keeps ganking our runs."

It was ironic that the gang claimed ownership of the very items they planned to steal. They used the stolen VitD to make the street drug called Shine. Arden huffed under her breath, knowing that no one else shared her amusement. Still, she understood the concern. This person was causing all sorts of problems. Going through the dangers of a run only to get there and not find any product was problematic and risky.

"Kimber has the latest intel, so I'll turn the discussion over to her," Niall said, waving Kimber toward the podium.

Arden had a visceral reaction to Kimber. She couldn't stop her lip from curling. Colin shoved an elbow into her side to remind her that showing her true feelings in public wasn't a good idea. She sat a little straighter and wiped the disgust from her face.

Niall and Kimber were sleeping together. The entire gang knew because it was a badly kept secret. Not that Kimber and Niall were actually a couple. It made Kimber's crazy worse every time he denied their relationship. Kimber was possessive and not in a normal way, more like in a crazy-obsessive way. Like keeping tabs on her not-boyfriend by hiding a tracker on him. Niall hadn't noticed.

Kimber clicked on the halo, the digital screen that projected vid-feeds. Her curly black hair had been pulled into a tight ponytail, and thick glasses dwarfed her small face, highlighting her perpetual frown. "We know very little of this person, nicknamed the Ghost." She scanned through a series of photos taken at planned heists that were thwarted, including a shot of the sun-star symbol, sprayed with dripping red paint in each case.

Arden found the Ghost's use of the sun-star hilarious. She wished she had thought about repurposing the symbol. It was brilliant marketing, designed to tick off a whole lot of people while making a political statement.

"In the last week, he's hit three of our projected heist locations only minutes before we got there. Our sources say he's giving the merchandise away like some sort of modern-day Robin Hood," she said with a sneer.

Kimber clicked off the screen, turning to face the audience again. "His thefts cut into our trade. We have no idea how he gathers his intel, but it's a source we'd like to exploit. Right now, the goal is to find the

Ghost and use him. Lure him to our side if possible. If not, he'll be dealt with."

She meant he would be killed.

Arden raised her hand. When Kimber acknowledged her, she asked, "Why are you assuming the Ghost is a 'he'?"

Kimber squinted, her mouth thinning. "We don't. The only clues we have to the Ghost's identity are grainy surveillance pictures lifted from the govie database." She turned back to the halo, booting up the surveillance pictures. They showed a figure covered from head to toe, any distinguishing features data-blocked by his nanotech mask.

"Based on the height, we're assuming the Ghost is male," Kimber said. "But you're correct, it could easily be a tall female. What is known is that this person always uses a red mask with horns and he, or she, doesn't speak. We do know that the Ghost doesn't sell what he steals. Instead, he gives it to local charities. We've decided to start our focus there."

Niall retook the podium. "Kimber will be running the Ghost detail, so if you're assigned to that duty, please see her. The rest of you, keep a lookout and report anything suspicious."

There was a general consensus of agreement in the group.

Niall's stance straightened. "Now on to the finer points of the evening. We need to move forward with our plans for Project Blackout."

The reaction was immediate. Voices spoke over one another, and several people half rose from their seats. Niall was losing control of the meeting, and he looked oddly happy about it. His hands gripped the podium as he smirked while watching the chaos.

He clearly wanted this uncertainty. Somehow it would help him put into motion whatever messed-up plan he'd set. Arden understood him enough to realize that. This was the way he'd run the gang ever since he'd taken over, pushing them into risky things. They weren't the only gang out there, yet his ideas ensured they made a name for themselves.

But the fact was, letting the gang run amok was dangerous. It made Lasair a target and crumbled the gang from the inside. She wasn't the only one who'd begun to question Niall's authority.

Arden stood, hating that she had to publicly confront Niall, but she knew that if she didn't, someone else would. If that happened, she wouldn't be able to direct the outcome. Maybe he could see reason before it was too late, because he was numbering his days with this move. She battled her conflicted feelings even as Colin sent her a glare.

The situation with Niall, as he systematically destroyed their gang, put into perspective how right Colin had been. Days were fleeting and precious. If she didn't break from the gang soon, she'd be dead along with everyone else when this nonsense Niall cooked up played itself out. It didn't stop her being constantly sucked back into the gang's problems. How could she watch her brother mess up his life along with everyone else's and do nothing to stop it?

She raised her voice to be heard over the yelling. "I have something to say."

Colin groaned.

Niall meanwhile wrested the attention of the room back to him, pointedly ignoring Arden. "I have received intel indicating the best time to hit the joint refinery and processing plants will be within the next month. They have a transport due to ship out. If we hit before it leaves, the losses will have the greatest impact."

She spoke over him even though he clearly wanted her to sit down and shut up. "What's going to happen to this city if VitD is destroyed? Everyone will die."

Niall glared. "Lasair won't. We've stockpiled enough. We'll be the only ones with a surplus. It will be enough to give us time to make a play for the city."

"The govies won't let you do that. Once the drugs are gone, they'll take emergency action." Besides, when did the gang have aspirations to take over the city? Since never. That road could only lead to disaster.

Niall ignored the rest of the room now, speaking directly to Arden. "We're not fighting the govies. They'll be as lazy as they've always been and back whoever has the power."

Unlikely. But keeping on this track wasn't the way to convince him, or anyone else. The gang could be swayed to his thinking.

"What will happen to everyone else once the drug trade stops?" she asked. "What about the children? They're innocent and shouldn't be condemned to death."

Niall shrugged. "If they don't like it here, there's always the Wilds."

Arden pressed on, not wanting to think about the large swaths of undeveloped planet in between the cities where the soil was fertile but nothing grew without the help of artificial sun lights. Or the animals that were either poisonous or liked to eat humans. Even if the danger from being eaten wasn't enough to put off someone from crossing it, most of the Wilds territory was too dark, the static cloud too thick to see anything. To go there would be a death sentence. It was the reason people didn't leave this city. There was no way to get to another of the planet's cities without a transport ship. "Our stockpile will eventually run out. What would happen to us then?"

Voices got louder as others started to question Niall's plan. Arden couldn't help but catch Colin's pained look.

Niall's voice rose over the room's chatter. "VitD will eventually be delivered through another supplier from another city. These things self-regulate."

Shipping it in, after they found another city with a surplus, would take time. There wasn't a lot of travel between the cities or a guarantee that another pharma could make excess VitD to supply them.

"And if it doesn't get here in time?" Arden asked.

"At least it would take out one or more of the Solizen families."

People were going to needlessly suffer and die, for what? Greed? If she let this injustice continue, could she really live with herself?

"That's a big gamble," she said. "Especially with innocent lives."

"It's for the greater good," Niall said.

Arden's mouth hung open. Really? When had human life become so easy for Niall to extinguish? And yet, the tide of the room had shifted, the group actively nodding at Niall's statement. Her breath felt tight in her chest. "What if the Solizen fight back? Even if the govies don't join the fight, we can't hold out against all the families if they band together."

Niall's expression turned feral. "Why would they? We've already destroyed one family. Their Tower sits in ruins. None of the other families came to their rescue, so there's no reason to think they'll stand behind one another now. Their weakness is in their inability to work together." He addressed the whole room then, pausing for dramatic effect. "We are united. Anything that comes against us will be crushed."

The room cheered.

Niall paused for the praise, then added more loudly, "If we ever want to have freedom, we need to level the playing field. There can no longer be castes among us. We all deserve to feel the sun on our skin. It shouldn't be reserved for the wealthy."

Arden couldn't argue with that.

# CHAPTER FIVE

"I want to speak with you before you avoid me for another week," Niall said. He'd cornered her as soon as the meeting had ended. Arden had tried to slip out, but he'd caught her and pulled her to the back corner of the room.

She'd expected it, yet she didn't hide her annoyance. Every bit of anger and resentment she'd let fester quickly rose up. She focused it all on him. Arden turned her back to the room and gave him a death glare. "What do you want?"

"I need you to do the club business tonight. I have a personal run," Niall said. Close up, he looked worse than she'd realized. Stress lined his face, and his hands shook. In another few weeks, he'd probably smoke himself into a coma.

"I'm not a dealer. You promised I didn't have to do that anymore." They'd negotiated her stepping away from direct sales. She'd had to do a lot of shady things to get that concession. If Niall couldn't be trusted to keep his word, Arden wouldn't play nice.

Niall shrugged. "That was then, this is now. I need you."

"So that means that I'm at your beck and call?" She folded her arms over her chest. "No way, Niall, try again. This is my night off."

"No one's stopping you from partying. Sell and play at the same time. It's not like I'm asking for something impossible." Niall looked around the room, the tap-tap-tap of his fingers against his pants distracting her. Then he turned his glazed eyes back on her. "And it's not like you haven't done it before."

Arden spoke through her clenched teeth. "I'm not doing it."

"If they want to get high, why do you care?" Niall scowled, his face coming close to hers. "You act like you're better than us. No one wants your judgment."

His unspoken "especially me" was loudly received. Well, too bad. She had to live with herself. It was one thing if adults wanted to get high. She didn't mind selling to them, kind of understood the need for the escape it offered. The addicted kids were a whole other matter. Seeing it firsthand tore at her soul a little more every day. But what did he care? He was as addicted as they were.

None of that mattered, though. He'd promised her, and he had to keep his promises. Otherwise how could she trust him? Arden squared herself, ready for a fight. "No."

"I don't understand how you can separate the business into compact boxes in your head. It all fits under the same umbrella. Selling to the tweenies makes us cash. It's how we survive. It's not our fault if they get hooked. No one forces them to use." Niall's expression hardened. "Be a team player."

He had a way of making her feel guilty. Not on his account—he was mostly a jerk who'd caused his own problems—but for everyone else whose lives hung in the balance of his decisions. She wouldn't see them burn because he was too macho to admit he didn't know what the hell he was doing with the gang. Or with their parents for that matter. He'd gotten them addicted to Shine to keep the pain of Violet Death at bay. Destruction followed Niall.

She shook her head, wanting to argue some more, though she knew that it would be pointless. At the end of the day, he was the boss. He'd force her to comply.

He came to the same conclusion. "Enough, Arden. It makes me look weak when my sister gives me as much crap as you do. You know what will happen if I'm challenged for leadership? Do you want that?"

They'd kill him. Of course she didn't want that. And he'd kill her if it saved him. Neither option was an outcome she wanted. Especially the second one.

"Fine," she agreed, wanting to get away from him. "I'll do your dirty work."

But she didn't have to feel good about it.

# CHAPTER SIX

Dade walked into the space they were using for the photo shoot. Someone had snagged an empty apartment in the Upper Levels, a surprising find since there was rarely a vacant location in the city. Probably it had been rented, the occupants paid handsomely to move their stuff out for the day.

There were people inside, standing around when he walked in. They all stopped what they were doing and stared. While that was unfortunately normal, it made Dade uncomfortable.

The dressers descended on him with grasping hands. They ripped his clothing from his body before he could get behind a changing screen. It made him feel violated, a feeling he often associated with his social responsibilities. He had little say over most aspects of his life, and that often included simple things like dressing himself.

When they finally deemed him acceptable, they showed him to a seat at the hair-and-makeup table that had been set up in one corner of the living room.

Clarissa was already at the table, lounging in a chair and looking as amazing as always. She smoothed her clothes with an absent brush of her hand. She wore a long bright-pink-and-orange silk robe, the front opened to her navel and showing off lots of tanned skin, while the back fell into a long bustled train. A fuchsia synth-silk tie wrapped around her waist. Beneath it all she wore synth-leather pants, displayed by a split in front.

Absent was the phaser she usually kept strapped to her thigh. She probably still had knives tucked into her boots, though. It was an assumption he could safely make because she was as devoted to her weapons as she was to her friends. He was sure that her missing weapons wouldn't be too far away, just as his had been left with Saben nearby.

He tugged at his neck band. They'd dressed him in a charcoal tunic with a high collar that reminded him of a noose. The outfit was heavily embroidered with silver ivy leaves that made him itch. Thick chains looped his neck, heavily pressing against his sternum while jewels glittered on every finger. The ensemble was ostentatious and ridiculous, and it looked nothing at all like his normal clothes.

Clarissa blinked one spidery eyelid open to inspect him. Her voice sounded like thick gravel in dark syrup when she said, "You should wear that tonight, you look hot."

He appraised himself and couldn't imagine endless hours dressed in this horror. "I look like I stepped off a fashion runway. A really gaudy one."

"Which makes it perfect. I'm sure your mother will have nothing negative to say about it for once."

Dade silently agreed that would be a plus. The ziptext he'd received from his father had required Dade's presence at his hosted dinner that evening. Coupled with specifics about formal dress, behavior, and expectations, the message held the promise of a long, regrettable evening.

The hairdresser went to work on his hair, while the makeup woman finished with Clarissa and switched to Dade. He hated wearing cosmetics. It made his face feel as if layers of weird clay were sitting on top. The feeling was different than wearing a synth-mask, which was so thin, he almost forgot it was there.

"I don't want to go tonight," he groaned. "We need to figure out an excuse to skip it."

"No way, I've got plans, and you have to help me."

Caution made Dade slow to reply. "With what?"

Clarissa looked at him from under the thick fringe of her bangs where they cut straight across her forehead in an unwavering line. Her eyes glittered, and her lip twisted at the corner fractionally, warning that he wouldn't like what she was about to say. Yet her glossy red lips stayed sealed.

The women finished with his makeup and hair. Clarissa waited until they'd packed up their things and walked away before she leaned toward him. "You know I wouldn't ask you for a favor if I didn't really need it. And in this case, it benefits you too. It's a win-win."

Groaning, he made a "get on with it" gesture. She was already selling him the outcome without divulging her plan. Never a good sign. "What horrible idea are we enacting for this evening's entertainment?"

"I need to tag Chief Nakomzer." By "tag," Clarissa meant that she needed some kind of device planted without the chief's knowledge.

"Of course you do," he said with a sigh. Tag the head of the govies in front of his family and hers, as well as any number of politically involved Solizen. They might as well hang a sign saying that they wanted to be caught and charged with treason.

He didn't bother asking why. She would tell him, but then he'd have to get involved in her plotting. To be honest, his own conspiracies were enough. He didn't also need to worry about hers. The unspoken tenet of their relationship was: "Help when requested, keep your mouth shut otherwise, and don't ask questions." It had been that way since they were kids. There was no reason to change it now, even if this might get him arrested.

"He'll be there tonight," she confirmed, then gave him a sly look. "I'll take care of him, but I need you to tag Sophia."

"No way." He considered Nakomzer's assistant to be a monster, and she hated him equally.

"I won't be able to get near her, not like I can with Nakomzer. You, on the other hand . . ." She bit her lip and tried not to laugh. "She likes you."

Dade gagged. "Stop."

Clarissa clapped her hands together in delight. "Fine, she hates you enough that she'll ignore you, which makes you perfect for the job."

He couldn't help but admire her enthusiasm. Dade was decisive about things, but he didn't have quite as much fun. She enjoyed everything about the destruction of social order.

The photographer walked over, interrupting their conversation. He stopped in front of them, looking them over critically, as if they were a painting or a work of art. His hands pressed together in front of his mouth as though he were in prayer as he stared at them.

The entire process was extremely uncomfortable. Dade didn't know if he should say something. Wasn't that common courtesy?

The scrutiny didn't seem to bother Clarissa. If anything, she slipped easily into her society persona, the one that was perpetually bored with everything.

"Yes, this I can work with," the photographer finally said, more to himself than to them, and then he hummed a little happy sound under his breath. His accent was heavy, he was obviously from another of the planet cities, and the dark skin of his bald head reflected in the harsh overhead lights. "You are such a lovely engaged couple. I'm going to make you look amazing."

Clarissa gave the photographer a dazzling smile. "We're so pleased you were available. When I heard you might not be in the city, I didn't know what we'd do."

"Who else could take these pictures but me?" he agreed, clearly pleased with the praise. He stepped forward to grip her hand, giving it a squeeze as he pulled her from the chair.

"No one, of course." She slipped her hand into the crook of his arm as they walked through the apartment toward one of the bedrooms where the set had been constructed.

Dade inspected himself one last time in the mirror. He looked ridiculous, rich, vapid, with way too much money and zero common sense. It was probably exactly the look they wanted. Dade sighed, getting up out of the chair to follow.

When he reached Clarissa and the photographer, they had stopped in the middle of what had once been an empty bedroom. They had their heads together while they discussed poses. The photographer gestured with his hands. Dade didn't know the guy's name or his work. With the way Clarissa was cooing, Dade supposed he was famous.

Dade stopped at the edge of the bright lights. He didn't know where to look first. At the red walls that reflected an unattractive glare, the gold-painted chairs that screamed gaudy and uncomfortable, or the random colored throw pillows stacked up in piles.

Clarissa beckoned him over. She patted his back reassuringly as the photographer described his vision.

But honestly, the whole thing gave Dade a headache. He nodded where appropriate and was thankful when the crew piled into the room and business finally got under way.

The photographer directed them. "Hips together." His hands gently steered them closer. "Wrap your arm around her back," he instructed Dade, then placed Dade's other hand on Clarissa's waist.

They knew what they were supposed to do. How they were supposed to act in public. So it wasn't a big deal to stand close together now and act like a couple.

Clarissa leaned into the pose. Her hands found the exact spot on Dade's chest that the photographer wanted, because he began to murmur, "Yes, exactly that."

Then the photographer stepped back to look them over with a wider view. He made a pleased noise while taking the camera from his assistant. "Okay, kids, forget the camera. Focus on each other. Let your love ooze."

Forgetting the cameras would be next to impossible. And oozing love? That sounded like an industrial accident. Plus, Dade didn't know how to pretend he was in love with Clarissa in the first place. He figured that if he wasn't frowning, that would be good enough.

Awkward did not begin to describe the next few minutes. The lights were hot. He felt the caked-on makeup melting off his face. The popping of the flash blinded him with each click of the shutter. And the stares from the crew tightened his shoulders.

Clarissa, on the other hand, looked in her element. She twisted for the camera, parting her lips slightly so that her face appeared relaxed. She offered sultry expressions.

All while Dade moved robotically beside her.

It must have been bad, because the photographer lowered his camera and frowned. "Let's try for a different look."

When he turned to his assistant to discuss a new pose, or possibly how they could make Dade appear less awkward, Dade pulled Clarissa closer to whisper in her ear. "We keep putting this conversation off, and it's obvious we can't anymore."

Clarissa let out a soft hiccup sound, as if she found him both ridiculous and adorable in one. "How do you propose to break our engagement now? It's not officially a day old."

"You keep reassuring me that we'll take care of it before this goes too far." He felt a little desperate. It was inevitable now. He couldn't pretend it wasn't happening. "You don't think this is too far? Because I think we've stepped over the line."

She gave him a sidelong look. "You knew we couldn't negotiate the contracts forever. They were going to eventually agree to the terms, and then we'd have to announce the engagement. This was the natural progression of things."

Dade scowled. She was being deliberately indifferent, and he didn't know why. It should have never come to this. They shouldn't have let themselves be bullied into this relationship in the first place. Once the momentum of their parents' schemes caught, it became too complicated to untangle.

"You promised we'd take care of it by now," he said.

"No, I said we'd figure it out."

He let out a surprised whoosh of air, and his eyebrows shot up. "What's that supposed to mean?"

"They're not going to let us out of this easily," she said dryly. "Especially now that they're making it public."

"Which is why we should have stopped it months ago."

"How do you propose we could have done that? Our hands were tied then just as much as they are now." As she'd spoken, Clarissa's shoulder's tightened, and she'd leaned into his space. When he didn't back down, she let out a sigh, her body deflating in frustration. "You're not looking at this logically. We should consider going forward with the wedding. At the very least, ending our engagement right now is wrong for us in the long run. We work better as a team."

The suggestion startled him. He'd assumed she was with him on this. After all, they'd spoken about it nonstop since the idea of their marriage had been presented by their parents as a way to unify their families, and thus their businesses. But now as he thought back over those conversations, he realized he had been obsessed about fixing the situation while she'd been silent.

So yes, it was disconcerting that she'd want to continue with the farce, yet he should have realized she'd intended this all along. Clarissa was an expert at manipulating circumstances to best fit her. She'd simply postponed dealing with it. That should have been his first clue.

It wasn't like they'd ever been a romantic item, or would ever be. They didn't like each other that way. They were friends now and always, but they'd never be lovers. He cared for Clarissa. Still, under no circumstances did he want to marry her. He made a face at that, a half squint, half wince, while struggling to figure out her angle.

"Thanks," she said, a tinge of hurt in her voice. "I'm not a hideous ogre, you know."

"Sorry." Dade wiped the wince off his face. His intention hadn't been to hurt her feelings.

"It's okay. I know it's not personal." Her face softened, and she added in a placating tone, "Besides, you know it's not real. It's not like I'd expect you to be faithful."

"Then why get married in the first place?" It was the same question he'd asked ever since he'd first been forced to sit in on the contract negotiations. All the other relationships in his life—including the one with his parents—demanded something from him. The only exception was his friendship with Saben. Even his relationship with Clarissa had a sort of symbiosis that required him to keep their dynamic in place. When he married, he wanted it to be a real relationship. Based on the simple pleasure of being with the other person.

"You know why," Clarissa said, apparently determined to make him see sense. "We'd get independence, and more important, it would provide the opportunity to make a play for power. If we ever want to stop living under our parents' thumbs, we have to control things. I don't know about you, but all I've ever wanted was the ability to make my own decisions."

He wanted that too, but clearly they didn't see eye to eye on how to make that happen. Committing his life to her didn't seem like freedom. "I don't see how marriage will solve that problem. We're only allowing them to continue to treat us like we're chattel. I am worth more than that, and so are you."

"We could make it work for us." She shrugged as though what she suggested weren't life altering. "If I have to marry anyone to get what I want, I'd choose you for a partner. I trust you the most."

That flattered him, yet there was no talk about love. Not that he expected her to reciprocate feelings he didn't have. At the very least, he deserved to be with someone who cared about him romantically.

From the beginning, she'd been so much better at pretending this engagement was real. She hadn't batted an eye when it had been suggested. When the gossip cams had hounded them, she leaned on him and smiled for pictures as if it had been the most natural thing in the world. What she asked for was a lifetime of that, or at least several years until they could extract themselves from their parents' preordered destiny. Dade wasn't so sure that would be possible, though. No matter how many plans they set into motion, anyone who went against the Solizen power would lose.

"Even if you don't agree, now is not the time to call it off," Clarissa said.

"I know."

"No, I don't think you do." She tilted her head to the side and studied him. "Your father would be much more interested in how you spend your time if he thought you weren't with me when you disappear."

He couldn't help a quick intake of breath at her very pointed observation. It hit him like a punch in the gut. How had she known? Had she had him followed? Knowing Clarissa, she probably had.

He recovered and nodded, understanding that lying was futile, yet still making an attempt to play it off. "What are you implying?"

She gave him a patronizing stare. "I've known you my whole life. I know when you're up to things. Keeping secrets from me isn't in your best interest. I can't help you if you don't trust me."

"I do trust you." He pulled her in for a long hug. "What I'm involved in right now, you can't have anything to do with. It's too risky."

She slowly nodded. "Okay, I'll let it go for now. It's just that I worry about you."

"I'll be fine." He squeezed her to emphasize that point, then kissed her forehead in silent thanks for caring for him and always having his back.

He heard the click-click-click of the camera's shutter catching the moment and making him freeze.

"Yes, that is exactly what I want," the photographer cheered.

# CHAPTER SEVEN

Cocktail hour was already almost over when Dade and Clarissa stepped into his family's apartment in Sky Tower Two. Clarissa had talked him into running errands after the photo shoot since they were already dressed and could then arrive at his house together. He agreed because it meant putting off going home, and therefore avoiding any questions. They entered arm in arm, already playing their role as a couple.

Dade's father glanced his way with a frown. He looked pointedly at his watch to note the time, but he didn't acknowledge Dade beyond that. Most of the guests wouldn't have noticed his late arrival anyway. They were well on their way to being high on drugs or alcohol, or both.

His mother sat on the sunken circular couch in the center of the room. The cushions were deep, covered in blue velvet that popped against the plush white carpet. She sipped her pink-tinted, bubbled cocktail while gossiping with several women.

Dade's home was high-gloss, made to show off. Everything was arranged to demonstrate wealth, from the polished indigenous stone shelves of blue and silver, to the 3-D pictures of Dade and his parents. Music floated through the space, a soft, slightly whiny sound from a stringed instrument. Above them, orbs of poloosh lit the room. Poloosh was a glow stone that could be carved into shapes. Fifty hand-sized stones were clustered together to create a chandelier that continuously emitted light.

Dade wandered the perimeter of the room to the far side. Clarissa stayed on his arm until a waiter passed them. She reached out to snag two glasses, offering him one as they took up position against the window.

He tipped his glass against hers. "Cheers."

The Sky Towers had been constructed to allow for maximum sun coverage. Long sheets of glass made up the back wall with the balcony beyond. The other walls were painted in a pearlescent sheen to catch the light and reflect it back into the room.

He looked over the clear purple sky, wanting the peace that usually came with it. The blood-orange sun was just beginning to set as their two moons rose in the distance. Far below, a blanket of gray static clouds cut off the view, making their Tower feel separate from the rest of the city.

"What are you daydreaming about?" Clarissa asked. They stood shoulder to shoulder, leaning into each other to ensure their conversation didn't travel.

He shrugged.

"Well, get out of your head. We have work to do."

He couldn't shake his nervousness. Which was silly. He'd done things like this a hundred times. It was just that he tended not to do them directly in front of his father. It wasn't like his dad was unobservant. Dade had a healthy respect for getting caught. If he did, it would ruin all his other endeavors.

Clarissa pulled out two small clear disks from her tiny purse. Both disks fit into the palm of her hand and appeared to be not much more than bits of stray plastic. She handed him one of the devices. "Bat your eyes, and she won't see you coming. All the girls fall for it."

"You don't," he pointed out.

"That's because I'm smarter than most." She turned toward the room. "Are you ready?"

"Why do we have to do this here?" This plan was insane, even for her.

"When else are we going to get the opportunity?"

"It's like you're trying to get caught."

Her eyes sparkled with excitement, but she just shrugged and coyly said, "Sometimes things hide in plain sight."

That was the truth. The irony of the statement amused him as he slipped the disk into his pocket.

Dinner was announced, and the guests began to make their way into the dining room. Clarissa held up her empty glass, signaling to a waiter who hurried over to collect it. Dade followed suit, murmuring his thanks.

Her hands empty now, Clarissa slid her arm through his, latching onto his elbow. "Time to shine, darling."

The dining room was surrounded by glass. In the distance, the sun had begun to set, sliding ever-darkening purple light filtering across the room. A long table ran down the center, seating up to fifty. Tonight every gold-leafed chair was filled while the servants buzzed in and out of the kitchen with trays piled with food.

Dade took a seat next to Clarissa halfway down the table near Chief Nakomzer. He didn't fail to notice that his cousin, Rylick, sat at the head of the table closer to Dade's father. In exactly the place Dade should have been. He would admit—to himself, at least—that it hurt that his father favored Rylick.

But then, Rylick was also watched more closely too. That was not something Dade could deal with.

Dade looked up, surprised, as Sophia took the empty seat next to him. It couldn't have worked out any better if Clarissa had planned it. He looked to Clarissa, who offered him a wide grin. Almost like she could read his mind.

She winked.

Maybe she *had* planned it.

Clarissa turned her attention to chatting up Nakomzer, her target for the evening. Nakomzer was generally a cold guy, but around her he always softened up. In no time at all, she had him laughing and leaning closer to her.

Which left Dade with Sophia. Dade looked for an opening, but she kept her back turned toward him, talking with the gentleman to her other side. Dade shifted slightly to catch her attention, trying to get her to turn. "How are you this evening?"

Sophia slid her gaze sideways, leaving her body twisted away from him, so that she looked at him over her shoulder.

Dade cleared his throat and tried again, a little more hesitantly this time. He felt ridiculous, because she was making it obvious she didn't want to speak to him. He wouldn't want to talk to her either if he didn't have to. "I heard that you just came back from one of the outer cities. Did you have a nice trip?"

Sophia sniffed.

Was that an answer?

Normally he could at least squeeze out one-word answers from her, even as rude as she usually was. The fact that he couldn't even get that much tonight left him at a loss. He had no idea how he was going to pull this off. His attention slid to her purse. It sat in front of her plate, which meant that he could potentially drop in the disk when she wasn't looking. Except that she kept placing her hand on top of it.

Clarissa had watched the exchange, and it was clear she was amused. She smothered a laugh behind her hand, then coughed gently into her napkin. She couldn't hide the mirth in her eyes, though.

"It's not funny," he said, the words barely a whisper.

She lowered the napkin and agreed. "No, it's not. You're usually much better at this."

"At flirting or getting the job done?"

This time a laugh did escape. "Both."

Dade knew he was a constant source of amusement for her, so why would this situation be any different? He leaned back into his seat to let the waiter serve his first course, all the while eyeing Sophia's purse. He ran his finger under his collar as he'd been doing for the last few hours. Wishing it wasn't quite so hot in the room and that the high collar's embroidery didn't feel as if it choked off his air.

"Relax. You're acting tense, and someone's bound to notice," Clarissa said.

"I'm always tense at these things." That was true. He hated these forced niceties with his family, though it was also true that this time, his tension had more to do with Clarissa's request.

"Are you saying you can't do it?" she asked, her voice light and taunting. "I've already planted mine."

Leave it to Clarissa to make this into some sort of dare. There was no way he'd let her show him up. Clarissa was right that he was fully capable of pulling this off. Why did he shut down around his family? Dade needed to get out of his own head. Though that was easier said than done.

He glanced again at his father to make sure Hernim wasn't paying attention. Rylick watched him, though. Or maybe it was Clarissa he eyed. Either way, it meant Dade had to be cautious. His gaze slid back to the purse.

Dade's first opportunity happened after the second course, a soup made from indigenous icca greens. Sophia opened her purse and took out her datapad. She turned away, leaving the bag open. Now was his chance to make his move. Just as he reached forward to drop the disk into her purse, his father stood and tapped his glass with a fork.

The ringing of silver against crystal had Dade pulling back.

Hernim Croix cleared his throat. "Thank you for joining us to celebrate the upcoming nuptials of my son and Clarissa Hemstock."

The guests politely clapped.

Dade's hand closed around the disk as they became the center of attention. The mention of their engagement soured Dade's mood.

Clarissa leaned into him. She petted his arm and then gave him a pinch. "Smile."

Mr. and Mrs. Hemstock, Clarissa's parents, sat across from them. They accepted the praise for brokering such an advantageous match for their daughter by preening and thanking the other guests, as if they were the ones to be married. Mrs. Hemstock was short, her Asian heritage strongly evident in her coloring and features, whereas Clarissa's father was tall and willowy, and quite pale. An oddity for one of the Solizen, who were usually golden with tanned skin, a source of pride. The Hemstocks weren't warm people. There was always a rigidity that struck Dade as off-putting. He didn't trust anyone he couldn't read. The fact that they were a rival Solizen family was less significant.

The spotlight didn't leave Dade or Clarissa for several minutes. Various toasts were offered. Dade maintained a strained smile throughout, with the disk pressed into his palm. He felt every second of the stares trained on him. A light sweat started across his brow, but he didn't move to wipe it away. That would show weakness.

"Tonight isn't all about our children," Hernim said, taking his seat. The waiters moved forward to serve the main course as Hernim moved the discussion to the true reason they were there: the thefts they were experiencing.

"The gangs are becoming more aggressive. I've lost three shipments in the last five weeks," said a woman with tightly curled gray hair. She wore yellowed pearls around her throat, a demonstration of her power to own a priceless artifact from the Old Planet. The necklace moved against her neck as she spoke.

This was the part Dade found hypocritical. To the outside world, these high-ranking members of society made their money from legitimate prescription drugs. They did this by jacking up the prices and driving down the supply so that they could profit the most from it. They weren't trying to help people. Behind closed doors, they lamented the loss of their drug capital. As if they didn't collectively own 85 percent of the city's income. How were they different than the street gangs?

"Lasair," Hernim agreed, naming the biggest Undercity gang, and a thorn in their side. It wasn't the only gang that stole from them, but they were the loudest. They liked to taunt, to let the Solizen know that they were causing havoc. "They've increased their hits on Croix Industries as well. It's time someone took control of the streets and flushed them out."

"We have some leads on where they're meeting," Chief Nakomzer said. "But we're getting stalled by the lack of cameras that still work in Undercity."

Dade squeezed his hand. The disk tucked inside pressed into his flesh, reminding him that he still had a job to do no matter how distracted he was by the conversation. Talk of Lasair made him think of Arden. She hadn't said where she was from, yet his gut instinct told him she was from Undercity in spite of the fact that she shouldn't be able to travel to Above. If she were a member of Lasair, she'd have a way to do that, though. She'd been too capable with the knife, in a way only the streets could teach a person. And she had that desperate, determined look of someone with nothing to lose.

The need to see her again washed over him, making him both excited and anxious. He had to keep those feelings locked down, and instead come up with a way to plant the bug. He shouldn't be daydreaming of a girl he'd met only once and instead should pay attention to the danger he was in right now.

"If the government can't contain the city gangs, we need to look into other options," Hernim said.

"Now wait a minute." Chief Nakomzer held up his hand in an attempt to stop Dade's father from going where he was headed with that insinuation. "We can't condone vigilantism. Doing so would cause a widespread panic."

No one looked impressed.

Chief Nakomzer sputtered. "We have more than your internal thefts to worry about. The citizens in the Lower Levels are showing signs of mobilization. This is the greater threat at the moment."

"To whom?" the lady with the pearls asked.

Nakomzer frowned. "To all of us."

Sometimes Dade couldn't believe the things that were said at these parties. If it wasn't about money, the Solizen didn't seem to care. To them there wasn't an outside world that existed beyond their enclosed Towers. Public unrest wasn't on their radar. Only when it cut into their profits would it become a problem.

Sophia watched the reactions of the Solizen to Nakomzer's words, probably to discuss and analyze them with Nakomzer after the dinner. Her open purse was closer to him now. This could be the opportunity he needed, but her body was pivoted too far his way. Dade would definitely be in her peripheral vision. Which made it tricky, but maybe he should just go for it. Dade leaned forward, moving his body in slow increments to see if she noticed. If she indicated in any way that she did, he'd back off.

Meanwhile Nakomzer tried to convince the assembled Solizen that they had a far greater problem on their hands. "The civil unrest is far outweighing the peacekeeping corps. If this continues, you'll have a much worse problem than distribution. You'll lose your client base."

"There's always someone who will buy our products. There is no sun, after all," Dade's father said. "They need us."

"Maybe it's not Lasair or any of the street gangs who are agitating the situation," said a dark-skinned man from the other end of the table. His face pinched, making the weathered lines groove deeper around his eyes. "We need to take a look at the Ghost."

Dade tensed, his hand inches from the purse. He was just about to make his move and drop the disk in, but he found himself frozen. His breath caught in his chest, like the sharp prick of a knife right under his sternum.

Clarissa went still beside him, her body coiled. Though how she knew the implications of that was a puzzle to work out another time.

Nakomzer gave a short, stuttered laugh. "There isn't any such person."

"Of course there is," the pinched-faced man insisted, frowning at Nakomzer. "Rumors always have a grain of truth."

"It could just be any one of those thieving gangs looking to cover their tracks," Nakomzer hypothesized.

"Why would they do that?" Hernim asked. "They've been quite willing to claim all their activity up till now. How do you explain the footage of the lone character? He leaves his mark after every crime."

"A sun-star symbol," the lady with the pearls said.

Dade's mother gasped, her hands flying up to cover her mouth. "How dare they."

Nakomzer didn't look pleased when he confirmed. "That symbol has appeared on the streets in greater frequency. It would seem that whoever is doing this has appropriated the symbol and plans to use it to start a revolution."

"Mocking us," the pinched-faced man added.

The woman with the pearls spoke up. "It's because the people see him as a sort of Robin Hood character. Steal from the rich, give to the poor."

"What do you mean 'give to the poor'?" Dade's mother asked.

"The VitD this Ghost steals, it's not reformulated into Shine like it is with the gangs. It's given to charity houses," the pinched-faced man said.

A grumbling tension took over the table as the Solizen whispered among themselves.

Nakomzer spoke louder, trying to get their attention back. "If there is a Ghost, he's little more than a street thug."

"I make this promise," Hernim said, looking around the table, the threat in his voice clear. "When we catch this so-called Ghost, we will show him or her no mercy."

Agreement was swift and vocal.

Dade felt Clarissa's hand rest against the back of his. Her touch was light, shocking him out of his thoughts. He made a face, sending her a silent question.

She answered it by glancing down at where their hands joined.

When his gaze followed hers, he realized that the hand she'd covered had curled into a fist around his fork, his knuckles turning white. It took him a few seconds to consciously relax. He set his fork down and turned his hand over so that he could lace his fingers together with Clarissa's. Dade nodded his thanks.

Clarissa winked.

"In the meantime," Hernim continued, "we should focus on Lasair. It is the bigger threat. If we take it down, the other gangs will follow shortly behind, as will the Ghost."

Hernim motioned for Nakomzer to explain. Dade realized it was an olive branch, letting Nakomzer appear to take control. Yet his father would blame Nakomzer if the plan failed.

"We're in the process of sweeping the Lower Levels, looking for anyone associated with a street gang," Chief Nakomzer said. "We'll find someone and then squeeze them for information we can use."

Dade's stomach sank. That would mean catching Arden or one of her friends. The thought made him cold.

He wanted to see Arden, to warn her of the danger. It was irrational and stupid, but he couldn't put the thought out of his mind. If he could see her, see that she was fine, he could let it go, perhaps breathe easier. He knew he was fooling himself. That it was only a flimsy excuse to see her again. It would be a foolish errand. But in this case, he was okay with playing the fool.

Clarissa squeezed his hand again, regaining his attention. She tilted her head to Sophia's purse. Then she gestured, indicating that no matter what else was taking place, he had a job to do.

Right.

Dade didn't care about stealth at that point. He wanted this done. The servers began to pick up empty plates before bringing out the dessert trays, which meant that his escape would come soon. He moved forward to pick up his glass. Right before he reached for it, he dropped the disk into the open mouth of Sophia's purse. He watched as it fell, making sure it hit its mark, and then he sat back and took a drink. His job was done.

He waited till dessert was half-finished before he pushed to his feet and murmured his excuses to the table. His father glared, but Dade didn't care. He kept his movements fast and efficient so that there wouldn't be an opportunity to stop him.

Clarissa stood as well. It didn't surprise him. The fact she had his back meant that she also nosed into his business. She wouldn't let him leave without grilling him, not after the tension he'd displayed all evening. She followed him all the way to the front of the apartment.

There wasn't time to change. Dade grabbed his cloak from the closet near the door and swung it over his shoulders so that the fabric fanned out before it settled. Then he grabbed his phaser, strapping it to his side. His body vibrated with anxiety, so much that his hands shook. He flexed them, taking a moment to make sure he didn't leave the house missing something vital.

He felt Clarissa behind him. She didn't say anything till he stood at the apartment door, ready to bolt, his weapons strapped. "Where are you going?"

"I have to check on some things in the Zero District." It was the slummier part of Level One, where all the party kids hung out because drugs were easy to score and the govies generally ignored the area.

She glanced back toward the dining room, before pinning him with a stare. "It's not safe there. You'll be caught."

"It's better if I leave while they're distracted. Plus, if I wait, it will be too late." He grabbed her shoulders. "Don't worry, I'll be fine."

Clarissa narrowed her eyes. "You'll never make it past the Sky Tower guards."

"Then help me. Distract them. You've done it before." He gave her a pleading expression, willing her to understand that he needed to do this and that he would not be stopped.

"It's that important to you?"

"It is."

The tension in her face cleared, and she laughed. She raised a perfect eyebrow. "You've met someone."

"Not really. Maybe. I don't know." He sighed. "Yes."

Clarissa sent him a look saying he was silly. "Sounds like she's got you all twisted up. I don't have to meet her to know I adore her."

"Are you going to help me or not?"

Clarissa let out a grunt. "Yes, but you'd better ping me the minute you get home, or I'll go after you myself."

Dade nodded. "Agreed."

# Chapter Eight

Arden surveyed the dance floor from the floating moonglass balcony that overlooked the club. Colin danced beside her. He bumped and ground against her during the chorus. She'd occasionally throw him a glare, to which he responded by singing the lyrics at the top of his lungs.

Below, bodies gyrated in a tangled mess. They danced with their arms entwined, twisting together as they passed inhalers of Shine. The drug was encapsulated in a reflective disk that had a retractable mouth-piece. After they inhaled, they'd share smoky kisses with their partners and sometimes with strangers. The air took on its smoky scent.

"Dance," Colin yelled as he leaned into her ear. He pushed against her, trying to get her to move with him.

She took a sip of her glowing blue drink laced with pink cubes.

"You're such a party pooper." He moved away, sensually dancing and pressing himself against the see-through balustrade. The people below cheered, catcalling him to come down and join them. Colin threw kisses at them, continuing his antics.

The music vibrated through her, numbing her mind as well as her senses. Blind was the worst way to do business. Plus, she just didn't want to be here. There was nothing new and exciting in this. Maybe it was time to consider other options. Even as she had that thought, she pushed it away. What could she do, really? Become a day worker with no skills? The only skills she had were those the gang had taught her. She was pretty sure "ass kicking" wasn't exactly marketable.

"Does it seem crowded tonight?" she yell-asked Colin.

"No more than usual. You just haven't gone out in a while." He knocked his hip against hers. "We should go down and get sweaty."

"No." Arden touched her gold-sequined mask, a nervous habit because she knew the nanotech wouldn't let it slip out of place. She'd paired it with a matching gold dress. Her hair was down tonight, golden brown, untamed curls long against her back.

Everyone in the party scene loved masks. They'd become popular in the last year even though they'd been difficult to procure since the govies put restrictions on them now. The masks clung without being heavy, like a translucent sheen, so the wearer felt as if nothing were on the skin.

Colin pulled out a number of Shine disks from his pocket. The disks were single-use and dispensed Shine in an aerosol blast that was inhaled. "I have seven more. How many do you have left?"

"About the same."

The Shine had gone like hotcakes earlier, which was nice because it meant an early night.

"Ready for another round?" he asked.

"In a minute." Arden tipped her drink, showing him that it wasn't quite empty.

Turning back to the dance floor, she watched Uri dance with Mariah near the DJ booth. The pressurized floors changed colors beneath them. Holograms projected around them, flicking between rainbows of color. Mariah's back was pushed up against Uri's front, her head leaned onto his shoulder as they moved together. They looked happy.

Arden wanted that. She'd admit, to herself at least, that she was jealous of their relationship. They made it look easy.

Perhaps it wasn't the relationship she wanted, so much as the feeling of having someone to lean on. Metaphorically speaking, because she really didn't need anyone. Though it might be nice to have someone to count on, with whom she could share something deeper than friendship. And maybe experience a little romance.

"If you want to be productive, you should keep your eyes open for the Ghost," Arden said.

"Why would I want to be productive?" Colin asked. He took out an inhaler and slipped a Shine disk into it before taking a hit. "I bet you he's super hot underneath that mask. Like Batman."

"Or she. Like Batwoman."

"Why are you so insistent on ruining every fantasy I have?"

"It's a gift." This time when she looked over the club, she searched for the Ghost's signature red mask.

The red mask she saw made her catch her breath.

Arden knew exactly who she was looking at the second she set eyes on him. She'd watched that swagger for at least an hour earlier that afternoon. No amount of camouflage could keep her from recognizing Dade, because he had imprinted on her brain. He stood out like a shiny beacon in a sea of bland. And she had to admit, she'd been searching for him on the dance floor.

Dade looked amazing in a dress tunic. Which was exceptionally over-the-top for a club. And yet, his yumminess was indescribable. The boy should wear a dress tunic every day. The horns of his mask curved over his head, and he wore his longish hair loose. Why would he wear a devil mask? Everyone knew better. Perhaps he was too coddled in his Tower to realize its implication. That was funny, and yet heartbreaking as well.

He was also alone, again. Which meant he hadn't listened to a word she'd said. Why had she bothered giving advice if he was going to ignore it? The boy had a death wish.

"Is that?" Colin squinted, as if that would help him see Dade's face beneath the mask.

It would be impossible. From here she could tell that he was wearing a mask that would obscure his identity. The perception of his facial features hazed and shifted as she watched, the nanotech rearranging itself so as not to allow anyone to get a lock on his features. She didn't need to see his face to know it was him, though. She could pick Dade out from anywhere at this point simply by the way he carried himself. Confidently, like most siskin, yet there was a core of inner strength that burned brightly.

She could hear the surprise in Colin's voice when he said, "It can't be Dade Croix. Not slumming it like this." He shook his head, laughing.

But it was. At first she wondered how Colin would know it was him. Then she remembered Colin's obsession with the gossip-vids. He watched them every night with a bowl of popcorn while snickering at the screen. Of course he would also recognize Dade even wearing a mask.

"I really think it is." Colin turned to her, his eyes nearly bugging out of his head. "Do you think he's the Ghost?"

"No," she said, immediately dismissing the idea as insane. "More like he thought it'd be amusing to wear the mask as a joke."

"That's true," Colin conceded. "He does love to play tricks on the paparazzi. Still, how can you be sure?"

"Trust me, there's no way he could be the Ghost. He's too sweet."

*"Too sweet?"* Colin blinked repeatedly, making him look like he was experiencing an aneurysm. "Are you kidding me? Is that your siskin? The one you were playing kissy-face with? You didn't mention that you'd gone insane."

Arden's heart rate was already exceptionally high, but the reference to Dade as "hers" made her heart give a great thump in her chest. Excitement. This was excitement. It was a feeling almost foreign to her, as there wasn't much in her life to be excited about. She was usually consumed by work and revenge.

It was nice. Okay, perhaps she could admit that it was more than nice, actually. Something she could get used to if given the opportunity.

Even though she knew that having something that brought her joy only meant weakness.

"I wasn't playing kissy-face with him," she said. "We talked, is all. He's only a boy. You're acting like he's royalty."

"He is royalty," Colin choked. "It's not enough to moon over a sky boy—you had to pick someone from the Croix family?"

She found herself moving toward the stairs that would lead her below.

"I thought you weren't going to dance," Colin said, stepping after her but stopping at the top rung.

"I changed my mind."

"Are you going to congratulate him on his engagement?" Colin yelled after her, over the music.

She stopped dead, several steps down the stairs, then turned back, her breath frozen in her chest. "What did you say?"

"When you were cutting each other and making lovey eyes, or whatever the hell you were doing," Colin said, looking like an avenging angel, his hands on his hips, "did he happen to mention his fiancée?"

The words swirled around her, but they had no meaning.

"It has been all over the visicast for the last few months," Colin said. "The analysts talk about nothing but the consolidation of their families. How this would potentially affect the Solizen power structure. This shouldn't be news to you."

Her mouth worked, but no sound came out. Not that she knew what to say anyway.

"You really should pay more attention if you're going to have a psychotic crush," Colin said. Turning to contemplate Dade, he tilted his head. "I can see the attraction. I wouldn't mind climbing that."

"You need to back off." Her warning was flat.

Colin stared at her now, his jaw slack. "Wow, you really like him. Not just 'get in his pants, my hormones are raging,' but 'like him, like him.'"

She rolled her eyes. "Eloquent."

"Don't pursue this," Colin said. "This is going to end badly, I can promise you that."

He was right. If Dade did have a fiancée, Arden had absolutely no business seeking him out. Added to that, the nervousness she'd felt all night had begun to erode her confidence. She faced down men with phasers on a weekly basis, stole shipments of drugs, dealt to addicts, killed people when necessary, and yet thinking about approaching this boy had her second-guessing herself.

Ridiculous.

There had been something between them. She couldn't have imagined that.

"I don't want you to get your heart broken," Colin said.

"My heart has nothing to do with this."

Colin gave her a disbelieving look, before he started down the stairs after her. "I'm going to dance with Uri and Mariah. I don't need to watch while you make poor life choices. Just remember, I warned you."

"Play interference for me?" She didn't want to attract Uri's and Mariah's attention, especially if it could get back to Niall.

"Afraid they'll kill Dade and splatter blood on your pretty dress?"

"More like I don't want to deal with it." They reached the bottom of the stairs, and she turned to keep him from leaving. "Do it for me?"

"You'll have to tell them eventually."

Arden shook her head. "Only if I see him again."

That wasn't going to happen. This was a one-off. Well, a two-off. There was no way to pretend otherwise, even in her head. For some reason she couldn't explain, she had to know if it had been real: him or her reaction to him, her feelings—the confusion made her question herself, and she didn't like that.

She circled the room so that she could approach him from behind, just in case he'd shown up with friends. Her path took her through the dance floor. The intensity from the sweaty bodies felt more potent here.

People reached out, touching her arm. She had no idea who they were, but she knew what they wanted.

Arden slipped the last of the Shine disks out, making several quick transactions without slowing down. A slip of the hand, a swipe of her palm-sized wand-scanner, a lingering brush of a hand against her, silently asking her to stay and share in the party. But she dealt with them like she always had, fast and detached. Wanting to minimize her exposure to the lure of escape. She had finished that task, at least, if Niall asked.

She made sure to avoid Uri, Mariah, and also Colin, who winked at her when she slipped past. Arden hid herself in the shadows where the dance lights failed to penetrate. She waited on the outskirts of the dance floor, observing Dade's movements as she had done earlier that day.

He didn't dance, a solid statue in the midst of the undulating hedonism that moved around him. That alone made him stand out, made him more alluring than if he'd taken part in the promise of their bodies. He drew looks of awe from the crowd. Many recognized him, either thinking he was the Ghost or perhaps sensing his real identity. Either way, they kept a healthy distance. Dade never looked in any one direction for more than a few seconds. He was clearly searching for someone. If Arden found out who, perhaps it would answer her questions as to why he'd stumbled in here.

Dade began to walk through the crowd, never wavering from his intended direction and assuming that people would move. And they did, parting for him unconsciously.

She followed. Curiosity, lust, and excitement all mixed together.

He stopped in the middle of the dance floor. Dancers writhed around him. He remained still, poised like a hunter. As if he expected his prey to dart out in front of him.

Arden reached out. She brushed his shoulder, following the line of his arm down to slip her hand into his. A zing sizzled against her skin, making her suck in her breath.

Dade turned at the touch. Their fingers loosely joined. Then he squeezed her hand, pulling her closer. Sliding her other arm up around his shoulder, she fell into him as he tucked her against him, her body pressed warmly to his.

He didn't look surprised to see her. If anything, he appeared relieved. He smiled, big and radiant.

Arden didn't know what to say, deciding to enjoy the moment and letting the heat build between them.

Electricity sparked inside her as their gazes held. Time suspended, the moment perfect in beautiful connection. Their bodies began to sway together, becoming one with the music and each other. The bubble of space that surrounded them shrank. Dancers moved closer, swallowing them up so that they became a part of the living mass, hidden from outside eyes, safe in their own world.

All that existed was the music and him. For the first time that she could remember, Arden felt alive. That spark he'd lit inside her now rushed through her veins. Nothing else mattered beyond this. Reality would exist later once this magical moment broke.

He leaned in, so close that she could smell the mint on his breath and the deep spicy richness of his cologne. She wanted to press her face close to his tunic, perhaps lay her head on his shoulder. But she maintained sense enough to hold herself back. Barely. This feeling, as nice as it was, couldn't permeate her life. Because then she'd miss it when he left. Nothing good ever stuck around.

Dade's hand cupped the side of her face. His fingers trailed in flutter-soft strokes across her cheek, just below her mask. The touch left warm prickles of awareness. She shivered at the feel of skin against skin, wanting to press into it. Needing to prolong it somehow, to make it last, wanting to live in the moment before it slipped away.

Then he touched her hair. Dade fingered the tendrils a moment before his hand slipped to cup the back of her head. He moved her forward, as his mouth inched toward hers.

Arden turned her face up. Anticipation melted her, making the heat inside her spread like lava through her stomach and chest.

Just for a moment, his lips hung above hers, almost, but not quite, touching.

They connected. Dade's lips brushed hers, soft at first with the barest hint of pressure. Then he leaned in farther, pulling her until she grabbed at his shoulders to seal their lips together.

She felt as if all her dreams coalesced into heart-melting want. She could go on like this forever, sharing the same breath, touching, and being one together. Their masks brushed lightly, the nanotech sparks showering them in a cascade of fireworks light.

Arden pulled back and drew in a long breath. They stared at each other, while their bodies still moved. The music continued to play, yet the moment they were caught in was long and quiet. She slid her tongue across her bottom lip, considering going back for another kiss.

A piercing siren shattered the haze of her mind.

Arden drew away, startled. Her brain tried to catch up with the situation exploding around her. It took her a second to put the context together, to realize the club was being raided.

Govies stormed in from the doors, the windows, and through the roof. They wore their govie-greens: gender-neutral, sleek synth-suits in a material that helped to deflect phase-fire. Over this, they sported high-tech tactical gear and head cranials, with blue-phase shields that covered their eyes and provided them with night vision.

A concussion grenade exploded. The reverberating sound shook the dance floor. Smoke billowed, making it impossible to see. The club lights were cut, leaving only the glow from the govie phase shields to slice through the fog like ghostly beacons.

Arden tried not to breathe in the noxious fumes. Her body felt as if it had ground itself together, bone against bone, while her eyes watered and her head swam. The ringing in her ears from the grenade messed with her balance. She swayed, stumbling forward.

Dade caught her.

Club goers scattered, making the chaos worse.

"We need to go," Arden said.

He nodded. "I'm sorry. I meant to get you out of here before they showed up."

That stopped her cold. She narrowed her eyes. The odds were always in favor that the govies might strike the club. But he'd known. Had Dade set her up? "How did you know there would be a raid tonight?"

"I didn't, not really. But I knew they were upping their sweeps. I thought I had enough time to warn you."

"That's stupid," she said, while feeling a warm flutter in her belly. "You're not ever to risk your life. I already told you that once today."

Arden didn't know if she was more frustrated at him for being here or for caring. She couldn't trust him, but did it matter? He'd come to find her. That made him her responsibility. Even if he might be playing some other dangerous game, she couldn't leave him for the govies.

She grabbed Dade's wrist and navigated them through the screaming chaos. They reached a back hallway where a govie stood at the mouth of the egress, keeping people from escaping in that direction. She shoved a group of club kids into him. While he was distracted, she moved around them and down the hall.

She pushed her way into the men's restroom. Thankfully, it was empty. "We don't have much time. Lock the door."

Dade looked back the way they'd come before he stepped inside and did as she'd asked. His face was lined with worry, his shoulders tight. "What about those kids?"

"It's them or us," she said. "And I didn't want to kill a govie tonight. I try to save that for the last option." Arden aimed for a joke, but it fell flat because it was the truth. Neither of them laughed. She left it at that, hoping she'd made her point.

"We can't leave them. They're nobodies, just club kids."

"Which means they'll be released from custody soon enough," Arden said. "Let it go. We can't help them."

Dade didn't look happy, yet he nodded.

She walked to the other end of the restroom. There was only one way out since they obviously couldn't exit onto the streets. The Lasair members guarded their bolt-hole entrances zealously. Rescuing Dade was going against every rule the gang had. He could easily disclose the bolt-hole's existence, making that escape route inoperable.

She should not trust him. *Didn't* trust him. And yet, she found herself leading Dade to the janitor's closet.

He looked at her, his eyebrow raised. "First date and you're already shoving me into dark closets?"

Arden rolled her eyes and pushed him inside. "As if." But his words made her relive the brief kiss on the dance floor.

She followed, shutting and locking them into the darkness. From her pocket, she extracted a glo-wand, extending the tube and flicking it on to emit a low yellow light. Then she knelt down on the floor and unhooked a hidden latch that revealed a keypad. After she typed in the code to release the hatch, the floor slid open to reveal a set of stairs descending into the darkness.

"Tell anyone about this bolt-hole and I'll kill you," she said, gesturing for him to go first.

# CHAPTER NINE

"Why do you keep threatening to kill me?" Dade asked, his amusement clear.

"You seem to inspire that in me," she said, forcing back an answering smile. Normally she wasn't too entertained by people, but he was so honest and charming in his reactions, it was difficult not to get sucked in.

Arden shone her glo-wand on another keypad inside the tunnel lip. When she keyed that one, the lights inside the tunnel flickered on. She pulled the hatch the rest of the way open and then gestured again. "You first."

He didn't protest, moving past her while giving her a smirk. The kind promising a secret that said he would share it with her if she would only ask. It made her toes curl and her heartbeat stumble.

She shouldn't have been surprised at his cockiness. He'd come to the club knowing about the sweep, after all. That he was flirting even when they were in danger of being caught and she was literally leading him into a dark tunnel underground should be expected.

She followed, making sure to shut and lock the hatch behind her. The light on the panel turned from green to red. The tube felt claustrophobic, with a stench of unfiltered air. The temperature lowered as they descended. Arden hated traveling to and from Undercity. The press of the walls always reminded her of how trapped they really were.

They climbed down for a while, Arden's muscles beginning to burn with exertion before they reached the bottom of the tunnel. Dade looked around the small antechamber. He studied the blue-tinged brick walls as if committing them to memory. The Levels and the Sky Towers were constructed from metal and moonglass. Only here in Undercity were the walls made from the planet's soil.

Reaching out, he ran his fingers along the rough texture. "I never thought I'd see brick in person. It's fascinating."

Arden found his reaction humorous, but she managed to keep it in check. "Then you're going to love the rest of it. Come on."

She slipped her mask off, tucking it into a pocket. Then pulled up the hood of her cloak. "Keep your head covered until we reach the fields. There aren't many working cameras in this neighborhood, but there are enough."

"Right." Dade mimicked her movements.

There was another door on this side. The tunnel locked at both ends. She opened it, leading them into the basement of a food-package shop. The storage area was crammed with boxes and barrels. Arden didn't bother with the overhead light, relying on her glo-wand as they entered the back of the shop and worked their way through the store. The dim electric lights from the street outside cast a gloomy shine through the clouded, aged windows. Arden shut off her glo-wand, collapsing and pocketing it.

The store didn't have much in the way of decoration, like most shops in Undercity. Cell-powered lamps hung from the rafters as a precaution against frequent power outages. The floor had been cobbled together from natural stone collected from the Wilds and smoothed to make a flat surface. Cracks in the grout had been dug out and refilled several times in a variety of colors. But the surfaces were clean, and the place was dry. There wasn't the prevalent Undercity mold smell.

Food commodities were carefully monitored for distribution. There wasn't a lot for sale on the shelves. The items had been prepackaged individually in govie wrappers, and each sat with space surrounding it from the next item. They were high-calorie offerings made from meta-grains, their goal to sustain the body on less food. Prices glowed in suspended numbers in front of each shelf. Govie Buy Certificates were needed along with credits for purchase. This system limited the number and type of supplies, making sure there was a fair exchange of goods.

"We need to move quickly," she said when they reached the door to the street. "Stay in the shadows. If we're seen, run. I'll find you."

The streets were empty since they were currently in the middle of lockdown hours. Anyone on the streets now either had legitimate business with a govie pass or shouldn't be there at all. The likelihood of being caught was slim because there weren't frequent patrols in this neighborhood, but caution was still necessary.

"I'm not worried," he said.

"You should be." A little fear would be good for him, but as he'd proven over and over, getting him to understand that would be impossible. "If we're separated, you won't get out of Undercity without me showing you the way."

The food-package shop was located in a quiet section to the south of the town square. Arden led them past the row of storefronts and out toward the wheel of the city center where they could take the path that led to the farm district. From there, she would take him to a bolt-hole close to the Sky Towers. Then she would be done with him. Arden considered whether she'd use the next hour to figure out what made him so intriguing, then ruthlessly cut that thought from her mind.

Dade looked up to the ceiling that domed the walkways, enclosing all of Undercity. "There's brick everywhere."

"It's how they keep us from crawling from the depths into Above." She felt uncomfortable with his curiosity, like she feared being judged, and that in turn made her angry and embarrassed. No siskin was going to make her feel less than, even if he seemed enthralled by her world and hadn't uttered a single disparaging remark.

This was her normal, her home. For the most part, she barely noticed it. Of course, she saw the difference between the world she belonged to and Above, whenever she snuck up to run a job or manage a deal. It didn't mean that she wanted him to understand the difference.

"It's a long walk, so keep up. The subtrains stopped running a few hours ago. I need to be back by the early bell." She walked quicker, putting some strides between them and hoping that if they moved faster, he'd show less fascination with Undercity and then she could breathe a little easier.

"I don't understand. Wouldn't it be easier to wait a few hours and then return through the club?"

"It's too risky. The govies will be watching the streets. Standard procedure is to establish a perimeter before the raid that then stays in place for at least twelve hours after. You probably just made it inside." Then she added seriously, "I can't get caught."

"Have you been caught in raids before?"

"Not yet." Though she was sure she was in the database.

Not that she was only worried about being caught by the govies. She also couldn't be caught leading Dade through Undercity. If anyone from Lasair noticed her, she'd be in trouble.

Here, in the heart of Undercity, steel carcasses of what had once been enormous mining facilities rose out of the earth. They held the weight of the city above, providing the foundation on which the Levels had been built. Large sections had been reinforced with brick and more steel.

Along the apex of the ceiling where the brick met to shape the peak of the dome, squares of opaque glass filtered in light. These were worked into the sidewalk in Above, unnoticed by the hundreds of pedestrians who stepped over them daily. Moss, dirt, and cobwebs crept over their surface, and plants grew from cracks.

"Undercity is different than I thought it would be." He'd caught up to her long strides, matching them with little to no effort.

"What did you expect?"

"The vids I've seen are from before the Levels were built. I expected it to be like that, but older maybe. It hasn't been kept up as well as I'd been led to believe."

"The only thing anyone from Above cares about is that the infrastructure is sound. Wouldn't want the city imploding," she said. "Well, that and they want the food we grow."

Dade shrugged. "I hadn't given it much thought, I guess. I figured it would still look like it did when the planet was terraformed."

Arden snorted, half in amusement and half in disbelief. "You believed the history-vids that this is a 'perfect planet'? That our ancestors were lucky to find it?"

Dade didn't respond, but the tiny frown indicated that he probably had.

"This planet has oxygen, and the necessary minerals in the soil to grow plants. I guess if that's all that matters, it's perfect," Arden conceded. "But a perfect planet would have sunlight available to everyone."

Dade gave a half nod, not so much to her, but more indicating that he was deep in thought. He didn't voice whatever it was he was mulling over. Arden accepted that as response enough. He needed to come to terms with the true reality of the way things were.

Trash became a problem as they left the urban center and wandered into the less-densely populated lands where the food was grown. Debris had been pushed to the corners, ready for pickup, though that didn't run on any regular schedule. Along with the rubbish, there were also piles of broken brick and other scraps, ready to be repurposed for new projects. Water collected around these piles, as the streets were not properly irrigated to handle the rising water table.

Dade stopped at the edge of the electric fields. The power-wired fences were necessary to keep gleaners out. Food was too precious a resource, kept under surveillance. Beyond the fence grew hybrid corn, the stalks a greenish blue from the soil's minerals. The sun-strobes over the fields were turned off at this hour. He stepped to the barrier and reached forward as if about to reach through the fencing to touch the plant.

"Don't." She stopped his hand. "The amount of voltage running through the fence will knock you out for days, if you're lucky enough to survive."

Even the Lasair didn't steal food. The risk/reward ratio wasn't worth it. It was easier to buy food with drug money, coupled with black market Govie Buy Certificates, than to take it by force.

Dade put his hand down, still looking at the corn. "I only wanted to touch it. To see how different it felt from houseplants."

"Undercity uses less than five percent of this. We live on meta-grains generally. That and fiber bars."

Dade made a face.

Arden laughed. "Agreed, they're nasty."

He tipped his head, staring at her, and then asked, "Do you ever think about the Old Planet? What it must have been like to plant something and watch it grow without much help other than a little irrigation?"

Arden scrunched her nose. "I can't say that I have."

"It has to be better than living like this." He made a gesture to the fields. "You live next to the sunfields, and yet you can't eat the food that's grown here."

She became frustrated that he made a point of it. Maybe he was too privileged to understand that there was nothing she could do about it. "What are you suggesting? That I return to the Old Planet? If I even had the credits to leave this planet, I'd first have to find a spaceship heading in that direction, which you know would be impossible. And if I managed that, I'd be middle-aged by the time I got there. I'm not spending half my life in the belly of a ship. No, thank you."

"I wasn't saying you should go there. I only wondered if you thought about what it might be like to live in a world where anyone could grow food if they wanted to."

"I don't have time for playing the 'what if' game," she said, exasperated. "I spend too much time trying to survive."

He stared her down, unblinking, as if in the truth of what she said, she'd missed something important. "Just because I was born privileged doesn't mean I don't care."

She rolled her eyes and let out a laughing huff. "Spoken like a Solizen. I suppose you do charity work too."

He gave her a small enigmatic grin. "I do."

Like she believed that.

"Who says that the Old Planet would be any better?" Arden asked. "It's likely no one survived the last World War anyway. Our ancestors were probably lucky enough to colonize before they were exterminated. I'm not sure that if given the opportunity, I'd choose to go back."

They'd had food problems on the Old Planet too. The planet had been stripped of its natural resources, which had led to corporations' sending mining colonies into space to find what they needed and bring it back. Only, this city hadn't sent a shipment to the Old Planet in more than a hundred years. No one had ever cried foul. At this point, it was unlikely that they'd find anyone still inhabiting the Old Planet.

They used an old, decrepit bridge that connected the sunfields to the abandoned mines, crossing over a small river. She showed him where to avoid the crumbling sections. Beneath the bridge, the current flowed swiftly. The rising groundwater in the area had resulted in the need for several man-made lakes to divert the overflow from the city. There was a slight mineral odor to the water.

The mines weren't used anymore. They hadn't been since the Levels had been constructed some fifty years past. Precious metals that had once lined the tunnels were now gone. The silt and rock had long been carted off and used for concrete and brick. Many of the old mines were so unstable, they could cave in at any second. Most were blocked off, while others were located so far from the city, they were assumed not to be a risk for curious thrill seekers.

"Are you going to be in danger from bringing me here tonight?" Dade asked, picking his way along the edge of the bridge.

Arden shrugged. "I'm always in danger."

"If they find out I'm with you, it's a death sentence, isn't it?" he pressed, showing a great depth of understanding about the position she'd placed herself in.

"Yes." She didn't know if he meant the Lasair, or the govies, or even the Solizen, but all the answers were yes. "I don't regret helping you."

"This has been an experience of a lifetime. Thank you."

"You're welcome." The frustration she'd felt earlier had melted away. In a strange way, he understood and he cared. That knowledge left her feeling lighthearted.

Their destination was one of the original five entries to the Levels before Undercity had been closed off. It was located in an abandoned way station directly under the Sky Towers. Once the station was built, it quickly became apparent that this wasn't the best location due to frequent flooding. Which also meant that because of the danger, the Lasair used it only in emergencies.

She pushed against the door, the lock long gone. The casing was swollen, detaching from the rock walls and emitting a groan as it opened. The crumbling station felt like a ghost town, its roof mostly gone, giving a direct view to the Undercity dome. Inside, it was still filled with old seats and dead ticket machines, and behind the guest counter, transportation route information.

The quadralift to the next Levels had been taken out and the holes blocked. But the maintenance ladders were still there.

"This is not good," she said, shining her glo-wand around. Water pooled deep on the ground. Used tickets, maps, and other memorabilia floated in the water. The water level was higher than it had ever been this time of year. "It looks like we're about a half hour from flooding. The bridge will be unusable at that point. We'd better hurry if I have any hope of getting home tonight."

Dade frowned. "What if you don't get back across in time?"

"If I get stuck, I'll just go topside. There's another route that will take me home. I prefer not to use it, though. It's not safe for me to travel alone in Above at night." She shrugged. "Don't worry about me. I'll figure it out. I always do."

He pressed up close behind her. His hand came up to brace her waist, pulling her into him. Then he whispered into her ear, his breath heavy and warm, "I want to worry about you."

Arden leaned back for one weak moment, her body shivering. Enjoying that sense of comfort that she wasn't allowed often, if ever. Then she quickly pulled herself together. Stupid, stupid, stupid. She couldn't afford to lose track of what this was.

A moment in time that wasn't real.

Instead of staying there, she took a huge step forward, putting room between them. "Stay away from the walls—they aren't stable."

He followed her in the dark. She heard the splashing of his boots in the water and thought he'd let the moment go. And then.

"Why do you keep pulling away?" he asked. His words echoed, surrounding her in the shadows.

She could lie. Laugh it off. But even as she thought that, she knew that the only way to deal with this situation was to face it with the truth. "Because you confuse me." She kept walking. Refusing to stop to discuss this. "I don't trust you. Or . . ." She paused, thinking. "I *shouldn't* trust you. But that's pretty much the same thing."

"You keep saying that. And yet, here I am."

"Here you are," Arden agreed, sighing. She shook her head, pressing her lips together.

"You feel something for me," he said in a way that told her he already knew the answer and was determined to get her to say it out loud.

Why was he pushing this? She didn't understand him. "I'm intrigued is all. You're a series of contradictions."

"Meaning?"

"First off, don't you have a fiancée?" She stopped walking and focused the light in his face so that she could see him lie, as she suspected he would. "Why are you trying to pursue this thing between us if you're already promised to another?"

Dade's head tilted to the side. A wrinkle appeared in the center of his brow. "Yes, I have a fiancée?"

"Is that a question?" The absurdity of the situation made her laugh.

"I mean, yes. *Yes*, I do." He paused. "Sort of. But not really."

"It's either yes or no."

Dade shook his head. "Not with my life it isn't."

Arden huffed, turning back around and walking. "Just say what you mean."

"Her name is Clarissa." He paused, perhaps waiting for her to match the name with the face. But she drew a blank. Following current Solizen gossip was Colin's strong suit. "Our parents want to join our families together. Politically it makes sense in such an unstable climate."

Then he added as an afterthought, "It's a solid plan, even if it won't play out the way my father expects it to."

"If you're engaged, why are you flirting with me?" It was too easy to become infatuated with him. She constantly had to remind herself that he was spoken for.

"Because the engagement isn't real," he said. "It's political, like I said. Plus, the wedding hasn't happened, and if I have my way, it won't."

"Which means that you still have a fiancée and that you still intend on getting married."

Dade's expression clouded. It was the most frustration she'd seen from him all day. "You act like I have a choice. Don't pretend your life is so different."

"I've never been engaged to anyone," she scoffed.

"No, but you've done things you didn't want to do because you had to, because your family required you to. It's no different."

He was right. She'd done lots of things for her family that she'd regretted. And was still doing because they were required of her. But those things didn't involve crushing her heart, like Dade getting married to someone else after she committed herself to him. That would destroy her.

"Did you fight it?" she asked, realizing that the question gave away how she felt.

"My agreement wasn't required." He didn't seem fazed by that.

His reaction grated Arden. If he hadn't fought, at some level he must consider the marriage inevitable. Even though he sounded confident that he could end the engagement. He was a bad gamble. She could never date someone who was promised to another. And then she nearly kicked herself for thinking about dating him in the first place. The thought was preposterous.

Before today, she would have said Dade had everything, but perhaps he didn't. She considered his life in a way that she hadn't before. He lived in the Sky Towers. Saw the sun every day. Felt its rays on his skin. He didn't have to worry about food or the cost of life. And yet, he'd never have a life that was his own. His family had owned him from the moment he was born.

Like her life, but different.

Both equally sad.

Perhaps she had to readjust her thinking. Not all Solizen were bad, just as not all Lasair were good. No one was 100 percent either way. Not even her.

Yet she still pressed on with her questions. "If you can't find a way out of it, are you going to cave? Will you show up at the church and promise vows in front of God and everybody because there wasn't another option?"

"No." Dade stopped walking. The slip-slip of his shoes squelching in the water had quieted.

It forced her to stop as well. She turned to face him, keeping the light focused on the ground in front of him so she could see his face without blinding him.

He looked at her as if trying to read her expression. Something indefinable changed between them in that moment. Though she couldn't put into words what that was, Arden felt it. Knew that it was there as inevitably as she counted on her next breath.

"If it comes to that," he said, "I'll have to make other decisions. I promise you on my life, I will not marry Clarissa."

Arden swallowed and nodded.

He continued, his voice strong and confident. "I don't want that life."

Her heart caught somewhere near her throat. She had trouble speaking past the lump. "What is it that you do want, Dade? I've been trying to figure that out since I met you."

"I want you," he said.

Her heart started beating erratically. The air left her chest. Still, she denied it. "You've only just met me."

"That doesn't change how I feel."

Arden knew he was right, because it didn't change the way she felt either. He didn't fit into her life, and yet he felt as if he belonged there. She bit her lip, not knowing what to say.

"For the first time in my life, I want to be selfish," he said. "If that forces me to go against my family, well, that's what will happen."

That sentiment made her carefully consider what their outcome would be. She felt the same way. Yet being selfish led to danger. If she knew anything in life, she knew this.

Because of this, and in spite of how she felt toward Dade, she needed to stop what was growing between them. The box that she'd forced her thoughts of Dade into was getting horribly out of shape. Best to shove everything back inside and tape it up as best she could. It wasn't what she wanted, of course. But sometimes it was necessary to do things that might hurt in order to get the best outcome.

"There can't be a 'you and I,'" she said.

He stepped forward to take her hand in his. "There already is."

His touch made her thoughts fly. His hand was firm and warm, giving her comfort and making her believe that they could overcome the obstacles their families presented. But she fought against that, half dying inside. Insisting, "We have people we care for. I won't put mine in danger with my decisions." Arden studied him, hating each word that left her mouth and wondering whether they hit their mark. "It's unfair to them."

The sentiment was just as much for him as it was for her. She pleaded with herself to take her own advice. She wanted him. She wanted to throw everything away and chase these feelings.

"It's unfair to us," he insisted.

"We can't see each other again. You can't come looking for me. We're done, you and I. I'm no more than a fleeting moment that passed through your life." She pulled her hand from his, gripping it at her side. "You are never again to put yourself in danger to find me."

"You are so much more than a moment," he said.

She wanted to shake him. She had to get him to understand, even if that meant that she pretended not to care, even if she risked hurting him. And in the process, she must cut her own growing feelings. She turned and started to walk once more. "We're almost there."

Then she would say goodbye. Forever.

Conflicted feelings bubbled inside her as they stepped the last few feet to the entrance.

She keyed in a code on the entry pad and opened the door to the bottom of the ladder, then turned to him. The knowledge of the risk she'd put her family in came fast and furious. She felt frustrated at herself for allowing him such power over her, when he was so clearly the wrong choice for her life. It made her lash out with an icy voice. "If you ever tell anyone about our ability to move through the bolt-holes, I'll kill you."

"Again with the death threats," he joked. But then he added seriously, "I would never betray you. I hope that someday you'll believe that."

He seemed to take this whole conversation, and her, in stride.

It left Arden feeling unsettled. Why, when she'd said everything she should say, did she feel as if a knife twisted inside her? Why did it feel wrong, like dust in her mouth? This time with him, hidden away from the real world, should last longer, so she'd be able to tuck away every second into the corner of her mind to remember for later. But it couldn't last forever. This thing between them needed to end now.

Arden reached out to grip a rung on the ladder. "This is it. Hand on the ladder."

She waited for him to comply before tucking her glo-wand away, plunging the room into darkness. Then she began her climb, hearing the clacking of his boots on the rungs beneath her.

Before long, they reached the hatch, the dim red light of the switch-box serving as a warning not to smash her head. She felt along the surface for the control pad. With a few twists and a series of numbers, the hatch opened above her.

They exited into an alley adjacent to the Tower quadralifts. The policing in this sector was high because of the vulnerability to the Sky Towers. After the first one had been blown up, they didn't take any chances. So there wasn't anyone loitering on the street. It also meant that she had only a small window of time to disappear again.

Arden climbed out, stepping aside for Dade. She kept the door open next to them.

"The quadralifts to the Levels are just there." She pointed. "Don't go straight into them. There's a stairway here." She indicated the unmarked door they stood in front of. "Take the stairs to Level Two, then grab the lift from there. Leave your blackout bracelet on until you're in front of the quadralift doors."

Dade nodded in acknowledgment.

She didn't know what to say then. Words had dried up in her mouth. She turned back to the hatch to leave.

Dade reached out and grabbed her arm, stopping her. "I won't let you push me away. I want to see you again."

It scared her that she wanted that too. Scared her that they might not ever have this again. "Why?"

He frowned. "If you have to ask that, then you don't feel that unexplainable something that exists between us. It just means I'll have to try harder and wait until you do."

Her heart melted. She did feel the connection, which was the problem. It was ridiculous, though, that a feeling this powerful could happen so fast. Plus, the logistics would never work. He didn't understand how perilous it was for a sky boy to come to the areas she frequented. "You can't."

He pulled her close. His mouth inches from hers. His other hand sliding up to cup her shoulders between his hands. "If that is really what you want, then I won't go looking for you." He said it in a way that demonstrated that he clearly didn't share the same opinion. "But you must agree that if you change your mind, you will come to me. I want to see you again. You must know that."

He reached up to slide his fingers along her cheek. "I don't want to let you go. Not now that I've found you."

She wouldn't promise him. No, she *couldn't* promise him. But she couldn't deny him either.

He leaned forward, pressing his mouth to hers. And then they were kissing as if they needed each other to complete their next breath. It was raw, and needy, and hot.

Arden pulled back, gasping.

"This isn't goodbye," he said, stepping away.

She watched as he slipped inside the door and out of her sight.

# Chapter Ten

Arden's unit was near the top of the housing wall. A sea of doors, all mismatched, poor lighting, and the crumbling exterior made the apartment block look haunted. What the structure had been prior was no longer discernible. Brick extensions had been added between previous buildings, grouping what had been separate structures into one long wall that spanned several blocks. The streets had been domed for travel, with housing above creating cutouts where the walkways intersected.

Precarious stairwells dotted the structure. Some only accessed floors near the bottom, while others extended higher, bypassing the floors beneath. Inside the units, the floor plans didn't make sense, and the walls were too thin to stop neighbors from overhearing.

Inside her family's home, several shadows moved behind the murky glass. Their images were distorted like grotesque marionettes, illuminated by the dim glow of lights. It wasn't unusual to have visitors at this time of the morning. The Lasair members often used her house as a gathering place. It was a central location, directly in the middle of their town, but, more important, it had quick access to the outer spokes of the city where they could use the bolt-holes for the majority of their jobs.

Arden wasn't up for visitors, especially during the twilight hours of the morning. Not when she felt this unsettled. The pieces of armor she usually hid behind had cracked, leaving her feeling exposed and vulnerable. It worried her. All she knew was that she didn't want to face anyone before she could come to terms with what it meant.

Dade's kiss had shaken her to the core. Even though she still felt its high and the ghost of his lips on hers. The walk home hadn't cooled that any. Its memory made it harder to resist seeing him again. Already she wavered.

She firmed her resolve for the fifth or sixth time since she'd left him. She would not be swayed. That was it. She'd never see him again.

Pausing before the warped front door, she took a deep, calming breath to center herself. She lowered the hood of her cloak and straightened her shoulders, and then she pushed her way inside.

The minute she walked in, Arden knew something was very, very wrong.

Colin sat hunched forward on the edge of the faded orange couch. His head was bowed, resting on his fisted hand. What caught her attention was not his body wound taut, but rather the blood splattered across him. It dotted his clothes, a large swath over his middle. Long streaks had dried down his arms, and matted in clumps in his hair.

Arden's heart lurched. Followed by a pounding, pushing pressure on her ears. She found it hard to swallow. Colin hurt was her worst nightmare.

Then she realized little things. The blood didn't start from any specific place on his body. And he didn't appear injured. She was moderately reassured the damage wasn't his.

She exhaled.

Knowing that he wasn't in imminent danger of bleeding to death eased her anxiety. The pounding in her head lessened, and she was able to draw a full breath for the first time since she'd stepped into the room. It calmed her enough to absorb the rest of the scene.

Uri paced the living room. His path wound him in and out of the rickety furniture. He ran his hands repeatedly through his hair, making it stand on end. His face was drawn and haggard, and his skin was more translucent than it had ever been. She could see the blue veins running down his arms as he gripped and regripped his fists.

His body vibrated with suppressed rage. While he walked, he mumbled under his breath. And then he swung his fist out, connecting with the wall. He screamed at the same time, a heartbroken wail of a sound. Plaster fell where his fist connected. When he pulled his fist away, it was covered with blood.

"Uri?" Arden asked, not sure what she should say. Worrying that he'd crushed his hand, she shut the door and took a few steps into the room. She stopped short before she got close to him.

When he turned, she saw that his nose sat at a funny angle, dried blood underneath. His eyes were wild. Uri, who was always in control, always the bedrock of calm and unfailing strength, was gone. That scared her more than anything.

Arden swallowed. She'd missed whatever awful thing had happened. She'd been off traipsing around, kissing Dade, when she should have been with her family. Truthfully, she felt afraid to find out what had caused this panic. Because she knew it would change things. Reset her life back to where it had been. Just like she knew would happen if she let herself get sidetracked by a pretty face.

Where was Niall? Whatever errand he'd been on tonight should have long been over. Unless he had gotten caught in a raid. Confusion and fear over what that might mean sizzled up her spine.

Arden's mother shuffled into the room. She looked tiny and frail, her skin parchment thin. She'd lost most of her hair due to malnutrition and neglect. What was left of it hung in a stringy, uncombed cloud. She'd given up on life a long time ago. All Arden remembered was growing up with a mom who was just this side of a zombie.

Mostly, Arden attempted to reason through why her mother was broken. Sometimes she grew angry with her for it. She hated her mom for giving up, for not having the strength of character to face each day and fight back. Then she became ashamed of those harsh feelings.

Creating a circle of frustration from which she couldn't escape. Because of that, she tried never to let these thoughts bubble up anymore, though they did, and to accept that people weren't as driven as she was.

Her mom held a tea tray, with chipped and mismatched teacups. She set it on the tiny table in front of the sofa. Then she stood up, wringing her hands. "We're out of chamomile. I didn't know what to do." Her gaze darted around the room, never settling on anything. She didn't seem to notice that Arden had come home.

The boys didn't pay any attention to her either.

Uri stopped his pacing. His hand came up to his nose. With a crack, he snapped it back into place. Then resumed walking. The tissue around his nose appeared puffy. When the swelling went down, it wouldn't heal well. Not that it mattered. Uri had broken it several times before, so it hadn't been straight for years.

Colin continued to stare at the floor. Arden wished he'd look up so that she could figure out what was going on.

Her mother nervously went about pouring, her hand shaking as she tipped the spout, spilling more liquid outside the cup than inside. Her erratic behavior appeared more flighty than usual, indicating the onset of a breakdown.

"Um, I didn't know what to do. I heated the water. And I . . ." She blinked twice.

It was then Arden realized there was no tea at all. Just hot water, the liquid clear where it pooled in running puddles on the table. Her mother continued to pour despite the mess she made.

Arden jumped forward to stop her mother from emptying the teapot's entire contents onto the table. She placed her hands over her mother's, easing her back. "It's okay, Mom. I got it."

In the back of the house, her dad started hacking, a rough cough followed by a wet sound Arden knew was blood. She didn't need to see it to know what was happening. The same thing played out each night, only growing worse with time.

Her mother reacted to her father's cough with a small jump. She twiddled around, glancing to the back room, before turning again to Arden. Confusion clouded her eyes.

"I'll figure something out," she promised her mother. Not knowing herself if she meant the tea, or her father, or the situation between the two boys. "Why don't you take care of Dad?"

"Right." Her mom nodded absently. "I'll just . . ." She looked to the back room from where more hacking coughs emanated. "I'll see what your dad needs."

Her dad had suffered in the mines. He'd worked for years digging belowground, toiling as a mine rat. All he had to show for it was the mine cough. Then he'd started to display the more horrific symptoms of Violet Death, which had only morphed into an addiction to Shine that he'd developed in order to ease his suffering. He was now little more than bedridden. The symptoms were exacerbated by lack of vitamin D. He was too sick to visit the sunbeds. And the government had labeled him beyond help. Which meant that they'd no longer authorize the sale of VitD to him.

Her mother wasn't much better. The stress of caring for her husband along with her own use of Shine left her in a perpetual fog. Neither one asked where she and Niall acquired the drugs they brought home. Arden doubted either parent knew they were affiliated with a gang. They were completely unaware of her illegal enterprises. If they were asked, they'd say Arden participated in all the after-school activities.

Nothing could have been further from the truth.

She didn't feel guilt over this deception. It was easiest if her parents didn't get involved. If she were caught or her parents were grilled for information, the less they knew the better. It might even keep them alive for the little time they had left.

It also allowed the Lasair to hold meetings in their house. Her parents never asked about them. Like now, with two highly agitated men in her living room, no one questioned the oddness of this.

"What happened?" she asked.

Colin looked up, his eyes bloodshot. He opened his mouth, shut it, and then shook his head. Looking down again.

"They took Mariah," Uri shouted, hitting another hole in the wall.

"Stop," Colin said, sounding defeated. "Breaking your hand is not going to save her."

Arden knew she wouldn't get answers from Uri. He was too far gone in his crazy headspace. Instead, she concentrated on Colin. Arden sat next to him, getting him to look straight at her. "Start from the beginning."

Colin licked his lips. "We were on the far side of the club, opposite from the bolt-hole."

Arden nodded, not saying aloud that she'd made it to the bolt-hole with Dade, so she already knew that hadn't been their path of escape.

"Our best option was to blend with the crowd. We were almost out, but they . . ." He scrunched his brow, shaking his head. "They were expecting us. They knew who we were. They had intel on us, or our masks, or something."

That wasn't good. It meant that every member of Lasair had to change his persona and be more vigilant. That they'd even been marked showed a clear lack of security on their part.

"The govies let the others run by and focused on us. We fought." Colin shrugged. "I'm not sure what happened. Uri and I were in the middle of kicking some ass when I was distracted by a scream. I looked up and—"

Uri cut in, yelling, "They took Mariah."

The blood made sense now.

Arden's dad coughed in the background, breaking the tension of the moment. It was a reminder that they all needed to hold it together.

Colin cleared his throat. "Uri went after her. But there were too many of them. It was suicide." He shook his head. "I grabbed Uri, held him back, and we were able to fight our way out."

"I could have gotten to her," Uri said, turning his rage on Colin and leaning down aggressively. For a moment, Arden thought he'd lose it and take a swing at Colin.

Colin didn't help the situation. He stood, getting right up in Uri's face, and raised his voice. "No, you couldn't. We can't rescue two of you."

"Keep it down," Arden hissed. She didn't need to deal with two testosterone-challenged jerks coming to blows in her living room. Let alone drawing the attention of her mother. It would take more of Arden's energy to get her mother refocused and out of the way again.

This was her fault. If she had been with them, perhaps she could have helped Mariah. Yes, Mariah had been trained to fight as they all had, but sometimes backup helped. Yet instead of fighting with her family, she had been with Dade.

Worse, she'd taken him into Undercity.

Her head needed to get in this game pretty quick before they lost anyone else. Her self-flagellation helped clear her indecision and harden her resolve, if not her heart.

"Where's my brother?" Arden asked, her worry clear.

Colin shrugged. "I don't know."

Arden pulled out her datapad and sent a quick ping. The reply came almost immediately.

"He's on his way," she said, and exhaled. "Another few minutes."

She didn't put into words the rushing relief she felt that her brother was okay. Instead, she cleaned up the mess her mother had made and then went into the kitchen to make fresh tea. There was nothing more to do while they waited. If she didn't do something with her hands, she'd go crazy.

The tea took little time to boil and steep. Arden set the tray down on the coffee table, sat next to Colin, and poured herself a cup, again at a loss for what to do.

Colin whispered so Uri couldn't hear. "This shit is only getting worse."

"I know."

"If the govies turn up the heat, then Niall is only going to get more aggressive about his insane plan."

Arden nodded.

"If you leave, I'll go with you," he said. There was a plea in his voice that hit her in the gut.

Arden watched Uri continue to pace. She considered Colin's offer for half a second. Then guilt and family solidarity kicked in. "I can't." She hated herself for saying it. "You know we can't."

Colin frowned but nodded, not looking her in the eye.

The front door opened, and Niall walked in with Kimber. His entrance was loud and clunky, and he didn't look happy. They both appeared a bit strung out, their eyes glassy, pupils blown. Niall took in the room at a glance. Then he walked over and set down a smallish package on the coffee table. Arden knew that if she looked inside, she'd see at least thirty disks of Shine.

Her parents' drug use had spiraled in the last few months. Where once a box this size would last her parents a month or more, now it wasn't lasting the week.

Instead of being relieved that Niall had arrived, Arden found that her anxiety grew. With the way he looked, this could get ugly. Niall wasn't known for his gentleness and understanding.

She set down her mug. Pushing her shoulders back, she steeled herself for a fight. She'd faced worse.

Niall pulled out his datapad, turning it so they could see the screen, and pressed "Play" on a news-vid from Club Doom. There was smoke from the percussion bombs and chaos everywhere. Lines of govies stood shoulder to shoulder outside of the building in their govie-greens and riot gear, clear shields in front of them, stun-sticks at the ready.

Watching the scene made Uri go crazy again, his muttering louder now. He didn't seem to be paying attention to any of them. He kept hitting things. His knuckles now raw pieces of meat, splattering blood on the furniture.

Niall focused on Arden and Colin. Colin's anger at Uri had long fizzled out, replaced by an ache that felt palpable.

"How much did you mess up?" Niall asked. He directed the question to both of them, but she knew he was really asking her.

Arden wanted to argue that the raid couldn't possibly be their fault. She bit that back, though. She had been in charge of the op. And she should have been paying better attention. She'd failed her team. She deserved to be reamed out, or worse. Her performance was unforgivable.

Out with it. Pull it off like a quick-seal.

"The govies took Mariah," she said.

Niall's jaw bulged back and forth as he ground his teeth. He narrowed his eyes at Arden, saying to her, "I left you in charge."

She felt every bit of the weight of the criticism. The words hit like phasefire to the dead center of her heart. Her breath stuttered, and she lowered her eyes, not knowing what to say. Whatever she said would be an excuse.

"Did you see her taken?"

And there was the crux.

Arden shook her head, looking at him. "I wasn't there. Uri and Colin were surrounded."

Kimber made a noise that sounded like a disbelieving snort.

As much as she felt guilty, that angered Arden. Who was Kimber to pass judgment? She narrowed her eyes at the other girl, silently daring her to speak, or better yet, to say something later when they were alone.

"It's not Arden's fault," Colin said. "You know how it is in the clubs. We're not always together."

Niall frowned, neither forcing the issue nor letting Arden off the hook. "If Mariah has been taken, we have a limited window before they transfer her outbound."

If that happened, they'd never have the opportunity to save her. She'd be lost to them. Arden didn't want to imagine the torture they'd inflict on Mariah. It was better to focus on what they could do at this moment than the "what ifs" if they failed.

Kimber cleared her throat. "Staging a rescue would jeopardize our plans for the next shipment. We can't do that."

Uri growled, throwing a lamp. It smashed against the far wall. Arden didn't flinch, knowing the projectile wouldn't hit her. Still, it set her heart to racing.

"We have to think in terms of survival," Kimber pressed on, seemingly unconcerned with Uri's outburst and not even reacting to any of the animosity Colin and Arden were throwing her way. "We can't sacrifice everything for one person. Mariah knew the risks. She shouldn't have allowed herself to get caught."

Uri redirected his rage at Kimber. If he looked scary before, now he looked downright lethal. He took several steps toward her before Colin stood up to stop him. Niall stepped in to shield her as well, blocking her from Uri's line of sight.

Arden feared they wouldn't have much usable furniture left if this kept up. Or that Kimber would be choked, but that wouldn't be too bad. She deserved it. Still, they needed to get this conversation back on track.

"I'm going to rescue Mariah," she announced. It was, after all, her fault.

"I'm with you," Colin said, glaring daggers at Kimber.

Arden wasn't surprised by Colin's easy willingness to throw himself into danger alongside her. She was grateful even. Though that only increased the pressure to make this work. Or else she'd feel even worse.

Kimber huffed and flicked her hair. "I'm just saying, we need to look at this logically. How are we going to rescue her so close to the next heist? We don't have the manpower, for one. And an operation that size takes time to plan."

"I don't care about that." Uri turned to them, eyes blazing. "I want Mariah."

"We know," Niall said. He made no effort to falsely sooth Uri. "It's your op. How do you want to run this?"

Uri seethed. "We need to go in there with our phasers and take the bastards out. Mariah is all that matters."

"I said I'd get her," Arden said, standing and squaring off against the group. "That makes this my op." She turned to Uri. "Get a grip on yourself. If I can't trust that you'll maintain control, I can't trust you to have my back. And I will not put myself in danger because you can't focus."

That seemed to be the shot of cold water Uri needed. He finally backed down, his shoulders slumping. He blew a breath and ran a hand through his hair. "Sorry."

Arden walked over and placed her hand on Uri's back. "We'll rescue Mariah. I promise. We just need to figure out how."

# CHAPTER ELEVEN

Kids surrounded Dade as he sat cross-legged on the floor with his Ghost mask still in place. Their hands reached forward to touch him, dipping into his pockets to steal pieces of candy he kept there for that reason. They thought they were sneaky. They'd grin and laugh, hiding their prizes away to eat later.

He tried to make time to spend with them after he dropped off packages of stolen VitD. It was the best part of the job as far as he was concerned. The staff didn't mind that he lingered or that he kept his mask on. They allowed his visits while making sure the vid-feeds were turned off.

These kids were in flux status, refugees without parents. All were suffering from various stages of Violet Death, their skin marked with traces of the disease. They had been either trafficked from other cities or sometimes turned out by parents when they couldn't offer support. Because they hadn't had their data sensors implanted yet, it was impossible to match them back up with their families, and even more important, issue life-saving drugs. So they came to this clinic that helped abandoned kids who would die without his donations.

He always felt sad when he visited. While he enjoyed every second with the children, their situation made him desperate for change. The sadness inevitably turned to frustration and anger before he left.

What he did would never be enough. There'd always be more kids, and there would always be other facilities he couldn't support. His efforts were a drop in the bucket compared to the complexity of the problem. The tiny ripples he made didn't extend very far.

The thought made him frown, and he forced himself to stop and instead offer a grin to the precocious two-year-old who'd pushed her way into his lap. Her chubby hands grabbing his cheeks just under the edge of his mask, sending a sizzle of nanotech feedback to tickle his skin.

His comm link buzzed in his pocket. Dade fished it out, flicking his finger over the bio-scanner to pull up the ziptext.

*I need Shine,* Saben's ping read. *Will send location.*

Dade read it twice, thinking he'd misunderstood. He wondered why Saben had ziptexted in the first place when using an electronic trail was too risky. The nervous energy that bothered him all morning came roaring back. Everything had been off since they'd parted ways.

They'd planned to deliver supplies together, but at the last second, Saben had gotten a ping, and then claimed personal business and bailed. Which had never happened before. Usually, Saben stayed within the radius of providing assistance whenever Dade was on a job.

Dade had gone anyway, unable to delay his delivery. It hadn't been all that complicated to sneak out of the Tower alone. He timed his departure with the rotation of the guards and shuffled around some vid-feeds.

It hadn't stopped him from worrying about Saben, though. And now a ziptext on top of it? Whatever he had to take care of must be something important enough for him to resort to monitored communication channels. Added to that, Saben had requested Shine. That made Dade's instincts jump. Shine would be harder to come by than VitD. It wasn't Dade's usual trade, nor did he partake in getting high. He didn't have the kind of connections that could score him any. That meant to get a hit, he'd have to troll the streets for a dealer.

He pushed back all of his questions. They'd be answered soon enough. Hopefully. At least he was still in his Ghost disguise. If he got caught buying Shine on the city cams, it would be less incriminating.

*It might take some time,* Dade typed. He wasn't sure how successful he'd be at finding a dealer, much less convincing them to sell to a masked stranger.

Saben pinged back his coordinates. For the second time Dade was thrown off. What was Saben doing at the Center Clinic?

Dade left the dispensary amid disappointed cries from the children. They clung, but he extricated himself with a promise to try to visit the following week, careful not to give a specific day or time.

On the street, he looked for the darkest corners where the dealers hung out. Buying Shine made him think of Arden and the likelihood of seeing her again. Maybe he could figure out where she'd be and at least catch a glimpse of her. No, he had to wait for her to come to him. He'd promised that he wouldn't seek her out. It was the best course of action. One he wouldn't waver from, even though the temptation to see her again was almost too much. Arden would show up in the most unlikely places, he was sure of it.

It took a while before he scored. Turned out that no one trusted a man in a mask unless he was giving things away. Then he slipped into an area that he knew was a dead zone for the city cameras, so he could take off his mask and hood and cover anything that could be linked back to the Ghost. He kept his blackout band strapped to his wrist. To remove it would ping an alert of his location to his father on his scanners.

Dade checked the coordinates on his datapad to make sure he was headed in the right direction. He'd visited the Center Clinic only three times, and each time he'd accompanied his father. He felt vulnerable not only going to the Center as himself, which was a huge gamble, but also carrying Shine on his person.

The Center Clinic was a public hospital, so there was no reason for him to visit other than for shows of goodwill made by Croix Industries. Dade knew he would attract attention. He was always on the gossip-vids. His face a little too famous to pull off something like this. He'd be picked up on the security cams, and if questioned, he'd offer clunky excuses for his presence.

He liked a challenge, though. Besides, he owed Saben. Employee or not, he was first and foremost Dade's friend, trusted with unquestioned loyalty. Which again made Dade wonder at the nature of Saben's emergency.

The Center Clinic was located in an older area of the city, in the business district of Level Five. Rooms and offices had been built between existing buildings as the city fought to grow upward. This close to the city center, everything became congested and bottlenecked, the skywalks busy with pedestrians making their way home from school or work.

At the entrance, Dade paused, tipping his head to avoid the facial monitors. There were several govies at the door, their hands rested on the stun-sticks strapped to their sides. They looked into the faces of the visitors threateningly, not being subtle about it. Even if he hadn't been aware of his father's plan, he would have noticed their numbers increasing.

Groups of people jostled their way inside the lobby, seeming not to care about the scrutiny they received. Dade placed himself between several smaller groups entering the building, keeping his head down and walking as fast as he could without attracting attention.

Once inside, he split off from the groups, keeping his head turned and looking at the floor. Dade walked right past the reception desk and the mobbing visitors who distracted the employees' attention. No one noticed him or asked him to stop, so Dade kept walking.

The Center was split into several wings. Most of the visitors headed toward the public wing where the sunbeds were located. There, long lines of people waited to get their weekly allotted time with the only UV contact they'd ever feel on their bodies. Even then, it wouldn't be enough to keep their bodies producing vitamin D without help. It was just enough to slow their descent to death.

There were other corridors where people waited for news of their loved one's passing, and others for outpatient treatments or surgeries. He didn't look at the strangers as they cried softly or stared at the blank walls with glazed eyes.

It frustrated him that those who had power, who had the ability to change lives, refused to do so. Tech had never been the problem. They had the resources to figure it out. Their ancestors had arrived with a deep knowledge of space and the human body's reactions to various stimuli. The original scientists who'd helped terraform the planet were the leaders in their field. After all, the Old Planet was decades from the planet they inhabited now, and they'd managed to travel the entire distance without too many hiccups.

Over the generations, though, reliance on the scientists had shifted. Scientists who were so valuable in the beginning to set up the planet to sustain life, who created VitD as a stopgap to a better cure, now worked for the Solizen, barely earning enough Govie Buy Certificates to purchase food.

Dade headed for the long-term care patients. The ones who weren't going to make it but had enough money to go comfortably and not die on the streets. Death surrounded him. The farther he walked into the depths of the Center, the clearer he felt its presence. Its touch punctuated by wails of agony from those who suffered from Violet Death, seeking relief of the blessed dark that would come with the last coma state. There were fewer visitors here as he passed room after room of sick people. Nurses dressed in white silently roamed the wards, trying to make the patients comfortable.

He took the internal quadralift, then walked through a corridor leading to Saben's coordinates. The room was long and narrow, and rows of beds ran the length of either side. There was no color, everything white except for the silver of the machines that made low beeping noises.

There were no nurses here. The only other person in the room besides the patients was Saben. He sat hunched over a bedside with his back to the door. He held the hand of a dying boy as he whispered things Dade couldn't hear.

Dade walked closer. The soles of his boots squeaked against the shiny tiles. He felt out of place, intruding on a moment that was clearly meaningful to Saben. It made his steps hesitant, and he hung back until he was acknowledged. Saben would know he was there and would speak to him when he was ready.

He stood close enough now to finally get a look at the boy's face. He had almost identical features to Saben, same nose and same eye shape. He was perhaps a year or two younger than Saben, but with all the damage he'd suffered from the Violet Death, he looked much older. The boy's skin fell from his bones like syrup dripping off a spoon. Stretched too thin in places. He'd lost his hair from the medication they'd given him, his bald head making him appear frailer. Small rasping breaths rattled in his chest.

Dade hadn't known Saben had a brother, or cousin, or close relative—whoever this boy turned out to be. Saben had always been secretive about his former life, before he'd been chosen to be Dade's bodyguard. He'd said that sometimes things were meant to stay as they were and that old wounds could fester into greater things if reopened. Maybe this was what he'd meant.

The boy opened his eyes, the lids bruised deeply purple, to look at Saben. There didn't seem to be any recognition, just a blank look, like he was dead inside. Then he hacked a cough that sounded deep and wet, accompanied by a whine of pain when his body moved. Blood dotted his lips.

Saben leaned forward to wipe at them with a tissue as the boy's eyes rolled shut.

It was obvious why Saben wanted Shine. Besides the pain, there probably wasn't much time left. While the hospital tried to make the boy comfortable, perhaps the narcotic would let him slip off easier.

Dade felt as if he were intruding on an intimate moment, yet he stepped forward to hold the Shine disks out to Saben. Being here as a witness was painful. It squeezed his chest too tight. His hands shook. Adrenaline, frustration, and anger all mixed together until it became a pushing need to flee.

Saben didn't turn as he took the disk and clicked open the mouthpiece, holding it to the boy's lips. When he didn't make a move to inhale, Saben pinched his nose so the drug was choked into his mouth as he gasped for air.

Saben pulled his hands away when the dose was gone.

The boy stilled. His breathing slowed so the sheet barely moved, but there was no more coughing and no more blood.

Dade didn't know what comfort he could offer. He knew he should say something, but the words that came out weren't those he'd intended to say. "He's too far gone. The Shine is more likely to kill him rather than help."

"I know. I want him comfortable." Saben looked away from the boy to the empty Shine disk. His fingers twisted it, making it glitter in the overhead lights. "I would have brought it myself, but I didn't realize until I got here that he needed a push to the other side."

Dade nodded even though Saben couldn't see. It wasn't that he agreed, it was more that he understood. He also wouldn't be able to leave someone he loved to suffer that pain if he could help. Sometimes he even wondered if the small amount of VitD he did manage to distribute made any difference. When he saw this kind of pain, though, it firmed his resolve.

"We need to stop this," Saben said. He looked up, his eyes red rimmed and wet. "It's unfair."

"I know," Dade agreed. They couldn't change the social injustice, not really. What little they did only made a dent. But they could try.

# Chapter Twelve

Arden walked through the atrium of the skyport beside Colin. The design resembled a starburst with the atrium at the center. From there, spokes led out to the berths where the ships docked. The domed ceiling overhead, created from thousands of tiny triangular pieces of glass, used the small bit of light that was able to creep through the gray static to refract rainbows across the travelers.

She couldn't shake her tension. Her body vibrated. Meets were usually faced with a high degree of confidence, not unease in her gut that told her this didn't feel right. Mariah being taken had attached a level of alertness to her actions, keeping her ready for danger at any moment. So she couldn't tell if what she felt was based on the actual situation, or if it was lingering anxiety.

Strangers flowed around her as they made their way to assigned berths to board jumpers that would take them around the planet's surface. Flying was cost prohibitive, so passengers were usually only the elite: the Solizen and their top-paid employees. The majority of citizens never left the city zone. Not that anyone from Undercity would have the opportunity for escape, they remained locked up tight.

There were also berths that docked large transfer shuttles that connected with embargo vessels anchored in space, and smaller space pods that could travel between planets. Most citizens didn't know there were spacecraft that could carry them to other planets. There was no public access to records of any kind, so it was widely accepted that ways off the planet surface had long been shut off, or at the very least, could only be accessed through another city.

Being inside the skyport always reminded her that there were other places in the universe. Not that she'd ever be able to afford a ticket off-planet. She couldn't even afford one to city hop. Even so, when times got rough, she considered that option, thinking that maybe she could apprentice herself to traders in order to escape. Colin's pressing had reignited that line of thought.

Each brush of passengers' bodies against hers as they hurried on their way made her jump. The reaction was the complete opposite of the blending in she was supposed to do. One particular group jostled her so completely that she stopped moving, waiting for them to pass before getting her bearings back. She found herself standing still, right there in the lobby of the skyport like a target.

"Arden," Colin hissed from beside her, "walk."

The harshness of his words startled her into moving. She exhaled, telling herself to get her act together.

Her face felt hot under the synth-mask, so different from the masks they wore at the club. This one was part hologram, part tissue, and it gave Arden a different face rather than just covering it. She still kept her head down, though, letting the bobbed black wig swing forward to cover her new features and hide her eyes from retinal scanners. No matter how good the synth job was, there was potential for the cameras to get a lock on them and decode their true identity with facial recognition software.

The Lasair didn't use synths often. They were far too expensive and could easily be disrupted with an electrical current. But in cases like this, it became a necessity. Not only were they trying to stay off the govies' radar, but the traders they were meeting were untrustworthy too. They were, after all, smugglers of stolen and illegal high-level goods, which made them dangerous criminals. She was sure they weren't showing up wearing their real faces either.

Sometimes Lasair traded Shine in exchange for items that were easier to buy than to steal. This time, though, it was strictly a cash transaction. Arden and Colin should theoretically meet their contact, check the goods, and be on their way before the govies noticed that they didn't have legitimate business in the skyport.

"What is wrong with you?" Colin asked under his breath as he covertly scanned the area.

"Nothing." Everything.

Arden hated feeling this way. It wasn't the job. With Colin beside her, she'd be fine even if Kimber ran comms. It was everything else. She couldn't stop feeling her frustration over Mariah's situation, and guilt about Dade didn't do her any favors either. Thinking about him put her back on the cycle of want and exasperation that she desperately needed to end.

Normally things didn't affect her. She could be cutthroat and cold when she wanted to be. Since she'd met Dade, her world had begun to thaw, and Arden had to be ice. It was the only way to survive. She blamed him for softening her, but she blamed herself more.

Except if she worked it right, she figured she could do the two things she wanted most: to see him and to help Mariah.

"Do you see them?" Colin asked.

"No." Though it was difficult to get a good look at anyone. There were more people than normal traveling today. Add to that, the govies had doubled in number. They walked the atrium in their govie-greens, hands at the ready on phasers and stun-sticks. The entire city's security forces had been switched to high alert over the last week.

In her ear Kimber said, "Sun, Arden, get it together." Her voice was snippy, which was to be expected. It was clear she blamed Arden for Mariah's capture. Arden had thought Kimber had been difficult to deal with before. Now it was on a whole other level.

"I hate her," she said under her breath, knowing Kimber would hear her.

"She could be here with you instead of me," Colin suggested, laughing. He wiggled his eyebrows. "I'd be happy to listen in on that."

Kimber broke in. "You'd better be nice, or I'm gonna leave you without backup if anything goes down."

Arden rolled her eyes and huffed. Like she wouldn't anyway.

The situation reminded her to get rid of listening ears so that she could talk to Colin about her plan. Time was running out. If she had any hope of following through with the crazy idea she'd concocted, she needed to get Colin on board before the meet went down.

Arden looked at Colin and gestured to the comm.

He nodded, his mouth in a straight line.

"I have to use the bathroom," Arden said into the comm. "I'll be off mic." Then she clicked off her comm.

Colin raised an eyebrow and gave her a flat stare before he turned off his as well. "Why do I get the feeling you're about to ask me to do something foolish and insane?"

Arden put on her best smile, teeth and everything. "Because I am."

"What do you want?" He acted like he wasn't amused, a scowl on his face, but she could see the small quirk to his mouth.

It was enough to tell her that she had a shot. She gathered up her courage and said, "I want to break into Sky Tower Two."

Colin sputtered, "Are you crazy?"

"Maybe?" She'd already asked herself the same thing many times.

"Is seeing that siskin so important that you'd risk death? And I don't mean from the govies. If Niall catches you, he'll skin you alive."

"If you're in charge of the op, he won't find out," she said sweetly, batting her eyes. Sometimes she could sell a crazy plan as a fun joke. She hoped this would be one of those times.

Colin didn't buy it. "Why do you have this obsession with him? He's getting married, M-A-R-R-I-E-D."

"I'm not an idiot. You don't have to spell it out for me."

"Apparently I do."

Arden sniffed. "It's not an obsession."

He squinted. "Then explain it to me."

Okay, maybe it was.

"It's business," Arden said. When Colin gave her a disdainful look, she repeated, "It is."

"What 'business' could you possibly have with him? Please give me some kind of answer besides 'He's hot' or something equally as vapid."

She forced herself to relax. It wouldn't help her case if she started on the defensive. She was asking a lot from him. Treason against the Lasair was a death sentence no matter the reason. "I thought that maybe Dade could get info on where they're holding Mariah. Or perhaps he's overheard something that would be helpful. I have no other way to contact him, but if he can help us, it's worth a shot."

"Why don't you know how to contact him? Last I saw, the two of you were so close, your faces were in danger of needing surgical detachment."

Arden felt her cheeks heat, glad she hadn't told him about taking Dade into Undercity. That would be mortifying and, well, his reaction would be worse than this conversation. "I told him I didn't want to see him again."

"That's the smartest thing you've said all day," Colin said dryly.

"Are you going to help or not?" she asked.

Colin ran a distracted hand through his hair. "How do you propose to break in? The security at the Sky Towers is ridiculously tight. Which might not be a problem in normal circumstances, but with only the two of us . . ." He paused to see if she was going to offer up anyone else who'd be willing to help. When she didn't, he sighed and continued. "Going it alone presents more dangers than we could handle. Plus, where are we going to get the stuff we need to pull off a job that size?"

Arden grinned. If he was already calculating the possibilities, and probably running through the possible entry scenarios in his mind, she knew she had him. Colin would do anything for her. She appreciated that, while reminding herself that she shouldn't take advantage of it.

"Well, I'd hoped . . ." She looked around meaningfully, and then widened her eyes at him, not wanting to voice her treasonous thoughts.

"You want to steal from the shipment?" he asked. The way he said it, like he was surprised, had her laughing. It wasn't like they hadn't done all kinds of questionably immoral things before. Besides, was it really stealing if the items had been stolen in the first place? She liked to consider it more along the lines of realigning their accessories.

"It's not like they'll know any of it is missing. When we take the shipment back to the holding site, we'll just conveniently lose some stuff. No one will find out." Plus, if they stole some items, it would push back Niall's timeline for proceeding with Project Blackout. Maybe it would buy her the time to come up with another solution while he scrambled to replace the items she took.

Colin looked like he'd sucked something sour. "You don't need me to help you so much as you need me to keep you from getting yourself killed."

She nodded, smiling. "Exactly."

"Why can't I hear you?" Kimber yelled. "Did you idiots turn your comms off?"

Colin winced. Kimber's screechy voice directly in their ears caused an instant headache.

Arden switched her comm back on. "Sorry, didn't think you'd want to hear me pee."

Colin snickered, turning his comm back on as well. "I didn't realize mine was off." He didn't even try to hide the lie in his tone. Arden adored him for it.

Kimber growled.

Arden ignored her when she realized they were about to get company. "Incoming," she said for Kimber's benefit, hoping it would shut her up.

Colin snapped his spine straight and went into assassin mode.

Three boys and a girl cut through the crowd. They wore brightly colored outfits, dressed like travelers from another city. The cloth formed to the body so they'd be able to fight in them if necessary, a fact emphasized by the phasers strapped to their hips and backs. They made a powerful statement as they walked through the atrium, like a delegation of dignitaries. People treated them as such, parting for them and offering small bows.

The girl was noticeably smaller than the boys. She walked with a sway in her step, stealing the attention from her companions. She was pretty and petite, with curly dark hair, dusky skin, and wide almond eyes.

Around her, the boys were varying degrees of hulking. They walked in a ring, shielding the girl. It didn't come across as trying to protect her, but more as emphasizing she was their leader, the one who made the decisions. It was in the way she carried herself, the tilt of her chin, the way she looked Arden directly in the eye.

Arden had met many times with Mina, one of Lasair's black-market suppliers of weapons and tactical gear. Because of that, Arden had a healthy respect for her. The girl was someone to fear and not someone she wanted to make an enemy. Mina wore her lethalness like a badge of honor.

Mina stepped forward. She lifted her hands, palms up and cupped, the fleshy sides of her hands pressed together. Then she turned her eyes downward, and her head dipped in a bow. "Bright day to you." Her words rolled with silk-smooth tones and a foreign accent that Arden had never been able to place.

Arden repeated the greeting, giving a slightly deeper bow. "And to you."

They both reached out with their right hands, pressing their palms together, their thumbs twisting and connecting in a coordinated greeting.

When they parted, Mina tilted her head to the side. "I'm sorry we were late. There was a bit of trouble with our docking. It seems the berth we normally use is being repaired."

Arden jolted. She slid a sharp look to Colin. He blinked. The change from the normal berth was concerning, especially since that was the one they had bugged. Hopefully Kimber had been paying attention. She'd have to do a lot of work to break into the vids of a clean room once they were able to pinpoint which one. Until then, the meeting would be blind.

"If you will follow us," one of the boys said.

Arden and Colin fell into step next to Mina. Mina slipped her hand through the crook of Arden's elbow. Her body swayed into Arden's as they walked. Arden wished they really were friends. It would be nice to have powerful allies she could trust.

Behind them, the other two boys took up the rear of the group, boxing them in. Arden didn't like feeling pinned. She was capable of fighting her way out, yet anxiety closed her throat. She swallowed against it.

Kimber broke in on the comms. "Following you through the atrium, I've got eyes all the way through to the quadralift. When I figure out which berth they're using, I'll log into those vids."

On the lift, the boys stood closer than necessary, bunching the group in tighter. There was an uneasy shifting around the circle. Adrenaline flooded Arden. She mentally ran through the list of every phaser, knife, and any other possible weapon that each person had, cataloging how she'd take them out. She moved her fingers, loosening them so that she'd be ready.

Finally, the doors dematerialized. She pushed her shoulders back before exiting the quadralift into an eerily empty hallway. As busy as it had been in the atrium, the complete absence of passengers here confirmed that this was a setup. Anxiety that had strummed at a low pulse now beat with a full-out knocking on her insides. Her skin crawled, coming alive. She almost turned around but checked herself.

The back of Colin's hand slid against hers for only a fraction of a second. It was enough. Arden felt her calm slip back into place as she prepared to fight.

Kimber's voice became frantic, her comm fading in and out with static. "They have some kind of block. I'm blind. Trying to break into their feed—"

Arden was not surprised when the comm went dead.

The lead boy put his beefy palm to the scanner beside the berth door. There was a whoosh as the steel door slid open, the air pocket inside the room meeting the recycled air of the hallway. It popped Arden's ears.

"Is something wrong?" Mina asked.

"Of course not," Colin said smoothly, following the first boy into the berth.

Arden stood on the threshold. She looked at Mina. Her blank stare was unreadable. The other two boys stepped behind her, not touching, yet forcing her to make a decision. Arden turned her attention forward and walked into the room. The door behind them closed, whooshing again as the air lock reengaged.

That was when it happened. Mina stepped out of the way while the three boys surrounded them. The fight was pretty even, despite the boys easily having an extra fifty pounds apiece on them. Colin and Arden kept their backs to each other, kicking, swooping, and circling.

The brawl moved fast: arms, fists, feet landed with dizzying speed. At one point, Arden took a punch to the face. It knocked her sideways. For half a second, she couldn't make her brain work and then caught a second fist, this time to her lip. She felt her skin break, saw the blood spray from the connecting fist as the boy pulled back, and then her brain realigned and she struck out.

All the while Arden looked for exits. The door was shut and probably locked. Kimber hadn't made contact. Once she'd determined that the only way out was to fight, a calm settled into Arden.

Arden kicked out, landing her foot in the stomach of one of the guys bearing down on her. He grunted and fell back. Then she followed through with a second kick to his side. The extra boy lunged at her. She swung, landing a punch to his face.

Her body thrummed with pain. Sweat poured down her face, stinging her eyes. She felt the sensor on the mask blinking as it fought a losing battle to hold its illusion. Any second she'd be exposed.

Time to end this. Arden's hand moved for her phaser. As soon as she had a palm on the grip, the three boys doubled their efforts. She pulled the phaser free and raised it. A foot kicked it out of her hand. She watched it fly, already unstrapping her knife. She slashed out, her blade wanting to find flesh to sink into.

She spun away from Colin's back, grabbing one of the boys by the throat. As she tightened her arm to keep him secure, her other hand pressed the knife under his chin. In that next moment, the cold hard metal of a phaser kissed her temple.

"Drop the knife," the boy holding the phaser said. He pulled her hair in emphasis, and she felt the muzzle tap her head.

Arden tightened her arm against the other boy's windpipe, making him grunt, then dug the knife deeper into his skin. She sucked in a series of breaths heavily through her mouth, her chest burning, while she tensed her body. She wasn't going to let the boy go. She needed to keep some leverage.

On her right, she saw that Colin still fought with the third boy. He moved slower than usual. Blood stained his face and hands.

Arden's heartbeat thundered in her ears.

The boy fighting Colin kicked him in the gut, sending Colin flying across the floor to land on his back.

Mina clapped. "Very good."

Instantly she had the attention of everyone in the room. She gestured for the boys to let Arden go and not to reengage with Colin, who was slowly getting to his feet. The boy behind Arden lowered his phaser and stepped away.

Arden was much slower to release the boy she still had by the throat. She wasn't sure what had started the fight and couldn't trust that the confrontation was over. Tense, they all waited, sensing her hesitation. Finally she pulled her arm away, simultaneously pushing the boy away from her. Her feet danced back, putting distance between her and the rest of the room. She kept her knife in front of her, breathing hard.

Colin wiped at the blood on his face, making long red smears across his mask. Then he spat a glob of red saliva onto the ground. His teeth gritted, the white enamel now pink as he flashed a snarl at the boys they'd fought. He rolled his shoulders, loosening them.

Arden hadn't fared any better. Her body was sore, and her lip split and bleeding. Her left eye felt puffy and bruised. "What the hell, Mina?"

"I had to make sure that you're who you said you are."

Arden lowered her knife fractionally, her weight shifting. They'd met multiple times over the last few years, so why the distrust now? "Who else would I be?"

"I don't know your identity under the synth-mask and voice modulator, but I know the way you fight," Mina said, clearly impressed with Arden and Colin's skills. "Govies don't fight nearly as well or as dirty."

"That's what you're afraid of? That someone created a replica of this synth-mask to infiltrate you?" Arden waved at the blood-covered hologram on her face. "If we'd sent someone who was crappy at hand-to-hand, you would have shot her?"

Mina gave an elegant shrug. "Possibly."

Arden felt the heat of anger burn her skin. "You risked too much."

"Anyone could have synthesized your masks," Mina said. "I've known for some time that someone in your organization is leaking information. To that end, I've taken some additional precautions and included new synth-masks in the shipment that only the five of us will know about. We'll start fresh next time."

Arden understood where Mina was coming from, but it pissed her off nonetheless. Folding her arms, she pinched her lips together and squinted. Leaking information? She didn't know what to think of that bombshell since she hadn't any evidence of it. That would be something to think on later.

Mina didn't take Arden's angry silence as a challenge. Instead, she looked amused. "It's also why we made sure to cut you off from your comms."

Arden blinked.

Mina nodded. "We found the equipment you planted in the other berth. Don't bother to deny it was Lasair, I know my tech when I see it. I'm impressed with how long you managed to pull it off before we caught it."

Arden swallowed, feeling uneasy. Mina's praise was confusing. She didn't want to confirm what Mina suspected, but she didn't want to deny it and insult Mina's intelligence either. Instead, she walked over and snatched up her discarded phaser from the ground.

"I won't hold it against you. I understand the need for caution, but I won't forget either," Mina said. Then her voice turned dismissive. "Well, that's done. Let's get to the reason you're here, shall we?"

Mina led the group over to the hovervan parked beneath the ship docked in the center of the berth. The ship had sleek silver lines and a bullet-shaped nose, reflecting a distorted view of the group as they walked toward it. The loading dock was still down, showing off its vast interior.

Their goods had already been offloaded and placed into the hovervan. The back doors of the hovervan were open, so that Colin and

Arden could inspect the trade. Inside the van were rows and rows of phasers in all shapes, sizes, and scope, along with several boxes of electronic equipment that could be used to circumvent computer systems.

Two of the boys stepped around them and up to the back of the van.

"Go ahead and check the goods," Mina said.

Arden looked to Colin before they both walked to the open doors. She stood between the boys while Colin jumped into the back of the hovervan. He ran a hand over all the items, making a cursory check. Not that he could count the items there, but he could at least inspect the quantity and eyeball the inventory to make sure it was authentic.

Her heart thrummed with excitement. This was it. Soon, she and Colin would set her plan in motion. She'd find a way to save Mariah, and maybe figure out how to deal with her feelings for Dade at the same time.

When Colin finished checking the packages, she returned to Mina to deal with the payment.

"Everything look good?" Mina asked.

"Seems to." Arden held out a scanner strip that linked to a bank account Lasair laundered money through.

Mina wanded the strip, waited for the bleep, then nodded and pocketed the wand. She handed over the keys to the hovervan. "The vehicle ID tags should get you through the day, but ditch the van as soon as possible."

Arden nodded.

"Look," Mina added, her voice lowered so that only Arden could hear. "You take care of yourself, all right?"

Arden didn't know how to react to that. Was it a warning? Did Mina know something? Her gut had always wanted to trust Mina, even when she pulled crap like today. Arden found herself giving a reassurance that she didn't quite feel. "Don't worry, I will."

# CHAPTER THIRTEEN

Arden held a large vase of flowers in front of her. She wore a brown delivery hat, the brim pulled low over a pair of halo-glasses. Only a small strip of her lower chin and jaw was visible. She kept her head down in an attempt to avoid the facial recognition scanners that dotted the lobby ceiling in Sky Tower Two. She was relatively sure that she hadn't been placed in the FACE system, a computerized recognition program used to target and apprehend criminals. And she wanted to avoid being added.

A slow beat of anticipation thumped inside her as she walked across the empty lobby to the girl sitting behind the sleek glass desk. The steel wall behind her was emblazoned with the Croix logo.

There were two guards, both soft around the middle. One stood by the Tower quadralift, swinging his stun-stick with a twirl as he paced the floor. The other was positioned next to the glass doors leading outside. She didn't like having her back to him and fought not to let that discomfort show in her posture.

The girl behind the desk was young, her hair twisted in braids with silver beads that tinkled like little bells. She wore a shiny blue dress with the Croix logo embroidered on the collar. She popped her gum. The green wad peeked through with every loud chew. Her gaze flicked over Arden, quick and assessing.

The girl snapped her gum again. "Yes?"

"Delivery for Mr. Atherton in six-fifty-seven." Arden placed the flowers on the high counter, moving the vase to the side so that she could show her badge. The city certification number flashed neon along the bottom. Then she adjusted her halo-glasses to capture an image of the girl, including her name badge.

The girl clicked on the comm unit, pushing the buttons to ring the Atherton residence.

"Recoding the tone," Colin said through the receiver in Arden's ear as he intercepted the call. "Three seconds, two, one."

The line clicked over.

"There's a delivery for Mr. Atherton," the girl said, her demeanor changing from slouchy and annoyed to professional.

"Thank you, Maggie. You can send it up," Colin responded, using the receptionist's name noted on her tag.

Maggie clicked off the comm unit.

"You can go on up," the girl said, pointing to the lift.

The security guard set his palm on the scanner to open the Tower quadralift door.

Arden slipped in.

Once the door closed, she adjusted the collar of the work shirt, scratching at the cheap synth-fabric. Then she touched her halo-glasses again to access the schematics, switching to her visual-mapping program. "Entering target Level. Commence upload mapping protocol."

The glasses showed her the layout of the Level she was about to enter on a three-dimensional plane. The walls rose and spread forward, locating all possible doors and exits. She used her eyes to flick through the 3-D schematic: lines indicating walls, floors, and air vents. She scrolled to locate the door to the apartment. "Objective achieved."

"Affirmative," Colin said through her earpiece. "Activating heat sensors now. Will confirm targets in ten."

Arden wore the heat sensors on her body. Hacking the Tower surveillance provided a limited view. This was mostly because the Solizen didn't trust one another, so there weren't many cameras. Just one pointing to the door of the quadralift, another pointing down the hallway. It left a lot of room for error. Thus, by using the heat sensors, at least she'd be forewarned whenever another person was nearby.

Arden clicked the map to set a pin on the location of the apartment door. It marked it, and then began to list all available routes. She took note of the camera placement in the halls. Where they were directed and what areas they recorded. Labeling which ones needed to be taken out.

"The quadralift exit is clear," Colin said, watching security footage of the floor. "Security guard on north side walking toward you. Will be in target sight in three minutes. Get moving."

"Roger."

"Stay alert."

Arden smiled. It was his way of telling her that he was concerned for her safety and that he cared.

The excited feeling that always came right before a job flooded her. Arden stretched her fingers, making sure they were limber. She liked the adrenaline, the way it made her feel powerful. It turned her into something better than she could be otherwise.

Colin broke in again. "Setting the camera feed to loop in three-two-one . . ."

The quadralift dinged and opened into a vestibule. A sideboard sat across from the doors, framed by a mirror and a floral arrangement in reds, oranges, and yellows. Tiled floors reflected the overhead lights, making the space feel bright and open.

*Wasted space,* Arden couldn't help but think. She was used to cramped confines. In this vestibule alone, she could sleep eight people. It was a shame really.

Hallways lined either side of the Tower, forming an H shape. She focused on her target door and began walking down the sterile hallway.

Arden wasn't really heading for the Atherton apartment suite. Her mark was on the opposite side of the building.

Within minutes she stood outside the metal door.

"We have a problem," Colin said. "The scanner just picked up multiple heat signatures on the other side."

"Sun," Arden swore and stepped back, hands off the keypad for which she'd been reaching. "Get me an alternate route."

"Guard heading your way. We need to abort."

"We are not going to abort," Arden said with frustration. "If I don't do this now, I might not get another chance. It will be hell to get past that front desk again."

"Arden, it's not safe."

She hated standing vulnerable in the middle of the hallway with nowhere to hide. Arguing with Colin, no less. But she absolutely refused to leave. Dade was somewhere on the other side of that door. She was determined to speak with him.

"I won't be able to get in the same way," she said. "Next time I'll have to use a synth-mask, and if I do that, Niall will know. We both know that's a very bad idea."

"Who cares? When he finds out you're in the Tower without permission—plus asking for help from the enemy—you're dead anyway."

"Dead then or dead now, what's the difference?" she asked. "Stop messing around and get me an alternate route." Patience was difficult for her at the best of times. Right now she'd strangle him if she were close enough. Arden took a calming breath.

Colin's sigh over the line was full of sarcasm. "Trusting him is a bad idea."

"You don't know him."

"I don't have to know him to realize this whole plan is going to blow up."

"Thanks for the vote of confidence."

She needed to decide. Leave, with the possibility of not coming back? Or stay and play a game of break-in chicken with Colin? Arden gave it thirty more seconds.

"There's a suite of rooms below," he finally said. "It's not directly below the balcony you wanted, but close. Backtrack to the hall. First door on your right is the stairwell. Exit into the hallway, then it's three doors on your left."

She smiled and started moving fast. "Thank you."

Arden wasted no time making her way down the stairs.

"You'll have to climb up the exterior of the building," Colin said.

"Not a problem."

"I'm not worried about the climbing," he said, exasperated. "I'm worried that you'll attract attention."

"I'll be quick, promise."

Arden paused at the door from the stairwell back into the hallway, waiting for Colin's all clear. When she got it, she made her way down the hall to the suite below where she had stood before. She set the flowers down beside the target door so that she could access the scanner lock.

"There are heat signatures there as well," Colin said, "but not in the two closest rooms to the door. You should be okay. Just don't waste time."

"I won't." She pulled out her datapad, connecting it with flash wires into the scanner hub. "Uplinked."

"Running program now."

Her datapad spun with numbers, taking forever. Arden started getting antsy. "Hurry up."

"Almost done," Colin said. There was a pause. "Guard coming your way in forty-five seconds."

The scanner stopped spinning, the numbers blinking twice, and the door slid open. She disconnected her datapad, picked up the flowers in one arm, and slipped into the room. With her other hand, she pulled her phaser from her hip.

She deposited the flowers on a table just inside the door. She kept the phaser at shoulder level, ready to use. Then, walking farther into the apartment away from the entryway, she rounded the corner into the living area, leading with her shoulder. Her shoes sank into the plush carpet, silencing her footfalls. She could hear noise coming from farther in the suite.

In the living room, the light shone through the windows. It flooded the room, bouncing off the white walls and refracting off strategically placed mirrors.

Arden squinted.

She moved through the living room and out the glass doors onto the balcony. Stepping outside was like stepping into another world. The warmth touched her skin in a heated caress. Perspiration beaded on her skin. She allowed herself a moment to suck in a breath thick with heat and humidity. It settled heavy in her lungs, warming her from the inside out.

The Tower frustrated her with its opulence. Knowing it existed in theory was one thing, seeing it was another. This much free space, in the sun, was the height of excess. How could only a small group of people own such a thing just because they had money and power? The sun was meant to be shared.

A vacuum switched on somewhere in the back of the apartment. She slipped the door shut behind her.

Small groupings of furniture were placed around the deck. There were also several chaise lounges, for a long lie-down in the sun. Lush growing things were everywhere: vines and flowers, plants that served no greater purpose than to look pretty. The scent they gave off was thick with sweet perfume. She reached out to touch a leaf, rubbing its silky stem between her thumb and finger.

A moonglass railing encased the balcony, making it appear as if the floor went on forever. She walked to the edge, looking down into the static cover. Dark and ominous, the smog swirled, shielding the view of the city below.

Arden turned back to the Tower, covering her eyes, so that she could see the terraces jutting off the Level above. The design of the Tower structure was sleek, allowing for very few footholds. She was coming up with possible scenarios for her climb when a noise startled her, the slide of metal scraping against a hard surface.

She looked toward the sound.

Someone lounged on the balcony above, a boy with sun-browned golden skin and long, lean muscles. An arm thrown over his eyes as he lay back cut the view between soft bright hair and a strong chin. There was a bit of leg on display and a chest with very defined muscles with lots and lots of delicious skin.

Arden swallowed, pushing down a flutter of excitement. She knew exactly who that was.

His arm fell from his face, and he turned his head. The light caught in the blond of his hair, haloing it, making him shine like an angel.

Her indrawn breath must have been loud enough to catch his attention, here in the sky, where there was nothing but silence. His eyes blinked open, and a frown marred his forehead. "Arden?"

"Um, hi," she said awkwardly.

He gave her a huge grin. "It is you."

Dade got up and walked to the edge of his balcony. He stood close to the glass, showing off everything. He wore the skimpiest pair of shorts she'd ever seen, his heavily muscled legs packaged up in red fabric with a white piping. There he stood, half-dressed, as though doing so were nothing out of the ordinary. No one she knew went around without layers and their cloaks. Without sunlight, it simply was too cold.

He appeared as if he owned the world. Perhaps he did.

"I'd hoped you'd come," he said. "I thought it would be impossible, but I knew if anyone could figure out a way to do it, it would be you."

The sun glared down into her face. Arden squinted, looking up at the balcony, her gaze landing directly on his package. The sun, caught behind him, made his gorgeous body glow.

She swallowed, then glanced away, embarrassed.

This wasn't working. Seeing him messed with her resolve. She should leave now, disappear, and not look back. Figure out another way to get the information she needed.

And yet her body moved forward as if answering a siren's call.

Arden lifted herself onto the moonglass wall. The wind blew stronger here than under the cover of the patio. A gust nearly sent her over the edge. Arden wobbled, catching herself, and planted her feet farther apart.

Dade sucked in a breath. His hands gripped the top of his balcony wall, leaning his body over. His face had pulled tight with worry. "Two moons, Arden, don't fall."

"Keep your voice down," she said.

He leaned farther over the balcony. If he didn't watch it, he'd be the one to fall over.

"Get back," she said.

"Keep your voice down," he mimicked, then rolled his eyes. "I'm fine. Now get up here."

The balconies, configured like floating platforms, had space between them, jutting over the world below, too far to reach across. Along the bottom, there was a gap between the floor and the glass. About six inches, enough for her to slip her hands into.

Arden didn't allow herself to second-guess.

She crouched down, balancing on the balls of her feet, then pushed off in a jump, stretching across the empty sky. She reached the balcony, but the momentum kept her moving forward, then jerked her back. Her fingers slipped to the edge, then gripped down, stopping her slide but leaving her dangling over the dark clouds below.

Dade made a noise of distress.

Arden glared up at him.

He held his hands up in surrender. "Sorry. Carry on."

Her hair whipped around her face. She tilted her head, flicking it so that she could see. She swung from side to side to gain momentum, then lifted herself so that she could slip her foot beside her hand. She got a toehold and wedged herself up. Once she got her other foot on the balcony and her hand on the railing, she was able to hop over the glass, landing next to Dade.

She realized her tactical mistake immediately. It felt even better being close to him. His naked skin looked warm, as if it had soaked up the sun and now radiated its heat. She barely held herself back, her fingers itching to touch and her body wanting to press against his. All she had to do was take off her gloves so she could reach out and run her hands all over his chest.

How could she resist temptation? It seemed impossible.

Dade smiled fully, without reservation. The skin crinkled around his eyes. It spoke of welcome, security . . . home. In that moment, she was confident that he cared for her. That it wasn't just platitudes or hormones. He wasn't caught up in political agendas or family squabbles. To him, she was what mattered.

She also knew without any doubt that she couldn't stay away from him. It didn't matter how many times she reminded herself what a horrible idea this was: Dade was her drug, a more dangerous and potent version of Shine. And she wanted to get high.

"I can't stay," she said. Belying her words, Arden stepped closer to him. His skin smelled of a combination of cologne, sun, and a sweet fruit. She wanted to really touch him, yet was afraid to give in to the temptation. Lingering would compromise the mission. Already she wondered why Colin wasn't squawking in her ear.

Dade reached up, taking her hands in his. He squeezed her fingers. "For a bit?" He tilted his head and gave her an inviting look. It was soft and full of understanding with enough yearning to have her move yet another step forward. They were almost touching now.

He was practically naked. Naked, naked, naked. The word bounced around her head with the speed of a laser ball. His exposed chest glistened from a combination of sun, sweat, and oil. His muscles flexed as he tugged her so that her body fully rested against his.

Dade reached up to take off her hat, dropping it to the ground. Then he slid her halo-glasses onto the top of her head. He caressed his fingers along her cheek. "I was daydreaming about you. And then, suddenly you appeared. I could get used to my dreams becoming reality."

Arden felt her cheeks heat. What could she say to that nonsense?

He leaned forward so that his lips skimmed the skin of her cheek. He pressed against it, a light caress, before he let his breath, warm and moist, tickle her. "Tell me you've thought about me."

She wanted to deny it. Yet she found herself nodding, a slight movement that she halted as soon as she realized she was making it.

Arden felt, rather than saw, his smile as he brushed his mouth against her cheek once more.

"I like that," he said. "I like that you think about me."

He pressed his body more firmly against hers.

"Wait a second." She placed her hands against his chest, rubbing a minute, before pushing him back half a step. "I need your help."

His eyebrow rose. "You need my help."

"Don't be sarcastic." Arden huffed, amused herself. "I need information, and I hope you can get it for me."

He nodded slowly, while taking another step away. "I'll help you if I can."

She didn't like his hesitation. Nor how he was putting distance between them.

It made her suspicious.

"That night at the club, a friend of mine was detained. I need to find out where the govies are holding her."

He reacted to what she said, but not in the way she expected. Instead of vague interest, he registered horror. It set off alarm bells in her head.

"What do you know?" she asked.

He shook his head. "Nothing."

"I don't believe you."

He gripped her upper arms, giving her a gentle squeeze. "I really don't know where she's being held."

Arden made a frustrated sound. Stepping away from him, she turned toward the glass wall. "Before you said you'd help me. Are you going back on that?" She wasn't really upset with him. She knew she was asking him to betray his family. Mostly she hadn't stopped being angry with herself. Asking him to lay his neck on the line for someone he didn't know was too much to presume despite whatever was growing between them.

Then she immediately felt irritated for giving him an out. This was her job, her responsibility. When had she started thinking of him as a person she cared for deeply and not as a Croix? She needed this information no matter what it cost him. Keep this up and she'd be on the verge of getting pinched by govies herself.

Arden gripped the railing, her fingers turning white.

"Perhaps it's worse than you think," he finally said, coming up behind her. He laid his hand on her lower back and began to rub soothing circles.

She turned again to face him, forcing him to step back while her hands went to grip the rails at her side. "What do you know?"

"Nothing of their plans," he said. "But what I have heard is troubling. The govies have been given a directive to extract information in any way possible, including torture."

Arden's body tightened. They both knew that meant if the govies accidentally killed Mariah during the interrogation, they wouldn't be held responsible. Which made it all the more imperative that she find Mariah right away.

He nodded. "I don't know if I can find out where she's being held. That kind of thing is not information that I can easily access."

"You have to try," she said. He was her only hope at this point for redemption regarding Mariah. She couldn't accept a no.

Dade stared at her a long time. "I'll call in some favors."

"Promise me."

"I'll do my best," he countered. "If the information can be sourced, I'll get it for you."

His words didn't inspire Arden's confidence.

Dade leaned in, his hands sliding around her waist. He nuzzled a spot under her ear before he whispered, "It's going to be okay. We'll find her."

Arden liked the way he felt. It was comforting. Easy. Making it possible to forget her fears and to simply feel. She leaned into him.

"I know." She trusted him. Had from the beginning, or she wouldn't have risked everything to come here.

"I want to see you again, more than to give you the information. I want to spend more time with you. I'll do whatever I need to make that happen." He sighed into her hair, hugging her close. "It's been too long since I last saw you. I hate not knowing when the next time is going to be."

Arden closed her eyes, wishing the same thing. "Dade, it's not a good idea. I thought we agreed to that." But the way her voice trailed off was not convincing.

"Right. Well, you'll need to contact me to get whatever information I find." He'd pulled away enough for her to see his face. He looked sad. "It's too risky for you to come here again, especially if I start investigating."

"What do you suggest?"

"There's a ticket station outside the transport grid on Level Four, just south of Washington Street. Do you know it?"

"Yes."

"Outside is a set of benches. I'll spray-paint a red halo on the back of one when I have information for you."

That sounded easy enough to watch for. She knew a vid-camera in the area she could reposition and hack into in order to keep tabs. "Okay."

"I'll meet you at midnight in the West End Church the night I leave the signal," he said. "There's a back entrance halfway down the alley, marked by a blue cross. Knock twice. When the priest answers, tell him, 'May the sun shine for all.'" He quoted the traditional greeting of the Lower Levels.

"He'll know that I've sent you," Dade said.

Questions flooded her mind. Why did he keep secret company with a priest? What exactly was he up to? Had it anything to do with his initial hesitation to help her? And yet she didn't ask. He had offered to help her. That was all she needed from him. If she pressed too much, he might not get her what she wanted.

He could keep his secrets.

"Can I trust this priest?"

"With your life," Dade said. "But understand that by coming into his church, you're swearing to protect him should he ever ask."

"Understood." She fidgeted, looking around, then said, "I need to go." Not really wanting to, but knowing that the longer she was here, the greater the likelihood of her getting caught.

"Not yet."

He leaned down to place his mouth against hers. Kissing her in a way that tied her ever closer to him. Twisting her up inside. She wanted this.

Reality couldn't be forgotten, though. Eventually she pulled away, her mouth wet and puffy. "When I'm with you, I feel as if I could touch the sky."

"It's the same for me." He brushed his mouth against hers with teasing kisses. "Let's not stop."

Arden ran her hands over his shoulders to bring him flush against her, letting him deepen the kiss again. Allowing herself to float on the bliss that he stirred inside her.

Colin clicked in her ear, interrupting the moment. "Where are you? Your exit window was ten minutes ago." Nervousness strained his voice. "Your failure to return to the lobby has been noted. There are two guards in the hallway."

She pulled herself from Dade's embrace. They stared at each other, a wealth of words in the silence.

Arden touched the mic. "Be ready for pickup."

Colin sounded relieved when he answered. "Five minutes."

She focused on Dade. "I'll look for your signal."

He nodded.

Then, before she could give in to her weakness to kiss him again—or worse, tell him how much she looked forward to seeing him—Arden turned and balanced on the railing. She danced to face Dade. Shaking off her uniform shirt, so that she could access the sky suit beneath.

Dade laughed. "Next time you'll have to take me with you."

"It's a date."

Arden lifted her arms, engaging the light wings attached to her back. They unfurled, and Arden clipped herself into the control cuffs around her wrists. Then she fell backward into the purple sky, before she flipped to a dive, sliding the wings back to catch the current.

# CHAPTER FOURTEEN

Dade shifted from side to side, frustrated to be standing still so long. His legs had gone numb, and he really needed to use the restroom, his escape hampered by the bolt of white silk draped over his body that would become his bridal tunic. The back room piped in an excessive amount of heat for customers' comfort. Only instead, it produced a sweltering atmosphere that was nearly unbearable, leaving Dade feeling bored, hot, and irritable. Not a good combination.

Plus, it didn't make him any happier that the wedding plans were continuing, regardless of how he felt. He should have figured a way out of this mess by now. That he hadn't yet done so had him focusing more on maintaining his temper and not snapping at innocent people than on using the time to work out his problems.

"Please, sir," the clothier said around the pins jutting from his mouth. "You need to stay still." He twitched the fabric at Dade's feet, readjusting the hemline for the tenth time in as many minutes.

There was a disturbance in the shop beyond the thick draping. He couldn't hear what the voices said, only that they were loud and animated. Then Clarissa breezed into the back room. Several shopping bags draped her arms, and a few more were woven through her fingers. Her hair had been slicked into a faux hawk, displaying glittering gems at her ears and throat.

"Good morning, gentlemen," she said, offering a gorgeous smile.

Speak of the devil. Dade didn't know if he should be pleased or irritated at her interruption. With her here, it would take much longer to get this appointment finished, but at least she could keep his mind off how uncomfortable he was. And he did need to speak with her.

"Miss, you're not allowed back here," the clothier said. "This is a gentlemen's shop."

"Nonsense. There's nothing here I haven't seen before. Do go on." Clarissa made a little "continue" wave at him before she dropped off her bags in the seating area next to where Dade stood. Then she fell back onto the chaise with a dramatic, overly exhausted flourish.

The tailor looked extremely put out. He huffed and grumbled, and in doing so, spat out the pins from his mouth. Dade shifted to avoid them falling on his toes.

"It's fine," Dade told him. "She'll leave in a moment."

That seemed to make the clothier more disgruntled. Dade knew that it was difficult for someone to understand who wasn't used to hurricane Clarissa. That she'd shown up, when he hadn't been able to get ahold of her for several days, didn't sit well with Dade either. Combined with her current theatrics, he was suspicious of why she had cornered him publicly.

Dade frowned into the mirror, adjusting the various parts of his tunic, and asked her, "Do you answer your pings?"

She raised a perfectly manicured, overlined eyebrow. "I'm here now, darling, and it's nice to know you missed me."

Dade focused back on his tunic, wanting to take the whole thing off and call it a day. "How did you find me? I don't remember ziptexting you my schedule."

"It wasn't difficult. I saw the big hulk outside, and I know he never strays far from you."

Saben. Of course.

Clarissa relaxed into her seat. Leaning back like the veritable princess in an ivory tower that she was. Even here, in the market district, she let her subjects attend to her. She sent him an exasperated look. "You're in a mood."

He was. And she didn't deserve any of it. Dade turned back to pulling at his clothes again. "Sorry."

She made a noise in the back of her throat like she didn't believe his apology.

"Did the paparazzi follow you?" Dade asked. That was a complication he didn't want to deal with today. He'd been very careful on his way over. The closer their wedding came, the more intrusive the paps became. It was a logistical nightmare that had gridlocked most of his business outings.

"Please. I could outrun the pap-vids before I was thirteen."

"And yet you don't." He relaxed into their friendship, knowing that she wasn't here to upset him. He felt agitated over the situation, not with her. "I thought you liked having your picture on the gossip sites."

Clarissa shrugged. "It's not bad. As long as it suits my purpose." She paused, her tone changing subtly. "That is precisely what I'm here to speak with you about. I've come into possession of some halo-images I'd like you to see."

"Why didn't you upload them to my cloud?" Dade asked, confused.

"Because I don't know who monitors your digi-stream." Her eyebrow went up in a significant look.

Dade glanced at the man at his feet. His presence was nearly invisible, but Dade could tell that he was actively listening. Gossip about the two of them could fetch a high price on the open market. Anyone could sell him out.

He said to the clothier, "Could we have a moment, please?"

The man looked up from Dade's feet, gathering the scattered pins into a pincushion. His attention shifted from Dade to Clarissa and back, and he did not appear happy. After a moment's pause, he stood, offering a small bow to Dade. "Call when you've finished."

Dade tipped his head. "Thank you."

Clarissa's bubbly personality fell away when the man left, replaced by a serious expression. She scowled, her red lips tipping down. She reached into her bag to extract a silencer: a pewter sphere, tiny enough to fit in the palm of her hand. She dropped her arm to the floor, sending the ball rolling to the center of the room. When it stopped, the two halves detached, still connected by a blue pulsing light. The high-pitched vibration the sphere emitted couldn't be heard with human ears. Yet it would prevent any aux- or vid-tracks from being recorded within a twenty-foot radius.

"Don't be upset that I sought you out," she said. "I know you jealously guard your free time, but I wanted to keep this away from the Sky Towers."

"I could have met you for coffee, where I'd be more appropriately clothed."

"Finding you half-dressed doesn't bother me at all." Clarissa winked.

"Nice." Dade glanced down to make sure that all his bits were covered before he stepped off the dais and walked across the room. The tacked pants moved roughly against his body, pulling at his legs. Reaching her, he sat down gingerly on the chaise, careful not to cause any more damage. "Did you at least get the information I needed?"

"The girl who was taken at the club?" she clarified. When he nodded, she said, "I can't figure out why you're interested in that."

"Does it matter?"

"Maybe." She studied him. "The girl has become an issue. Everyone is talking about her, including the media. Though how they found out about her detainment is a mystery. Govies are usually more discreet, so it makes me think that there's more going on than you're telling me. If you're going to use her for information in any way, you need to get in line."

Dade pressed, "Where is she being held?"

Clarissa pulled her datapad from her purse. She tapped on it several times, then looked up. "I've sent you the encrypted file."

"Thank you."

She shrugged, then set the datapad in her lap and focused on him, taking his hand in hers. "A word of caution: If I were you, I'd let this go. Forget you have any business with the girl. They know she's Lasair."

"Who knows? The govies or the families?"

"Both," Clarissa said. "The families want to steal her before the govies break her and make her completely useless. Which means you're not the only one looking into her whereabouts. It's too dangerous to break her out, if that's what you're thinking."

"I'm not going to break her out," he said.

"Well, whatever you're going to do, think twice before you move forward with it."

"What does that mean?"

Clarissa gave a frustrated grumble, and then shot him a look so piercing, it made him pull back at the vehemence of it. "I'm not sure I trust you anymore."

"What?" Confusion was followed immediately by exasperation. He rarely could follow her thought process, and this was one of the times he found that inability highly irritating. "How can you say that? We're best friends."

Her mouth pressed together. "Best friends who apparently keep secrets."

"As if you don't keep secrets from me." Their relationship was built on loyalty, not honesty. "I'd never do anything to harm you."

"I wonder if that's true. The things you're doing affect me greatly." She let go of his hand and picked up her datapad once more. "As I said, I've come into possession of some interesting halo-images. I thought I'd share them with you."

Dade felt his stomach sink. Numerous possibilities filtered through his head, none of them good. She knew something, and had known something for a while. But for her to press like this, whatever she was in possession of, made him worry.

The last few weeks played through in his mind:
*Arden.*
*The club.*
*Undercity.*
*The kiss.*
*Her visit to the Sky Towers.*
*More kissing.*

None of the things he wanted her to have images of. Any, or all, of them would earn her condemnation. Yet those things were tame compared to his other extracurricular activities. He forced himself to remain calm and waited.

Fiddling with the programs on her datapad, she opened an encrypted file with two sets of codes and a palm print. Then she turned the pad around, offering it to him. The first image confirmed his fears.

The photos were taken with a concealed camera. The images were extremely grainy with a green tinge to the black and white, indicating they were taken using infrared. It wasn't the best setup to capture a clear picture, which made the subjects in them difficult to decipher.

At least, that would have been the case if the pictures hadn't been of him.

There were four photos in total of him and Arden in the club. They were side and back shots, their features obscured by other dancers and from the nanotech haze of their masks, which was fortunate. Added to that, the strobes in the club had cut the images with light, further mangling their features.

Then there was the fifth and final picture. A straight shot of Dade wearing the Ghost's mask. That was the money shot.

Even without a clear view of Dade's face, what could be seen was the formal tunic from their engagement pictures. There would be no way to deny it. It would be obvious to anyone who knew him that Dade was the Ghost.

Not that he would deny this to Clarissa. She was way too smart for lies. He was more worried about the clear fact that he was cavorting with the enemy. The pressing issue became who else had seen these. He hoped that Clarissa had scrubbed off any digi-feed.

"You had me followed?" Dade asked.

"I never promised that I wouldn't send someone to watch you." She paused. "I admit I was surprised, and not much can shock me."

"Just ask whatever it is you're dying to know."

"Fine." Clarissa sat back, crossing her legs while regarding him like a specimen in a glass jar. "Let's start with the girl."

"It's not a crime to meet someone in a club."

Clarissa raised an eyebrow and pursed her lips.

The reaction put Dade on the defensive. "She was pretty. I asked her to dance. So what? You knew I was meeting a girl."

"You're saying you didn't know that she's high on the food chain in Lasair?" Clarissa asked sarcastically.

He didn't say that. Though he was surprised. He had already figured out Arden was part of the gang even if this confirmation of her position had him rethinking his strategy.

"You're canoodling with Lasair, and then you're asking me for information on the Lasair girl the govies caught? What do you expect me to think?" she said with exasperation.

Dade cleared his throat.

She held up her hand, stopping him. "Don't bother lying. It's insulting. Especially with how you're acting."

"How is that?" Dade asked, curious yet offended. He'd never realized he'd had the ability to feel both emotions at the same time.

"Shifty. Like you're hiding something. You haven't answered any of my questions."

"Because you're asking things I can't answer." Not truthfully anyway.

"Why are you protecting her?" she pressed.

Because he felt like Arden was his to protect. Thinking that while sitting next to his fiancée was insanity, he realized, yet he couldn't help how he felt. He simply shook his head.

"Fine, you're not going to talk about the girl," she said. "Are you going to tell me about the other thing?"

"What other thing?"

She tilted her head and stared at him.

Dade forced himself not to speak. Not to make excuses or lies. Silence would have to do.

Eventually Clarissa took a deep breath, closed her eyes, and exhaled in a long sigh. "I've been tracking the Ghost for months, and when I finally get close enough, imagine my surprise when I see you. It can't be a coincidence."

"Don't ask me about it."

"I can't help if you're not honest," she said.

"I don't need help."

"I know you don't *want* help, you've made that abundantly clear. But you do *need* help."

The curtains rustled before the tailor stepped back into the room. "Excuse me, there's a gentleman here to see you. He says he's Mr. Croix's cousin."

Clarissa slipped into her social persona, as if they hadn't been discussing treason. "Thank you. Send him back."

The tailor bowed and backed out of the room.

"Rylick's here?" Dade asked.

"He asked me to meet him for lunch," Clarissa said. "I pinged him my location as soon as I found you."

"Lunch? I thought he annoyed you."

"He does. But he ziptexted me last night, telling me he was working on something for your father and requested that we meet." She raised her eyebrow and pursed her lips.

"Interesting." Dade frowned.

"I'd hoped you'd join us for lunch."

Rylick swaggered into the room. He always looked like he owned the universe and expected everyone to stop and watch him. Even if the audience was less than impressed, as Dade was.

"Cousin," Rylick greeted Dade before turning to Clarissa and kissing her on her cheeks. "I hate looking all over the city for you. I'm hungry."

"Charming," she said. "Dade's decided to join us."

Rylick frowned. "Very good. But for sun's sake, can we eat now? A physique this amazing requires regular sustenance."

Dade didn't point out that he hadn't decided any such thing. But then, gaining intel would be worth the price of having to endure Rylick's presence. "Give me a moment to change."

# CHAPTER FIFTEEN

Arden paced.

The church was empty at this time of night. She'd expected it to be locked up tight and was surprised to find the front doors open to visitors. A few stragglers had wandered in during the quarter hour she'd waited. One was in the prayer room and another had moved to the confessional box with Father Benedict.

She didn't like feeling exposed on turf that wasn't her own. Though she couldn't fault Dade for wanting to meet here. The city cameras couldn't reach inside church grounds, per numerous ordinances so wound into the infrastructure of their society that not even the government ignored them. Yet when she'd knocked on the back door and Father Benedict had ushered her in, she'd come to the realization that perhaps the priest was the real reason that Dade felt comfortable here.

Arden slid onto a stone pew near the front of the sanctuary as the confessional visitor left. She leaned forward to rest her elbows on her knees and hung her head. Still, she couldn't stop her foot from tapping with nervous energy.

This was ridiculous. He'd said midnight, and now it was going from the quarter hour to almost half past. Had he been discovered? Was their meeting compromised? Was he in trouble and needed help?

She checked her datapad to confirm the time. If he didn't show in another ten minutes, she'd leave.

Arden hadn't seen Dade in almost a week. She'd been far too busy dealing with the fallout from Mariah's arrest. They hadn't made any inroads into figuring out her location. Knowing that time was limited, Arden had sourced all of their contacts in case Dade didn't come through. The hustling for leads had helped to keep her distance from Dade.

Because she'd been so focused on her work, she had been surprised and excited when she saw his signal. It made her realize how delicate her resolve actually was. The fluttering in her heart started the second she'd known she would see him again. It hadn't lessened in the hours since. In fact, it had grown into a full-fledged storm.

Father Benedict stepped out of the far side of the confessional. She heard the soft clip of his shoes against the stone floor as he walked to the front of the church. He slipped into the pew next to her. He was dressed in drab brown robes, a yellow rope knotted about his generous middle. "You appear to be weighed down by your thoughts, my child."

Arden considered him, sad for this man she didn't know. Purple bruised his eyes. His nose was raw from continued leaking. Sores had started to creep up, at the base of his throat and spread over his hands. The sores would cover him soon, and then they'd break open, oozing pus. The later stages of Violet Death sucked.

She knew she couldn't confide in Father Benedict, but there was no denying his assumption. "It's just life, you know?"

Father Benedict had an aura of knowledge and calm peace about him. As if he understood more than what she was saying. He nodded and reached forward to pat her hand.

She relaxed into the bench a little more.

"He'll be here shortly," Father Benedict said. "Don't worry. If he said he'd be here, I have every faith that he'll show."

"Is he usually late?" It didn't seem like Dade. She would have expected him to be punctual.

"Not usually. But there have been times he's run into trouble."

That undid any calm she'd managed to achieve.

Father Benedict must have seen her shoulders tense, because he added kindly, "He's never had a scrape he couldn't get out of. He'll be here."

Arden frowned. Everyone had a final time when they didn't make it. She considered Father Benedict's words, though, and their intimacy spoke of a deep friendship with Dade, along with a softness akin to a familial bond. She'd also noticed that Father Benedict had never directly referred to Dade by name. To protect him, or for another reason, she wasn't sure.

"Thank you for letting us meet here, Father." Then curiosity made her ask, "Does he meet people here often?"

"You're the first," Father Benedict said. "He has spoken highly of you."

She fought not to let the pleasure of that assurance show.

"He asked me to help, should you ever need anything," Father Benedict continued. "Please don't hesitate to find me. I'll help you in any way that I can. And, of course, if you need to talk, I'm here to listen." He sounded sincere, as if the love he felt for Dade somehow extended to her.

It was a tremendous offer that left her floundering. "Thank you."

Father Benedict rose from the pew. He reached over to pat her shoulder. "There are a few things I must do now. I hope to see you again, my child."

Arden nodded and watched him walk away.

Alone again, she found that her anxiety returned. It was another twitchy five minutes before Dade showed, alone. He entered the same way she had, through the back to avoid any surveillance that would link them together.

The minute she saw him, her restlessness melted away. Now that she knew he was safe, breathing felt easier. Arden rose from the bench and walked to him.

Dade, heart-stopping and gorgeous, grinned at her. Grabbing her hand, he towed her to one of the empty confessionals. Pushing her inside, he squeezed in with her, shutting the door behind them. It was dark in the tiny vestibule. The only light, shining through the hatched grid on the door, splotched light on his skin.

They stood close, pushed together, almost sharing a breath. Touching from shoulders to hips. Arden reached out to place her hands against his chest. Dade gripped her waist, anchoring her.

"I'm sorry I'm late," he said, his words tickling the side of her head. Then he brushed his lips against her skin. "I had trouble getting out of the Tower. They posted more guards. Apparently someone dressed as a delivery girl tried to break in. It's got everyone stirred up, trying to figure out what she was doing there."

Arden chuckled, while making a mental note to retire that costume indefinitely. "I have no idea who would do such a thing."

"Me either."

She pulled back to look at him. "I didn't think you'd signal."

"I said I would try my best to get the information. It took some time, I'm sorry about that. But I'd always planned to see you again."

She pretended to ignore the flirting. "It must have cost you." A lot considering she'd been unable to pay off anyone for the same intelligence. She had no idea how she was going to tell Niall how she'd acquired it.

"They're keeping her in the South Grid Lockup. She's scheduled to be moved to the City Reeducation Center tomorrow."

The South Grid Lockup was where they held prisoners who were a potential threat to national security. And the City Reeducation Center was more a black hole labeled as a place for mind-level reconditioning. Once you went in, you never came out. Being sent there was as good as a death warrant.

The news was not good. Arden had hoped they wouldn't perform the interrogation in an official govie location. Somewhere off-site would be easier to get into. Both the South Grid Lockup and the City Reeducation Center were virtually impenetrable, with the level of security there equaling that of the city vault. Not to mention that the govies were authorized to use deadly force on any break-in attempts or escapes.

"She's not going to be in good shape. They're only moving her because the facility she's in doesn't provide the tools they need to break her."

"Extreme torture, you mean." Her heart sank.

Dade made an aggrieved face. "Unfortunately."

Arden drew a breath but managed to keep her face impassive. It seemed excessively harsh a punishment when the only thing they had to hold Mariah on was her having been beyond Undercity without authorization. "How can that be legal?"

"It's been sanctioned at the highest level," he said. "The govies are frustrated. They see the problem as a general disregard for the Level system and the drug use a sign that the gangs want the economy to fail. The govies will do anything at this point to stop the unrest."

"Let's not forget that they're also getting their pockets lined," Arden added sarcastically. "The Solizen are pushing the issue. Crime is as bad as it's always been. Nothing's changed."

Dade nodded. "You're right, money has a lot to do with it too."

"So now it's okay to torture for monetary gain?"

"Don't yell at the messenger." Dade held up his hands in surrender. "I'm agreeing with you, if you haven't noticed."

Arden exhaled. "Have they gotten any info from her?" If Mariah managed to keep quiet through the first round of torture, Arden could see why the govies were ticked enough to move her to the CRC.

"I have no idea."

Arden thought for a moment, considering this information. She'd never cased either location, as her gang members always focused on drugs and were thus far successful at not getting caught and needing to break out of a detainment facility. "What are the weak points of the locations? Any way I can run this like a smash-and-grab?"

Dade shook his head. "Your window for rescue will only be about two minutes. She'll be guarded from the door to the transport, but that is the only point that's vulnerable enough to make your move. The CRC has a covered in-doc area. So you can't hit there."

Arden nodded. "Okay."

"If you miss your window, there won't be a second chance."

"Got it." Arden licked her lips, then said, "I really appreciate your help. It's unusual that people keep their word. You did, and I'm grateful."

Dade's head tilted to the side as he considered her. "I need to ask you something."

"All right." She didn't like the tone he used, but he deserved an answer to whatever it was. They'd reached a new level in openness. It was time for her to reciprocate.

"I need to know how . . ." He paused to search for the right word. "How involved you are with Lasair?"

Her first reaction was a sharp intake of breath. She shouldn't be surprised. It wasn't like he couldn't put together obvious clues. She had to stop thinking of him like a spoiled rich kid. He'd proven himself to be a smart, worthy opponent capable of getting information she couldn't. Plus, even though he knew she was with Lasair, he had still been willing to help her.

"Niall Murray is my brother."

Dade frowned. "It was too much to hope that what I'd heard was incorrect and that you were just a foot soldier, huh?"

"I sell drugs, Dade." She was sick of being evasive. Not now. Not with him. He had to understand. If he kept pressing for this relationship, he needed full disclosure as to what he was accepting. "I steal them from your family, and I sell the drugs on the street, mostly to kids. It provides for my family. Keeps my parents alive. Occasionally I kill people because it's necessary. If it comes down to me or them, I'm always going to save myself. It's not what I want out of life, and I'm not proud of it, but that's the truth. I will sacrifice anything for my family."

"I had hoped that maybe . . ." He let his voice trail off, and his brow scrunched adorably.

"What? That I didn't actually get my hands dirty? I'm sorry to disappoint you." The response was a bit aggressive, and he certainly didn't deserve her anger. Mostly it was embarrassment that caused her to strike out with her words.

"No." His hands went to her shoulders, rubbing her arms soothingly. "I just hoped that you were lower on the food chain, is all. It's difficult for me to understand how you can perpetuate the disease."

"What?" She was flabbergasted.

"Sustaining the drug trade is no better than what my father does."

"I may sell the drugs on the street, but your family and the rest of the Solizen maintain ninety-five percent of the city's wealth and resources. Do you have any idea what it's like to scrape in order to survive?" She might play fast and loose with her morals, but she wouldn't be ashamed of it. "This is a war. And there's passive resistance and active resistance."

"Hooking kids on Shine isn't patriotism."

"No, but it breaks the system. Every drug that's on the street questions the need for VitD in the first place. There is no difference between prescription drugs and street drugs. They were hooked on VitD before I sold them Shine. I'm not the one creating a generation of addicts. I'm just being honest about my part."

Dade squeezed her hands. "I'm not passing judgment."

Arden breathed out, letting the tension go with it. "I want to believe that you and I can work. But it's conversations like this that make me question how different we are."

"Not so very different." He paused. "In the effort of full disclosure, I do understand what it's like on the street. I may not be there myself, but I see plenty of people who suffer."

"And how would you see that, locked in your Tower?"

"I'm the Ghost."

"What?" It took her a full moment to compute what he'd said. Two moons, Colin had been right. "You're just full of surprises today."

He gave her an embarrassed grimace.

Though she really should have known. Dade was compassionate to a fault, even if that meant stealing from his own family to give to the poor. Because who else would give away lucrative drugs without thought to the money he could make?

He pulled her closer. "By giving you this information, I've chosen a side. You are my side. That means I want us to be honest with each other from here on out."

She paused. Not disagreeing but needing to clarify, she said, "I can't give away Lasair's secrets."

"I'm not asking for that," he said. "I'm asking for you to call off your personal vendetta against my family."

Arden scrunched her face, not following. "We steal from you, in case you missed that part."

"That's not what I'm talking about. I mean the bigger plans to destroy us. I don't want you personally involved in that."

The implication caught Arden off guard, giving her pause. Was he speaking to a specific threat? Had he heard something about Project Blackout? Did Lasair really have a mole?

Dade rolled his eyes. "Don't pretend there's not a bigger play. Lasair wouldn't be content with sticking to the drug trade. Eventually they'll want to destroy us like they have other Solizen families. And I'm telling you, it's a mistake."

"I don't make those decisions."

Dade shook his head. "You're not hearing me. Something is being planned between the families and the govies. That's why they're pushing so hard to extract information from your friend. It would be a mistake to fall into their trap. I don't want you personally involved in that."

"There's always a plan. If it's put into motion, there's nothing I can do to stop it. I don't make decisions for the gang. And if I'm called to act, I have to do my part."

"There's always a way," he said, as if it were that easy. "No one else needs to die. Between the two of us, we can figure out a nonviolent way to stop the corruption."

"You're a dreamer."

"A dreamer who's doing something."

She couldn't argue with that. Admittedly, as the Ghost, Dade was doing more to help society than she was.

They were really going to do this, she realized. Make a real effort at this relationship and at fixing the problems that plagued them both. Together. It was crazy. And yet, she was happy. Go figure.

She wanted to ride this high for a while. But duty always came first. She needed to get the information about Mariah back to headquarters and plan her rescue if they had any chance of pulling it off. "I have to go."

"I worry about you," he said softly. When she started to protest, he added quickly, "Not that you're not capable of taking care of yourself. It's just, I don't like not knowing when I'll see you again."

His words twisted her heart. She leaned forward, tilting her lips up and pressing them against his warm mouth.

"Soon," she said. "When we figure out how to be together."

# Chapter Sixteen

Arden tied her hair back, twisting it into a braid before pulling up her hood. The fabric molded to her head like a second skin, made to lessen the heat of phase-fire while allowing for movement. It was part of their skintight running uniform made of individually formed body armor inside a synth material. A simple black mask would go over her face, but she wouldn't bother with it until they entered the grid.

They were in the Icebox, so named for the chilly steel-lined rooms where they kept their weapon caches. There was no heating system, and Arden shivered in spite of the synth-suit that was supposed to help regulate her core body temperature.

Lasair had weapon caches like this one all over the city. The soldiers knew the locations of the armories assigned for their use. Only the inner circle had the details about caches located in other quadrants. It made it easier to ensure their weapons weren't seized if a Lasair member was caught and tortured.

Each weapon room was kept filled to capacity. Phasers of every sort and size racked the walls on hooks, filling up the space so that there was nothing but glinting metal everywhere. On the ground were racks and bins of various other weapons categorized by type and size.

Most of the items were grab-and-go. A gang member could take what they needed when a situation presented itself. The harder-to-come-by items were logged and kept in a cage that required a thumb-scanner.

They were a gang of thieves, after all. Best not to play to their strengths. Especially when those items became critical and no one could recall where they had gone.

Benches rounded the space where they sat to strap up. The room also came equipped with a vid-projector for going over their missions.

Usually they talked and joked before an operation. Missions were thoroughly planned, so all they had to do was hit the target and go home. Not this time. They were moving on this information right away. Arden didn't like that. Neither did anyone else, and they all made sure she knew it.

Arden knew she had to be right about this intel. If she led them into a trap, it was one they couldn't escape. They'd never hit a target so well guarded before. The knowledge sat like a boulder in her stomach. She was betting their freedom on her relationship with Dade. Which wasn't fair to them and sure as hell was dumb for her. She hadn't yet come to grips with how much she blindly trusted him. Which made her a fool, honestly.

Colin sat too close to her on the bench, not respecting her space and generally driving her crazy. "It's not your fault."

Arden grunted. He'd been telling her a variation of that line for weeks. She was sick to death of hearing it.

"Mariah would have been taken that night anyway," he said. "You would have made for the bolt-hole like you did. Nothing would have changed. It's not your fault we picked the wrong exit."

Arden ignored him, pulling on her metal-enhanced boots. They reached her upper calves where her suit had no armored plates. She began the arduous task of lacing them up.

Colin took her silence as a signal to continue trying to convince her she shouldn't feel guilty. "You have to let it go. If you go in like this, you're likely to get yourself killed or someone else killed. You know that."

He was right. She'd been internalizing a lot of bad stuff lately. She missed the good old days of just doing her job and flying on an adrenaline high when they pulled off a run. All before Dade. Now there were equal amounts of anxiety and the rush she wanted.

Yet she didn't regret meeting him. She wouldn't have described herself as innocent then, but looking back, perhaps she had been. She'd changed so much, so fast. As if seeing a different way of life had opened her up to the possibility that there was no right and true side to this fight.

"What if she's not there?" Arden asked, giving voice to her tightly held fear.

He shrugged. "Let's hope we find her. Uri's about to crack, and your brother's not far behind."

She looked up to watch Uri pace. He cracked his knuckles repeatedly. He hadn't spoken much since Mariah had been taken, and Arden didn't trust him to keep a level head.

Niall was worse. He was as high as a kite. His eyes were glassy, and he mumbled as if hearing voices in his head. When she'd tried to speak with him earlier, he'd stared through her. She couldn't stop him from coming on this rescue mission, though. She didn't have that pull. Not yet, at any rate. Though it was looking increasingly every day as if she'd have to take control, if only to save him.

That pissed her off even more. She wanted to save Mariah, but had hoped that she could do so with people she could trust.

Her boots were laced now, so she sat up and turned to Colin. "This gang is imploding."

He threw out his hands and exhaled in exasperation. "That's what I've been saying."

"Treason," she muttered under her breath. They'd been dipping their toes in the treason pool a lot lately.

Kimber sailed into the room, cutting off their conversation. She'd be on comms for this operation because they needed Colin on the run.

They were going in small: just her, Colin, Niall, and Uri. Kimber walked to the vid-projector and inserted her data drive. A large map opened on the screen, showing the inside of the South Grid Lockup. "Huddle up."

Arden and Colin ignored her. They both chose to keep their butts on the bench, leaning back like they were too lazy to get up.

Uri walked over to stand beside Kimber. His face rock hard and mean. The running suit he wore emphasized his muscles as he crossed his arms and glared at the projection. "What's the plan?"

"I've gone over the schematics a dozen times. When they say that the Lockup is impenetrable, it is," Kimber said. "I can't find a single way to get inside without setting off a dozen sensors and starting a full-scale war."

"Which means we'll have to take her when they move her to the transport, like I told you," Arden said.

Kimber shot her a glare and then changed the projection from inside the facility to the port deck and the surrounding area of the Lockup. All the possible avenues for escape were labeled. Then she said, as if Arden hadn't spoken or come up with the plan in the first place, "Arden's intel was that Mariah will be relocated to CRC sometime today. We'll have to stake out the docking pad to be ready for when that happens."

Arden didn't stop herself from rolling her eyes.

Colin stood up and walked closer to study the map. "We're grabbing her and splitting up without cover?"

"We didn't have enough warning to set anything more elaborate in place. Nor do we have clear intel. That's not on me." Kimber threw another look over her shoulder at Arden.

Two moons, Kimber stole her plan and then stabbed her in the back at the same time.

"It also means anything can go wrong," Uri said. "Snatching her only gives us a minute to a minute and a half at most to make our escape."

Kimber gave Uri a hard look. "Do you want to get her or not?"

"You think you can shut off the cameras?" he countered.

Obviously Uri had as much faith in Kimber's skill set as Arden did. Though in this case, it didn't matter. Their time frame for the job was too small. If they were seen, it wouldn't make that much of a difference.

Niall studied the projection with a frown. "I don't like it."

"It's our only choice," Arden said.

Kimber slid her gaze to Arden once more. "Why doesn't Arden tell us where she got her intel? I'm sure that if we knew we could trust it, we'd feel a lot better about it than we do now."

Not being able to be honest about it had turned into a huge pain. Arden understood how they felt. She would hate to go into a dangerous situation without knowing all the details. Especially since she'd voiced the same doubts herself. "She'll be there."

Colin sent her an amused look.

"You had to get the intel from somewhere. Who did you use? How did you pay them?" Niall pressed.

Arden sealed her lips tightly together and glared at him. She raised a single eyebrow.

"We'll be sitting there with our asses hanging out," Niall said. "All because we should trust you without any proof? Have any of us ever asked you to do the same?"

Wasn't he sort of doing that now? He was high and unsteady. How dare he accuse her of being the one who put them in jeopardy.

Arden swallowed back her frustration. She wasn't all that successful. "Let's focus on the plan, okay? They won't be expecting us. We've never done this sort of thing before. It should be easy enough to take out the cams, take out the guards, and jet out of there."

"Oh yeah, easy," Niall agreed sarcastically.

"Mariah shouldn't put the rest of us in danger," Kimber said. "We're going to get ourselves killed trying to save her."

"Screw you," Uri shot back at her. "Nothing is as important as saving Mariah."

Niall shook his head and walked away.

# Chapter Seventeen

Dade could see just fine from beneath the synth-mask and hood. He'd not gone out as the Ghost in days. Even though he was privy to the knowledge of his father's increased security measures and managed to avoid the worst of them, it had grown too risky. His father's determination to catch the Ghost had become an obsession.

Dade had tried to let things cool off and get back to normal before he committed another theft. Yet here he was, sneaking into the joint refinery owned by all the Solizen families. It was a factory he was unfamiliar with, and he was here against his better judgment and Saben's vocal protestations. Dade knew this was taking a chance, but he didn't have another choice. The dispensaries he usually gave VitD to were running dangerously low on their supplies.

If he could score a larger haul than normal, it would buy him enough time to figure out how to bypass the new security and get back on an easier theft cycle. He'd hoped changing to a new location would work to his advantage and that he'd find some easier ways to steal VitD. So far that plan hadn't worked. Security was tighter here than at any facility he'd ever hit. Every floor was worse than the last.

He crept along the yellow-lit halls on the floor where he believed the latter stages of the drugs were processed before they'd go into packaging. It was a calculated guess since he couldn't locate the schematics in any of his family's cloud systems.

Dade turned a corner, sticking to the sides of the hall and moving as quickly as he could without drawing attention. This hallway was empty, another in a long line of nondescript hallways within the mazelike facility. The plain walls were broken up by metal doors with small round windows on both sides. He glanced in as he passed to see if anything inside the rooms looked like what he wanted.

He wasn't used to being lost. And would have asked Saben for directions, but the comm had gone silent some time ago. He tried to focus on his task, worried about what that meant.

So far he hadn't seen anything that looked like VitD. Most rooms were filled with machinery or people or both. No one noticed him, their attention focused on their work.

He'd also managed to avoid the guards. Sometimes he'd see them in the hallway. When that happened, he'd either choose another direction, or wait until they moved on.

It wasn't the guards who concerned him, though. It was the new squads of mercenaries who now marched up and down the halls in groups of two or three. They were big and thuggish, strapped down with firepower and clearly ready to do battle.

Dade looked into a window and was about to sneak past it when the right corner of his mask's eye scanner shimmered, taking on a slight red haze. He immediately stopped. The sensor noted things like air quality, temperature, and movement. He wasn't quite sure what this anomaly meant. He twisted his head this way and that, but the shimmer never repeated.

Suspicion kept him still. Just because he couldn't see something didn't mean it wasn't there. His gut told him that he had to figure out the problem fast. Before he was cornered by a group of mercenaries.

He pulled out his datapad and opened the program that scanned for anomalies. Once he set the scan in motion, it only took a few seconds to measure a reading. There were no abnormal qualities to the electro-fields in the hallway. Convinced that there had to be something there, he switched programs. He checked the air first. Then he moved the datapad along the wall and tested. Everything still came back normal. He couldn't let the flicker go, though. He crouched to the floor, placing his datapad on the surface, and reran the test. This time the biofeedback measure was a flat zero. Even the ambient electro-currents that were always present showed no readings.

That wasn't possible.

The floor looked normal. He would have walked across it and not thought twice if he hadn't seen that red haze. Dade put away his datapad. He stared at the floor, thinking, his vision unfocused.

The lack of focus made him notice a faint light coming from the grout where the tiles intersected. He inspected it closer. It appeared to be a fibrous filament that was not quite shiny.

Perhaps the floor was a series of grid sensors. He didn't know what they would do, but he had a few guesses. They could simply ping his location, or burn him on the spot with vape-fire.

He expelled a sharp breath and frowned. Perhaps it was time to call this mission off and figure a way out of the facility. His internal clock had steadily been ticking louder and more insistently the longer he delayed. The pressure of getting out unseen now eclipsed anything he'd come to do.

Dade decided to try at least one more corridor, hoping that there was an exit at the end of it. Because he knew for sure there wasn't one in the maze behind him.

Touching his wrist, he activated the suction grip on his gloves. Then he kicked the floor with the back of his heel, releasing small hooks from the toe of his boots. Up he climbed onto the wall. That made it a hundred times more difficult to bypass the windowed doors, and made him vulnerable to anyone who happened to turn the corner into this hallway.

His body strained, exertion making him sweat under the cloak and synth-mask. Grunting, he released himself from the wall and fell to the ground at the other end of the hall.

A foul mood had set in. Dark thoughts surrounded Saben's silence and Dade's awareness that he needed to get the hell out of there. He huffed, his breaths deepening while his body flexed with agitated worry.

He gave up on trying to find VitD and instead started looking for anywhere that could be used as an exit, an airshaft he could pry open, a window in an empty room that he could crawl out of. He turned the corner into yet another identical-looking hallway. He let out a strangled growl. This was not good. There were no guards or mercenaries, however, so that worked in his favor.

Halfway down the hall, he peered through a small round window into a dark room. It was the first empty room he'd come across in the last half hour. Dade couldn't make out much. From what he could tell, it was some kind of supply room full of boxes. He decided on a closer inspection, hoping for a window to the outside.

The door used a biometric scanner. Dade pushed the thin bio-print on the thumb of his glove. It matched a random employee he'd chosen who had access to most of the facility. The digital reader scanned the synthetic that mimicked skin, searching for not only the print but also the heat and ridged texture. A string of codes flashed across a small monitor before the light next to the door switched from red to green and the door slid open.

Dade pulled his phaser from his hip before crossing over the threshold. It was still inside the dark room. No sound but the thumping of Dade's heart as it reverberated in his ears. The door whisked shut behind him.

He'd made it to the first set of boxes when a voice said, "We'd hoped with a little encouragement you'd take the bait."

Dade stiffened.

A hired mercenary stepped out of the shadows on the far side of the room. The man was dressed in black, his face partially covered by heat-shielded synth-fabric. He held a phaser aimed at Dade's chest.

Then another mercenary, this one a young girl, stepped out from a stack of boxes across the room. She looked every bit as menacing, holding her phaser steady.

Dade was caught in the middle. He took a few steps back, then a few more, keeping his own phaser up. Trying to gain a little wiggle room and some time. The only exit out of the room was at his back, and he knew he couldn't make it there without being shot.

They matched him step for step, keeping their phasers pointed, one at his chest, the other at his head. Their gazes took Dade's measure.

The man shot first, a rapid succession of three blasts.

Dade had seen the twitch of the man's finger on the trigger seconds before he pulled, giving Dade enough time to dance to the side before dropping and rolling behind a stack of boxes. He returned fire, exchanging volleyed shots. Several came close enough to singe the fabric of his cloak. Boxes disintegrated around him.

A sense of peace came over him. He let go of the danger and instead focused on the moment, his every breath, each shot, moving steadily across the room while he stayed behind a barrier of boxes. He inched his way toward the door.

But the girl, seeing that, slipped between him and his goal, blocking his way out. She grinned.

Dade shot at her, satisfied when he sent her scurrying.

The room was blown to hell. Everything that had been in the boxes had been pulverized, creating a cloud of debris that choked him.

"You need to put the phaser down," the man called out from behind the stack of burned and crumbled boxes that he used for cover. "It's your only chance to leave here alive."

Dade responded with another round of phase-fire before jetting from behind the boxes that were no longer hiding him sufficiently. He jumped on top of what was left, then launched himself across the room to land where he knew the man hid. The mercenary's face registered shock seconds before Dade fell on top of him.

Not a moment passed before Dade got to his feet and kicked out with his booted heel against the man's wrist. The mercenary's phaser shot wildly, scorching the ceiling. Dade kicked again, dislodging the phaser.

The man got to his feet and swung at Dade.

Dade ducked, while twisting his body to shoot at the girl who came up behind them.

The girl's phase-fire hit Dade close enough to singe his protective vest, blowing a hole through his cloak. He shot back, hitting her in the right shoulder.

She screamed and dropped her phaser.

Meanwhile, the man jumped onto Dade's back, attempting to apply a choke hold. Dade twisted, flipped around, and used the butt of the phaser to knock the guy out cold. Then he moved across the room to stand over the girl. She was reaching for her phaser when he clocked her on the back of the head.

He heaved in air, sucking it heavily through his lungs. Dade stood up straight, taking a step toward the door when it burst open. Three more mercenaries, bigger than the last two, entered the room.

Dade swore as he raised his phaser, swallowing his panting breath. His gut hurt, his face hurt, his chest where the phase-fire had scorched his vest burned like a continuous electrical shock. There was nowhere left to hide. Dade was exhausted, but he wouldn't give up.

That was when he glimpsed Saben entering behind the mercenaries. No more than a shadow, a silent specter they didn't see coming. His friend moved soundlessly, knocking out two from behind before grabbing the leader by the throat and choking him until he passed out.

"Thank sun I found you," Saben said, his face tight and his mouth set in a grim line. He was worried, and that worried Dade.

Now that the adrenaline was leaking from his body, Dade felt embarrassed that his mission had gone sideways. He wasn't this sloppy. "What happened to you?"

"I had no other choice." Saben took a pack off his back and pulled out a foul-smelling pile of brown fabric. He shoved the clothes at Dade. "You weren't getting out of here unless I figured out an alternative route."

Dade recoiled, but stepping away did little to stop the stench of the clothing from burning his nostrils. His eyes watered as he coughed. "Where did you get those nasty things?"

"I borrowed them before I came inside." The way Saben said "borrowed" had Dade envisioning a naked guy knocked out somewhere.

"You couldn't find anything cleaner?" Dade asked.

"I took the first thing that would fit. Don't get prissy."

"What about the cameras?"

"I took out this Level before I came in with an explosive because it seemed the most expedient." Sabin stressed, "Now hurry."

Dade peeled off his hood, mask, and clothes, then pulled on the new clothes. He tried to breathe through his mouth and not his nose. Not that it helped—the scent was putrid.

"Tell me what happened," Dade said.

Saben set about dragging the mercenaries to the back of the room and then began to put the remains of the boxes in front of them so their bodies wouldn't be seen from the door. "A silent alarm was tripped. The factory went into lockdown. They shut down all networks in the building, which cut our comms and autosealed all exits."

"How did you get in?"

Saben laughed. "Same way we're getting out."

"What should I do with my things?" He couldn't very well leave them.

Saben looked around. "We'll have to burn them so they can't trace your DNA."

Dade looked longingly at the mask and cloak. He loved them. Yes, he could get newer ones with better gadgets. But this set was the original, and because of that they meant something. He was going to lose them without managing to procure any VitD. What a waste of time and resources, and he had no one to blame but himself.

# CHAPTER EIGHTEEN

Arden's body sang with its usual anticipatory music. She could already feel the high of the adrenaline rush hit her body. When they'd reached the ledge between Levels Two and Three, they worked together to ensure their speeders were well hidden from city scanners. The craggy outcropping of the buildings wasn't made for parking, even the temporary sort. There wasn't much room to maneuver four bodies and their vehicles.

She had her mask on. The heat from the feedback made her skin tacky with sweat. The suit she wore would keep her body warm and nimble in the frigid cold that blew against them. They stood in the swell of the air current as it rushed between the open sections between the Levels, the temperature here several degrees lower than normal.

She'd strapped her supplies to her back in a slimline pack that hugged her body. Arden engaged the grip sensors on her climbing gloves, then began to scale the building's gray concrete walls, aiming for a hoverport cut into the structure halfway up the building. Now that she had the lay of the land around the South Grid Lockup, she wasn't sure this plan would work. It had appeared much different, wider, from the aerial photos, whereas in reality, there was less room through the buildings than expected to maneuver their escape.

The others climbed behind her. They moved swiftly and silently, hands grabbing and bodies exerting as efficiently as possible. Stealth would be the key to pulling this off. Right now, as they hung from the side of the building, they were at their most vulnerable until the rescue plan was set into motion. Even with the thick static cloud that billowed around them, swallowing them up, they were still exposed to anyone who happened to look too closely.

Arden felt the push of the air stream as it whipped past her. It rushed through the open Levels, thrusting her against the hard surface of the wall. She inched around the side of the building, following available footholds. The air shifted, then sucked her body backward like a vacuum. She gripped the cold, unforgiving concrete and metal, the sensors on her gloves barely keeping her grip intact. Clinging, she curled her fingers to catch whatever lip she could as her feet slipped, searching for a toehold.

She crested the rise to the hoverport and crawled over the edge. The gray swirls of static cloud blew across the tarmac ominously. Her body low to the ground, she ran, the others following behind. They set up behind a section of hovervans. Pulling the packs off their backs, they began to extract their phasers and other items.

Niall put his hand out for Arden's binoculars, then slid to the end of the van to peek around the side. There was the whiz-whiz sound as he adjusted the digital sliders on the side of the view caps. Humming as they caught focus.

Everything was in position, and yet she couldn't get rid of the pit lodged in her chest. She rubbed it, pressing the heel of her hand tight against her sternum to try to release the pressure.

"What's wrong with you?" Colin asked.

Arden dropped her hand, gripping her fist tight at her side, and blew out a long breath. "Nothing."

*Do something,* she reminded herself, so she wouldn't look like a complete noob worrying over the outcome of their rescue. She checked the charge of her phaser. Trying to will away the tension that had taken her over.

Niall returned.

He handed Arden's binoculars back to her. "All clear. It's a go."

Arden nodded. Then Niall and Uri were off, heading in opposite directions.

Using the binoculars, Colin watched the other two get into position. "Your jolly mood seems to be spreading."

"Give me the binoculars and shut your trap," she said playfully, fully expecting the punch in the arm he gave her. She put the binoculars to her face and did another sweep of the hoverport.

When the door finally opened fifteen minutes later, three people walked out. Mariah was in the middle. Her hands bound with electro-cuffs: three-inch metal bracers covering her forearms, bound together by magnets. Her head was down, her face covered by her hair.

On either side walked two guards. They wore govie-greens, phasers in their hands at the ready.

"See? I told you she would be here," Arden said, feeling a rushing relief. Dade's info had been correct. She owed him big-time.

Mariah lifted her face into the cold blast of wind, her skin littered in bruises. Both eyes were nearly swollen shut. Her hair hung in stringy clumps. She was still in the same outfit she'd worn to the club, though now it sported rips and tears. What was left of it was heavily stained with blood.

At least she was walking under her own power. Broken bones, torn skin—those could heal. Dead meant Mariah couldn't come back.

Arden sucked in her breath, feeling each second of torture they'd put Mariah through as if she'd been the one battered. It made Arden determined to pull this off. No one was going to mess with her family.

"I'm going to kill them," Uri said through the earpiece. His voice shook with unhinged rage.

"Hold," Niall commanded.

Arden focused the binoculars on where Uri hid. Assuring herself he was going to stay in place. His body vibrated, yet he didn't make a move toward the building. She released her breath. This operation would blow up if he went crazy. He'd ruin their one shot, not that she blamed him for his anger.

The trio made its way to the transport hovercraft, the guards on high alert. Both of them repeatedly scanned the area, their phasers slowly panning the surrounding deck. The back door of the hovervan opened on their approach, accompanied by a series of beeps.

Arden slid away her binoculars, strapping them into the pocket of her suit. She leveled her phaser, training it on the guards, then relaxed her shoulders and body to get into the right mind frame to take a shot if needed.

They waited.

Seconds ticked, seeming too slow. And yet Niall still didn't give the signal. Their window was closing, and they all felt it. Adrenaline pumped through Arden. Her fingers were itchy, and her body strained forward. Beside her, Colin also kept his body ready, coiled with anticipation.

"If we wait any longer, they're going to take off," Uri said. If that happened, the rescue was over.

Arden agreed. They needed to move.

"Not yet," Niall said. "Wait for it—"

There was a split second when the first guard moved toward the driver's side and the second guard turned to the back of the vehicle.

"Now," Niall said.

The order hit like a crack. They were on their feet within the next heartbeat. Arden and Colin ran the length of the trackway. They kept their approach partially concealed, crouching as they ran, moving between the hovercars. Phasers were level and out, powered on high.

Colin came around the front of the car, surprising the first guard and catching him with a fist to the gut before the guard could raise his phaser in return. Then he rounded a kick to the guard's hand, kicking the phaser out. It clattered to the ground.

Arden focused on the other guard. Coming up behind him, she squeezed his neck, pushing on the trachea. He squirmed, knocking her in the face. She held on, climbing his back, her hands staying in place until the lack of air caused him to pass out. It would have been easier to shoot both of them, and they would have if necessary, but they couldn't alert the rest of the govies that something was happening outside.

When the guard slumped to the ground, Arden checked back with Colin, making sure that he'd subdued his guard. He nodded to her, moving forward to help with Mariah. Together they urged her to the edge of the hoverport.

Behind them, Uri focused his attention on a line of govie speeders, having already taken care of the hovervans. He quickly went down the line, on each one using a silenced charge, designed to take out their electrical system. Meanwhile, Niall ran to the door of the South Grid Lockup. He blew out the door scanner with several phaser shots. Which triggered the alarm.

Sirens blared. The loud pulsing beat hit Arden's ears, the vibrations nearly driving her to her knees, as they were designed to do. She forced herself to keep moving.

Niall ran past Uri, yelling, "That's only going to hold them for a moment. Let's go."

"I'm not finished." Uri blew out another speeder in the line, before he started running too.

"Move." Niall ran to the end of the hoverport, where Arden and Colin were jostling Mariah, and jumped over.

Niall landed on the platform where they'd parked the speeders. Colin and Arden followed. They were getting onto their speeders when Arden realized Uri and Mariah hadn't jumped. She looked up and watched an unspoken moment between Mariah and Uri.

"Hurry up," she screamed.

That snapped Uri out of whatever fog he was in. Uri moved, then jumped over the side, landing in a crouch.

Mariah was supposed to be next. Uri stood below, arms out to catch her since her balance would be off from her still-shackled hands. Yet she didn't jump, instead standing there frozen. The wind tossed her hair into her face as she looked over the edge with a vacant look of terror. The moments trickled by, seeming like hours.

They all began to scream at her—urging her to jump.

The deck flooded with govies. They'd managed to circumvent the door. Firing round after round, they ran toward Mariah. She ducked to avoid the shots, yet still wouldn't make the leap.

Uri hopped on his speeder, bringing it up and around close to where she stood. He had his phaser out, shooting back at the govies as he neared the platform to grab her. But he was going too fast, his trajectory off. Arden could see there was no way he'd be able to pull Mariah onto the speeder with him.

He missed by inches.

Niall and Colin were already heading out to deflect the govies who'd managed to find undamaged speeders. They probably hadn't seen the exchange. There wasn't time for Uri to circle around to try again. It was up to her to get Mariah.

Arden aimed her speeder for the edge where Mariah stood. She leaned into her driving, aiming for the angle she'd need while avoiding incoming phaser shots that were hitting hard and heavy. She trusted that someone else would take out the govies, so that her whole focus could be on Mariah. Changing direction on a dime to avoid incoming phase-fire, she zoomed by Mariah, catching her around the waist and hauling her on board.

Thankfully, Mariah came to life then. She wiggled and adjusted herself so that she could straddle the seat behind Arden.

"Are you okay?" Arden yelled over the wind as they changed direction away from the platform. She saw Mariah nod but couldn't hear a response.

The others pulled away from the platform, falling into line behind them. Unfortunately, there were more than a few govies able to get on workable speeders. The chase was locked within two Levels. Dropping below Level Three would be certain death, since the Lower Levels were far too populated to drive safely.

Retreating to Level Four was a possibility, but with a high likelihood of failure. Public transport was a problem there, since the skytram moved at too high a speed for the speeders to avoid if they found themselves on an intersecting path.

Anything above Level Four was out altogether. There was a plasma barrier to keep out any flight traffic. It would fry the speeders within seconds.

So the only way to shake the govies was to outrun, evade, and hide. Easier said than done. But there was no way Arden was about to be caught. Not after having Mariah back. She would see everyone safe or die trying.

A speeder came too close. The govie shot a blast of phase-fire, the blast missing them by inches. Arden turned between two buildings, hitting the brakes while skidding sideways. Correcting at the last second, millimeters from hitting the wall. She took off again, shooting out of the bottleneck like a rocket.

"Get me loose," Mariah screamed from behind her.

Arden nodded.

Uri had the magnet clips. He'd taken a left two buildings back. Arden corrected her route to intercept his speeder, running hers right beside his.

Mariah waved her cuffed hands, trying to get his attention.

Uri withdrew the clips, tossing them into the air, before he hit the brakes so that he could pull their tail off, allowing them time to get situated.

Arden caught the magnet clips, handing them back to Mariah. She pulled up to a higher Level, separating from Uri. Two govies followed her. They flew higher. Arden's ears hurt with the change in pressure. She could feel the hum of the plasma net in the air, a silent warning to steer clear.

She dodged another speeder, correcting in time. The other speeder continued past her, hitting the side of a building and exploding. Using her phaser on another, she shot it out from beneath the driver. The debris exploded and rained down on the Levels below.

Uri flew back into her sight, tailed by three govies. She lowered her trajectory, heading down fast to intercept them. Colin and Niall were nowhere to be seen, probably taking the rest of the govies with them. Which meant that between her and Uri, they had only the three govies left.

She saw the shimmer of the catch-net directly in front of Uri, a film draped across the sky to stop runners. Catch-nets were near invisible, only giving off a slight reflection, like water on glass, and they would knock drivers out, stunning them.

Uri headed straight for the net. Oblivious to the danger.

How the govies managed to put one out so quickly was anyone's guess.

There was no way she could scream loud enough or otherwise get his attention to veer out of the way. She pushed her speeder to the max, lowering herself over it. The machine whined beneath her.

She wasn't going to make it.

Uri hit the catch-net with a spark of colors. The speeder passed through the film, as it was designed, the netting disintegrating and falling away. Then Uri's speeder began to circle in wide arcs, like a top finishing its spins, while he slumped over the handlebars.

Two govies had followed him through, their speeders also chaotically spinning out.

Mariah threw off her electro-cuffs with a scream. "Get me close."

Arden handed back her phaser, so that Mariah could shoot the final govie behind them while Arden focused on getting them close enough to Uri without his erratic speeder taking them out for their trouble.

Mariah stood up in her stirrups, using her thigh muscles to keep her on board, while both hands held the phaser steady. She roared as she shot, taking out both the govie and his speeder in a volley of phase-fire.

"This is as close as I can get," Arden screamed over the loud whooshing of air.

"Get me another foot closer."

Arden did as she was told, swerving at the last second to avoid the back end of Uri's speeder as it came around, almost hitting them.

But Mariah was already jumping across the space, thousands of feet in the air, landing across Uri's slumped body. She crouched over him, her hands on the controls and her feet on the pedals.

"Go," she screamed, and sped off. Looking crazy with her hair tangled, face splotched with bruises, and wild eyes.

# CHAPTER NINETEEN

Dade couldn't look away from the footage.

News of the prisoner escape was all over the visicast, the coverage simultaneously projected in every room of the apartment, so that he couldn't go anywhere in the house without hearing the repeated drama of what had taken place that afternoon. Speeders had crashed into buildings, several city blocks were without power, and multiple families were now without homes because of the destruction. Yet he watched it all with his heart in his throat, hoping for Arden's escape.

Dade studied the footage again. He was sure the rider who'd grabbed the rescued girl and hoisted her onto the speeder was Arden. Watching it on replay to make him positive of it. He'd seen that speeder disappear from view, so she wasn't dead. At least he hoped.

"The group is still at large," the visicaster said, staring intently into the camera. The feed then cut away, flashing a picture of the girl's face, the one who'd been detained. "If anyone has seen this girl, they're asked to contact authorities immediately.

"While it has not been confirmed, we have received information that this crime may have been linked to the infamous Lasair gang."

Of course the govies wouldn't confirm it. It had been a demoralizing loss for them. They couldn't be happy with their defeat plastered on halo-screens for everyone to see. They also didn't want the public to know the Levels were vulnerable and that some of the Undercity gangs could move freely. The Lasair members were supposed to stay locked below. It made everyone feel safer.

On-screen, the visicaster continued to speculate how this could signal the start of a war between Lasair and the govies. That didn't concern Dade, though. The war was coming regardless.

The more pressing issue was that this attack against the govies had escalated the tension in the Sky Towers. It had been rising steadily ever since Arden had broken in, and then Dade hadn't helped his cause by almost getting caught at the refinery. He'd still managed to sneak in and out occasionally. Now, though, everything was on lockdown. The number of guards had been tripled, and everyone coming or going was scrutinized, their implanted data sensors double-checked.

He could probably figure out a way to make it out of his Tower without detection, but he wondered if it would be worth it. He'd already had to stop his Ghost activities. He felt guilty for leaving the children without VitD and hoped they'd have enough of a supply to last until he was back on his regular rounds. He couldn't risk being caught. It would end his efforts completely. There was nothing to do but sit and stew while watching the continuous news loop.

His datapad pinged.

Dade sighed, knowing exactly who it would be before he clicked the message center open. The ziptext didn't fail to disappoint. His father had been locked up with Chief Nakomzer all morning, and now it seemed he was about to turn his attention on Dade.

He slipped his datapad into his pocket, trying not to feel concerned about their upcoming talk. They hadn't spoken in a few days. Every time his dad went that long focused on something else, when he finally did remember that Dade existed, it was because of something big. And since there had been several "big" things to choose from in the last week, Dade expected the worst.

His father's office was located inside Sky Tower Two, in a different wing than the family's apartment. So while Dade didn't have to leave the building, there was still a fair distance to travel.

Chief Nakomzer had just stepped out of his father's office when Dade arrived. Nakomzer's face was red and wore a thunderous frown. Dade stepped to the side, allowing the chief and the two guards who flanked him to pass.

That meeting had obviously not gone well. Which didn't help to alleviate Dade's growing tension. He nodded to the guard outside of the office before he walked into the room.

Hernim Croix sat behind his desk. Constructed from indigenous stone and polished to a glass-like shine, it was a massive structure that didn't diminish the man in the least. He looked up as soon as Dade entered, pressing the button to close the door. He then indicated that Dade should take one of the chairs across from him. The wide-view screen on the wall projected a muted visicast. Visual images of the escape looped across the hologram.

Dade forced his gaze to stay on his father.

Hernim folded his hands together, his fingers loosely intertwined, and set his elbows on the desk. He appeared relaxed, inviting even. He leaned forward with his shoulders, creating an illusion of intimacy. "You've been busy."

The words short-circuited Dade's brain as warnings blared in his head. Even though he'd known an interrogation was coming, it had always been difficult to maintain an aloof appearance with his father. Yet he hadn't actually been caught, so he didn't think this was a fishing expedition about the refinery break-in.

"How so?" It made Dade happy that his words came out calm and confident with a hint of surprise, exactly as he'd wanted.

"I haven't seen you in the last few weeks. What have you been doing?"

Dade shrugged. He refused to offer any sort of excuse that could be picked apart for lies. Instead, he waited it out. If his father had any evidence, he'd have been crucified already.

The seconds ticked by, Dade's muscles tightening as each one passed. He struggled to keep his spine straight and not drop his gaze. The waiting seemed like an eternity. This was a longer pause than most, yet no accusation came. His father didn't blink, didn't present so much as a lie or a rumor.

His father had to know something. Maybe he couldn't prove it, but he had a strong suspicion. It was in his every movement. The way he spoke. The way he squinted his eyes as he studied Dade, as if waiting for Dade to trip up.

"It's time to stop hanging out with your friends and focus on something productive," Hernim said, surprising Dade.

"I have been productive, sir. I've worked at the factory and go to social functions whenever I'm required."

"At the factory," Hernim repeated with a grunt, his eyes narrowing. "Rylick confirmed you've been there. Still, it's time to get serious about your place here."

"I'm always serious."

Hernim began to tap a pen slowly against the desk. Tick-tick-tick. Then he allowed the silence to descend again—his father's favorite tactic. "We need to move into the next stage of our operation. Unfortunately, the govies haven't been able to keep up their end of the deal. That means we need to make alternative plans. We must all do our part, and that includes you."

Dade felt the noose tighten.

"I've given a lot of thought to your marriage."

Dade nodded slowly, struggling against the choking sensation closing his throat.

"I had thought that we'd give you a few months to settle into your engagement. But the events of the past day have moved up my timeline." There was cool determination in his father's look.

"What do you mean?"

"The Hemstock family requires a binding commitment before they are willing to stand with us on other issues." His father paused his pen tapping to make his next words count. "The govies are leaning on us now too, and Nakomzer is trying to distance himself. We're on our own, as it were."

Dade's throat was dry when he asked, "When is the wedding?"

"One week."

"Father, no." He managed to get the protest past his dry lips. His throat worked steadily as he tried to swallow.

"It's for the best. You were going to marry her eventually anyway." His father's voice had taken on a harsh quality. Then his eyes narrowed, and his nostrils flared. "I want the trouble you're causing to end now."

"I haven't done anything."

His father looked at Dade as if he could twist him from inside out. "You've been ditching your guard plenty. And don't think I'm unaware of your trips into the Levels. Care to tell me what those are about?"

Dade wasn't able to meet his father's gaze. "No."

Hernim snorted. "From now until your wedding, you're on lockdown. The only time you're to be out of the Tower is when your fiancée requests you accompany her or when you're on family business, as we must keep up appearances. I won't let this thing spin more out of control than it already has."

"You can't do that."

His father raised an eyebrow. "I just did."

# CHAPTER TWENTY

Arden waited with her back against the wall. Her phaser drawn, the muzzle tipped toward the empty hall with both hands clasping the grip. She watched the exits while Colin worked his ninja magic on the door lock with his datapad and decryption program. They'd made it into the pharmaceutical plant without incident, bypassing the guards outside while wearing docking uniforms to avoid tipping off the monitors. They were now on the Level below the labs, where the merchandise was exported.

The job was humming along as normal. Get in, get the drugs, and get out. No big deal. Sneaking through security had been tough. Worse than any other job she could remember. On the weekend, there should have been fewer bodies on-site, not four times the normal number. Maybe Dade had been right that something even more sinister was in the works.

It didn't feel right.

She tapped her foot and played with the safety on her phaser.

Off.

On.

Off.

"Stop it," Colin hissed. He looked away from his datapad where it connected to the electric lock, running its number sequence.

Arden's attention snapped back to the present. "What?"

"I'm going to lose my mind if you click that safety one more time."

She glanced down at her hand where her thumb rested over the safety. It took her a moment to realize what she'd been doing. She gave Colin a guilty grin. "Sorry."

"I've never seen you so nervous."

"Maybe because we're stupid to be here. Did you fail to notice the tightened security? They know something." She didn't add any of the other zillion reasons that crowded her head. "Plus, I can't shake this feeling."

"Of what?"

Her hands flexed and grabbed at her phaser. She pushed in and out a few breaths. "The weirdness. I don't know how to explain it. Like this foreboding sense of doom."

"You and your premonitions."

Arden released a shaky laugh, bordering on hysterical. "They're not wrong."

"Fine." Colin went back to the datapad. "But I can't help but think you're making it come true. Focus and we'll be okay."

"You're probably right."

Colin gave her his full attention. "If you think we should call it off, say so now."

It was nice that Colin was so calm. It helped her focus. She shifted her thumb away from the safety and thought about the implications if she did follow through with her reaction to this crazy feeling and it ended up being all in her head. Colin was right: they'd be okay. She just needed to get a grip. "Nah. We're low on VitD. If we don't get new supplies to make more Shine, Niall will have even more reason to go forward with Project Blackout." If she could buy a bit of time on that end, she could maybe figure out a way to keep her promise to Dade that she wouldn't harm his family.

Colin's datapad beeped. The light on the wall entry pad switched from red to green, and the door slid open.

"Easy," Colin said as he unclipped his pad.

Arden waited for Colin to put away the datapad. He took out his phaser, nodding that he was ready. Together they entered, moving through the room on opposite sides, checking for people. One side of the room held packaging stations, along with several assembly tables and conveyor lines. All turned off and dark, their metal racks shiny and new. The other half of the room near the bay doors consisted of shelving areas stacked with boxes of merchandise.

Once they made sure no one was there, Arden signaled to Colin. He nodded and opened the large bay doors that exited onto the loading dock.

Colin had placed the cameras on a twenty-second delay prior to entering the room. Arden rolled a silencer to jam any additional systems. Not as effective as breaking into the monitors and taking them over. But they didn't have the manpower to do that for this job.

Arden sighed. Yet another item to add to her growing list of failures on this mission.

Colin disengaged the bay doors. They slid upward, allowing Niall and Uri to back a stolen hovervan into the loading dock. It was used for deliveries, painted on the side with brown block letters that read "Croix Industries." Once out of the compound, they would park it in one of the abandoned metal yards and transfer the packages into less-trackable vehicles.

Uri came around to open the back of the van while Niall exited the driver's side. Then Colin, Niall, and Uri headed for the plain synth-board boxes with the Croix Industries pharmaceutical label, awaiting shipment out the next morning. Niall opened one box to make sure it contained VitD. Once that was confirmed, the guys began to load, working in silence. Every second counted, and they worked seamlessly together.

Arden took up her position as lookout near the entry doors. She stood, her body loose, but her mind wandered. How could she make a life with Dade when they would always be on opposite sides of the divide? Always stealing from each other. Trying to kill one another. How could there ever be anything between them? He'd said they'd work it out, and now she felt guilty on every run she made, both for betraying him and also for betraying her family.

"I expected you earlier," a voice said.

She felt the metal of the phaser tip against her temple as strong arms moved to surround her chest and pull her back, making her heart jump-start and the adrenaline run through her. She'd had one job, and she'd messed it up. This just proved it: her obsession with Dade was going to get them all killed.

Arden moved her head slightly to the side in an effort to look at her captor.

The boy wasn't that much taller than she was. He wore the same grin she'd seen in all the news-vids, his shaggy dark hair pointing every which way. She may not have ever met him in person, but she knew him. She was positive this was Rylick, Dade's first cousin.

Wasn't that just perfect?

She looked to her own cousin. Colin kept his body loose, his hand near the phaser at his side. Not quite reaching, not wanting to cause Rylick to react, while watching for an opening to move. He sent Arden a desperate look.

She blinked, and frowned. Trying to reassure him, but accepting that it was her fault. Not wanting him to make a move that would get him shot.

"Phasers on the ground," Rylick said. When they didn't immediately comply, he pressed his phaser harder into Arden's head. "I'm not messing around. I'll splatter her brains all over this room."

Niall was the first to comply. He placed his phaser on the ground, then slowly stepped back with his hands open and raised at his sides. Reluctance was evident in each movement. Colin stood still as if he wasn't going to obey. He frowned, looking around for a better option. Then, at a pointed look from Niall, he copied Niall's surrender.

At that moment, Arden realized Uri wasn't standing in the open. She had no idea where he was, but the fact that he wasn't in the line of fire gave her hope.

"You too," Rylick said into her ear.

Arden moved just as slow as the others had. She threw the phaser to the ground while keeping her other hand raised and visible. She kept her body loose, waiting for an opportunity to strike.

Rylick kept his arm around her, the phaser to her head the entire time.

"I've seen you," he said into her ear, low enough that the words wouldn't carry to the others. "I've followed him. Imagine his surprise when he sees you in chains."

She couldn't suppress the shiver that ran down her spine. Her heart beat loudly in her chest, filling her ears with the noise. She wanted him to shut up. Didn't want to hear his taunts.

"Maybe I'll tell his daddy about your fling." He chuckled. "Or maybe I won't." He leaned even closer so that she felt the heat of his breath practically searing her ear. "Perhaps I'll just kill you. You can't imagine how much pleasure that would give me."

"You don't scare me." But the fact that he could ruin Dade did. She tried to keep her spine straight. To swallow down the lump that had formed in her throat. To not let him know just how much he'd affected her.

His arm slid up from her waist to squeeze his hand around her neck. "It might be more amusing to watch when my uncle gets his hands on you."

Arden could only imagine. The stories of what Dade's father had done in the past were horrific. She wouldn't outlive the night, especially if Rylick told about her relationship with Dade.

He squeezed, cutting off her air. "He had her, and he chose you. Why?"

Arden fought against his hand, prying at his fingers. Struggling for an ounce of air. She couldn't wonder at his statement. Couldn't focus on anything but the darkness creeping around the edges of her vision.

Then Uri stepped out from behind the van. He fired multiple shots at Rylick. It wouldn't have worked if Rylick hadn't already been angry and distracted. He should have been expecting it.

Rylick startled enough that Arden was able to shove her elbow back into his gut, twist, and break his hold. Already moving, her body reacted before her mind caught up. She dropped and rolled, picking up her phaser as she went.

Phase-fire shot from all directions.

Arden headed for cover but wasn't fast enough. A blast of energy hit her left shoulder. Hot and intense, flashing pain flooded through her system. Moving despite the agony, she managed to wedge herself behind a large machine. Her back pushed to the wall, her good shoulder to the side of the metal. Pressing her fingers to the wound, she winced. Her breath came out in fast pants, and she thought she might be sick. She pushed the fabric of her suit apart to check the damage. It looked bad, but not life-threatening.

*Focus, Arden. Focus.*

She leaned out, taking a shot at where Rylick had sought cover. Pulling back when he fired in her direction. She looked the other way to check where the boys had disappeared. Uri was still on the other side of the van, while Colin low-crawled under the chassis. He wasn't quite on the other side yet, his lower half still underneath.

There wasn't any sign of Niall. That concerned her. She prayed he hadn't gotten shot and had at least made it out of the line of fire.

The next few seconds went faster than Arden could process, though later she would relive it until it made her sick.

Arden rounded the machine to shoot at Rylick. Uri rose at the same time from the far side of the hovervan, also shooting. Colin finally gained his feet and lurched around the opposite side of the van.

Rylick shot a few rounds toward her. She ducked back behind the machine as large chunks of debris went flying. Then he changed focus to shoot in Colin's direction.

She watched as Colin was too slow to shield himself behind the vehicle. Saw the moment the phase-fire hit him in the center of his chest. His eyes rounded, and his mouth dropped open. A large red hole bloomed in the middle of his body.

It lasted seconds, yet it seemed to take forever, moving slowly.

Colin's body fell backward.

Arden let out an anguished cry. Rage and disbelief filled her. She pushed out of her hiding space, sending out a series of phase-blasts toward Rylick. Uncaring that she was no longer shielded, she stepped forward, shooting as she walked. Tears streaked down her face. Anger, more than thought, propelled her.

"Arden, enough," Niall screamed loud enough so that she could hear him.

And then it was quiet.

Arden's chest rose and fell, her breath heavy sounding and harsh inside her ears. Focusing on the hitch it made was the only thing that kept her standing. Heaviness settled over her, making her numb. Her limbs felt like lead as the adrenaline burned off.

The "Stay with us" from Niall, from somewhere behind the hover-van, snapped her into motion.

First she checked that Rylick was no longer a threat. Keeping her phaser up, ready in case he was playing possum. She rounded the sorting machine he'd used as cover.

He lay on the ground, his body slumped at an unnatural angle. His torso leaned over his folded legs. She pushed him back with the toe of her boot, so that his body moved into a prone position. His arm splayed out.

His face was slack.

His eyes stared sightlessly.

Void.

Arden closed her own eyes, gulping back the nausea that threatened to bubble up from her throat as she lowered her weapon. He was dead, and yet she still leaned forward to press her fingers to his throat to make sure there wasn't a pulse.

She'd killed lots of people. Every life she took broke a little of her inside. But in this case it was more.

She'd killed Dade's cousin. After Dade had pointedly asked her to give up her feud against his family. How could he forgive her? She'd gone crazy at the sight of Colin being shot. How could Dade not feel the same?

The impact of what this meant, that she'd broken her promise to Dade, had her clutching her chest as she turned away.

She still gripped her phaser as she crossed over to where Colin lay beside the van. Niall knelt at his side, holding Colin's hand. He pleaded with Colin. "Open your eyes. Fight. You can't die."

Colin lay in a pool of blood, while more dribbled from the corner of his lip, shiny and slick. The fibers of his stolen uniform were burned, his middle soft and oozing. His skin grew paler as Arden watched.

He wouldn't make it.

She felt only terror and anger and overwhelming guilt.

His lips moved, forming words that he didn't have the breath to speak. Arden dropped her phaser, pushing Niall out of the way so that she could lean close to press her ear against Colin's lips.

"Choose."

Then the last of his air expressed from his lungs, and he was gone.

Emotion erupted inside her. Unlike anything she'd ever experienced. She cried out, sobbing and begging, pleading for Colin to come back. Knowing the whole time that she'd lost someone infinitely precious to her. Who left a void that could never be filled.

She felt her heart crack.

A hand shook her. "We need to go." Tears were cascading down Niall's face, and his voice was rough. But it was also calm and determined. She watched him physically pull himself together. He picked up Colin's body, moving him to the van where Uri helped to lay Colin in the back.

Arden didn't move. Couldn't force her body to cooperate. She stayed on her knees, focused on her hands, stained with blood. There was so much of it. Red. Wet. Everywhere.

Uri shut the hovervan door. The sound rocked through Arden with finality.

"Get in the van, Arden. We're moving out," Niall said.

Arden focused on the security of Niall taking charge. She nodded, yet only moved when he walked over to help her up. But her heart stayed locked with Colin, broken in the back of the hovervan.

# CHAPTER TWENTY-ONE

*Choose.*

Arden kept her gaze straight ahead, locked on the undecorated urn at the front of the sanctuary. The vessel sat on a tiny table covered with a gold cloth. Colin's body had been cremated earlier that day and now rested inside. This was all that was left, the totality of his life.

Beside her, her mother sobbed into a handkerchief. Arden's father had been too sick to attend. That, at least, was a blessing, because she couldn't take care of anyone else, much less herself.

She couldn't breathe. It hurt. Everything hurt.

Tears dripped down Arden's cheeks. She'd yet to figure out how to numb her pain. She didn't want to, but she knew if she let emotion sweep her away, there would be no way she'd ever be able to lock it in again. She would just let her anger take her to its inevitable end.

She refused to embrace this, the single most devastating moment of her life. It couldn't be real.

*Choose.* Colin's voice echoed in her head, making her crazy.

The rest of the Lasair gang filled the first few rows of the chapel, sitting in the areas designated for family. She felt them like a second skin. Surrounding her. Insulating her from the world outside the doors of the church. Whatever the final outcome, she needed them, especially now.

She felt so alone. There was no longer an emotional anchor in her life. Her safety broken, her family shattered.

Eventually they'd all die.

Wasn't that what Colin had said? He'd known that their only outcome would be death. He'd warned her. She thought about all his urgings to leave the gang. Wishing he'd taken his own advice. She wanted him back in her life. She'd give anything to have him back.

And yet, she still couldn't leave the gang. Now more than ever she was stuck. What did she have left without Colin? Lasair was the only family she could count on.

Colin's parents were on the other side of her mother. The sisters were holding hands. Grasping each other as if they could keep afloat in their grief. Arden was glad for her aunt's presence. There was little left inside Arden that could give comfort to anyone else.

She avoided looking at them. Couldn't handle sharing their pain.

She didn't know what to do. Be something. Do something.

Figure out how to live with no regrets.

The priest walked the circumference of the front dais, swinging a perforated gold ball on a chain. White smoke billowed from the holes. It smelled sweet, almost cloying. It filled the room, making the already insufferable temperature worse.

Several other priests stationed throughout hummed and chanted together in a prayer, maybe a benediction. Either way, the sound drilled a hole into her skull. She shut her eyes against it. Pushed her fingertips against her temples to relieve the pressure. And yet the tears managed to slip out through her closed lids, coating her fingers.

Finally the long service came to a close. She felt drained and empty. Lost.

Arden slid from her seat. She walked toward the outside of the church's scarred pews, past the yellowed plaster walls and broken stained glass. Head down, she focused on the tiled mosaic floor, not wanting to speak to anyone. She wasn't capable of small talk. And she certainly didn't want to exchange empty platitudes.

When she heard her name, she raised her head reflexively, then realized that Niall had cut off the conversation he'd been in the middle of and was now on his way to intercept her. Her heart rate picked up, rocking her chest with dread. He'd been acting irrationally since "the incident," as he was now labeling the disaster at the factory. Whatever he wanted to say certainly wouldn't be good.

She turned, hoping to push through the mourners, to escape into the streets for a few hours, or at least for as long as it took to get herself together before she was accosted with demands from the gang.

That wasn't to be.

Niall cornered her before she made it out of the sanctuary. He looked exhausted. The lines around his face had deepened over the last few days. Aging him. She knew he suffered Colin's loss as much as the rest of them. Yet he wasn't broken, not like her. Her world had ended. He'd found a face for his cause. Colin's death had made him more determined to move on with his plan. As if genocide were a sensible answer.

"Now is the time to strike." His voice was hard, and he spoke with little inflection. "They're suffering a loss."

"So are we." They were still inside the church with Colin's ashes cold at the front and his spirit probably looking on, disgusted. Couldn't they have this talk elsewhere?

Niall pressed. "They won't expect it. We'll have the advantage."

That he was using Colin's death to serve his needs made her sick. Her stomach swam. She pressed a fist to it, hoping to hold back the weakness she felt. "Niall, let's talk later, when—"

He cut her off, his hand slicing through the air. "This is it, sis. It's been decided. I expect you to be there." He didn't add that to ignore his order would be her death warrant. She'd end up number one on Lasair's hit list. "Take a few days. Get your act together."

Arden exhaled and looked away.

Uri chose that moment to interrupt them. He said to Niall, "We've got a situation."

Niall nodded and stuck his hands in his pockets, affecting a relaxed stance. He turned back to Arden, warning, "Be there," before walking away.

She looked to Uri, hoping for some words of wisdom. Maybe he'd offer another way out of this. Or at least he could talk to Niall to get him to hold off just a little more. "You're not okay with his plans, are you?"

Uri shrugged. "He's right, screw them."

"It's suicide."

"It's time," he said. Then he left too. Only when he took off, it felt like a door had been shut to any chance of a normal life.

The rage inside her began to eat away at her sorrow. Not replace. Her grieving for Colin would never be finished. Perhaps they were right, though. Making everyone pay would make her feel better in a small way. Not just the Solizen, but all of their society who'd allowed this inequity. They were at fault in this too, with the little value they placed on human life.

Arden sighed, swallowing back her need to cry out.

No, she couldn't display her rage in the way she wanted to. It wouldn't help.

If she were rational, she wouldn't even consider the idea. Colin wouldn't have liked it. He'd be the first person to tell her that she was taking out her anger on innocents. She needed to get a grip and refocus. Find her way out of this darkness. She needed to talk to someone who would set her straight. Remind her that there was still hope. That she could count on things getting better.

There was only one option.

Dade.

He'd give her the perspective she needed. Calm her down. Dade cared about people. It was the best thing about him: he was a shining light she could trust to tell her the truth. To calm the storm inside her.

If only she hadn't killed his cousin. Arden swallowed back bile. She certainly wasn't looking forward to facing him.

# Chapter Twenty-Two

Arden, hidden amid the food carts, stood across the street from the moonglass-and-steel cathedral. She watched the mourners come and go from Rylick's wake, the Solizen in their dark finery, faces contorted with pain. They clutched at one another as they gave in to their grief.

Two days had passed since Colin's funeral and six intense days since Rylick's and Colin's deaths. Days filled with agony and regret. Of trying to figure out what she needed to do to make sense of this mess. The grief had given way to anger, then to despair for Colin, for Rylick, and for herself. Watching the mourners made the rawness inside her feel bruised. Emotions she wasn't ready to deal with wanted to creep out from the space she'd coiled them into. She swallowed, pushing back the tears. Strength was what she needed.

And what she didn't have.

Dade stepped out of the doorway amid the crowd. He paused at the head of the stairs. Bitter wind blew at his hair and tugged at his cloak. From this angle, she could see sadness even as he held his shoulders back and his head high. Beside him, Saben acted as a buffer for those who sought to speak with Dade. They descended the steps together, flanked by two additional guards.

She followed the group to the quadralift closest to Wild Jacks casino. That lift always malfunctioned when it reached the Fourth Level. The light doors would dissolve and regenerate regardless of anyone waiting to use it. Which meant in order to catch up with him, she could go through Wild Jacks, up the internal casino quadralift to the Fourth Level, and cut across to meet him when the doors opened.

Her stomach did a flip as she took off at a run.

Arden's shoulder still burned where the phase-fire had caught it. The wound was deep, but the phase-fire hadn't done permanent damage. She'd allowed a doctor to dress it and had taken a bac-shot to avoid infection. Arden liked the pain. It was penance for her sins. It reminded her she deserved to feel anger. That she was alive.

She raced inside Wild Jacks, cutting through the gamblers, not that they paid any attention. Then exited onto the platform of Level Four, huffing a bit. Arden paused there, out of the way, yet in direct sight of the quadralift door. She hoped that when Dade saw her, he'd want to talk. He had to make the move. With the extra guards, she couldn't get him alone. Not if he didn't help.

If this didn't work, well then, she'd just have to think of something else. She had to talk to him whether he wanted to see her or not.

The door opened.

Arden was strung tight. As if every nerve ending in her entire body began to sizzle. She held her breath.

Dade stood in the center of the hoverdisk inside the quadralift, facing out with his head down. The guards flanked his sides. The only one paying attention was the hulking brute who followed Dade everywhere. His hand rested on the phaser at his hip, while he darted his gaze around the platform.

*Look up. Look up. Look up,* she silently begged Dade.

The door of the quadralift began to turn hazy as the plasma solidified starting at his feet, working its way up.

She wanted to scream. Wanted to wave her hands or use any other means of gaining his attention. Yet she stayed silent and still, even as adrenaline thrummed, shaking her insides. Her foot tapped. Her fingers flexed over and over, drumming an incomprehensible beat.

*Come on, look.*

And then he lifted his head.

Their eyes met. The electric charge that always arced between them sparked and burned, a live connection that jolted her.

For a second, fear took control. He might not forgive her. Might not ever want to see her again.

She swallowed down the bile rising in her throat, steeling herself for rejection.

How else could star-crossed love end other than death and destruction?

Arden reached up to pull down her hood. Letting her features be seen, both by him and by whoever happened to be monitoring the cameras. It felt powerful, like a declaration of intent.

Dade's face registered several emotions in quick succession: surprise, confusion, anger, resolution, hurt. It was the last that squeezed her stomach, made her heart ache as the doors solidified between them.

Then she waited. Anxiety became a living thing inside her. Whispering doubt. But she stayed because she had faith in him, in *them*. He would come to her.

When the doors opened once more, he was there. Alone. It was impressive how he managed that.

She exhaled in relief, feeling as if she'd shed a huge weight. Whether or not she could explain what had happened in a way he could accept, maybe even forgive, remained to be seen.

He walked out of the quadralift. She walked forward. Both watching the other as they took measured steps, to meet in the middle of the bridge connecting the two platforms.

She wanted to reach for him. Touch him. Assure herself that something she cared for had survived when she felt as if everything else had been taken away. Yet he didn't make any move for her, so she kept her hands to herself, pressed tightly to her side.

"I only have a moment," he said. "I stepped back into the quadralift before it closed. They'll be here on the next hoverdisk."

She nodded in understanding. There wasn't much time to convince him, then. She took a deep breath, ready to plead her case. But he spoke once more.

"They're looking for you." He'd kept his voice low, yet didn't lean into her as he'd always done before. That hurt. His distance knifed through her far worse than the pain in her shoulder. "I asked you to stop the vendetta against my family. And now look what's happened."

"I know."

"They said you were the one who killed him."

She didn't want it to go this way. Wanted to ease into the confession. Nevertheless, she had to be honest, even if it meant losing him. Arden took a deep breath, keeping eye contact. "I did," she said clearly as she pulled herself up straight and waited for the fallout.

A look of betrayal clouded his face.

It nearly tore her in two, but the reaction was exactly as she'd expected. They didn't have time for this, not if she wanted him to understand. "You knew the truth of it before you decided to speak with me."

"I'd hoped it was wrong."

There was nothing she could say to make Rylick's death better. She offered, "I'm sorry." And she meant it.

Dade's gaze strayed to her shoulder where the bulk of the bandage pushed out her cloak. "You were hit."

"It's nothing," she said, because she had her life. This would heal.

"It doesn't look like 'nothing.'"

Behind him, she could see the disk in the glass tube slowly descending, ticking away their time. "This isn't what I want to speak about."

"What is it you wanted, if not to beg forgiveness for my cousin's murder?" Dade asked, letting her feel the full brunt of his anger.

"My cousin died as well," Arden said softly.

"You shouldn't have been there. I warned you." He was shaking now, his eyes narrow slits. "If you weren't at the factory, none of this would have happened."

"You knew we were going to steal the VitD," she accused, unsure why she was pushing it. "We had to."

Dade's lips pressed together. He closed his eyes a long moment and then opened them. "There's always another way."

"There's not." She poked herself in the chest. "I live in this world, Dade. It's seedy and cruel, and horrible things happen. I didn't make the rules. I just survive any way I can. And sometimes"—her voice broke—"we lose people."

"It's not about the VitD. I steal it too," he said. "It's about your insatiable need to crush my family."

"Not my need." But still, there was that push from Lasair. He was right that she felt anger, and she wanted to make everyone pay.

"I sympathize that people are suffering. I've done what I can to help them," Dade said. He looked even more furious now than before, and Arden knew she was losing ground. "But that does not mean I can accept your desire to hurt people. What have you done to help them? It seems to me that you've just accepted the way things are. You're not looking for change."

She felt those words like a kick in the chest. They practically stopped her heart. Arden lashed out. "So I have to turn against my family? Is that what you're saying?" She wanted to shake him. Make him listen to reason. "Don't blame me because I'm doing what's necessary. You may think stealing your family's meds and giving them away makes you a better person than me, but it doesn't. You had all the power to begin with."

Arden regretted the words the instant she said them. She knew he cared. And yet, she couldn't force herself to take them back. She was every bit as caught up in this mess as he was.

His reaction was unexpected. Instead of yelling at her, he frowned. Looked more distraught than she could ever remember anyone being. "Why are we fighting?"

She paused. "I don't know."

"I don't want to argue with you. I want you safe," he said. "This thing between our families is not over."

Arden nodded. "I know."

"Many more people are going to die." He grabbed her hands, holding them in his and squeezing them. "We need to find a way to stop this. I know Lasair is planning something, just like I know my father is. It's up to us to end the war."

His words broke her heart. "I don't know if we can."

Dade frowned.

The quadralift was almost there. She could see the bottom of the hoverdisk. "We're out of time."

"I know." He pulled her close then, reeling her in with his hands. Then he leaned down and pressed his mouth to hers. His lips felt soft, just a flutter of a touch.

He kissed her as if saying goodbye.

Because she knew what goodbye felt like.

Her heart broke. Shattered into pieces right there. He may have been holding her, but he felt far away. She broke his hold to grip his arms and press in. Pushing the kiss harder. If this was to be their last one, he would remember it.

All of her anger and hurt came surging forward, all her loss and guilt. The unavoidable end of her relationship with Dade. Her feelings flowed from her in the way she touched him. She wanted him to understand her pain.

Then he pulled away. He looked at her hard. "This is not the end."

She nodded, not believing him.

"Go." He pushed her away.

She looked behind him, realizing that their time was up. She could see the murky outline of the three guards. The hoverdisk, still translucent, was not quite low enough to make their faces visible.

From the way they held their bodies, she could tell they had their phasers out. Arden needed to leave.

He hadn't forgiven her, and yet he was still pushing for this relationship. She was now more conflicted than before they talked.

"Are we going to survive this?" she asked.

"I don't know."

She turned around then and walked away, disappearing into the bustle of the city.

# CHAPTER TWENTY-THREE

Arden had no idea where to go. It had been a few days since she'd spoken to Dade. She'd needed a little time to think and didn't want to be around Niall or the gang. There was too much in her head that she needed to sort out. She'd used up all her non-Lasair hideouts. Niall would find her eventually even though she'd shut off the locator on her datapad. Arden still wasn't ready to face him. But she knew she couldn't put it off for much longer.

She approached the church from the back. It was the last spot she'd figured Niall would look for her. When she'd thought of it, she almost didn't use it because of Dade. Then had thought better of it. If Dade knew she needed a quiet place to think, he'd be the first person to offer up the church.

The robed man who opened the door appeared to know who she was.

"May the sun shine for all," she said, offering him a slight bow, her palms pressed together.

He didn't speak as he ushered her into the church and led her to a sparsely furnished sitting room. She sat on the decayed couch, pulling her cloak closer around her. There was a fire, but it did little to quench the draft. Plus, she had a feeling that the cold seeped deeper into her body than the temperature. It was in her soul. From the moment she'd walked away from Dade, she hadn't been able to stop shivering.

Father Benedict arrived not long after. He didn't look the least bit surprised to see her. "Welcome," he said, standing just inside the sitting room door. Violet Death had eaten away at him since she'd last seen him, his color now gone and his skin taken over by open sores.

"I need a place to stay," Arden said awkwardly. "Not for long, just . . ." She fiddled with the hem of her cloak, figuring out what to say without lying. It didn't feel right to lie to a priest, even if she didn't belong to this religion.

"You are welcome here, my child. Be at peace. God's house is open to anyone who seeks shelter." Father Benedict gestured for her to follow him. "Come, let us find you a room, though the comfort here is not found in materialistic offerings."

Arden exhaled a mirthless laugh. "It's fine. I'm not used to comfort anyway."

He took her to a windowless room that reminded her of a prison cell. The walls were made from stone, and there was very little furniture: a small cot and a table with a stool.

"As I said," he turned to look at her, giving her a soft smile, "the comfort we offer within these walls is spiritual."

She pulled off her coat because it felt awkward not to, and it gave her something to do besides fidget. But she regretted it almost immediately when his gaze strayed to her shoulder.

"When is the last time you had your bandage changed?"

Arden looked at it. "I don't know. A few days?"

Father Benedict frowned. "I'll be back shortly with a med kit and something to eat."

She wanted to tell him to save his medicine, to use it on himself. Though she knew that at that point he was as much as dead from his infection.

Instead she said, "Thank you."

When Father Benedict left the room, the silence became oppressive. A single bulb shone a glazed light, which made the room appear smaller than it probably was. She'd slept in worse. Closing her eyes, she lay back on the cot and tried to reach a calm place. She couldn't shake the feeling that something had been wrong when she'd spoken with Dade. Anger she'd expected. However, she'd been surprised at the distance she'd felt from him and the sadness in his final kiss.

There was something she'd missed. It pricked at her consciousness like an irritating burr.

Arden felt stuck in her life. How was she supposed to do as Dade asked and not target his family when she knew that it would hurt her own? It wasn't fair to ask that of her. She didn't know how to proceed. She didn't have a plan, a direction. It wasn't like her. Dade had mixed her all up.

The realization that she felt defeated came as a surprise. Arden had never lost before. Never failed at anything she'd tried for. She had always been confident in her intuition. That ability had saved her life more than once. Second-guessing led to death in the most literal sense.

Now that confidence was shaken.

If she started to doubt herself, how could she trust that she'd be able to take on any challengers? If she went rogue, anyone could cut her down.

There was a knock at the door before Father Benedict pushed it open. He carried a tray of food and set it on the small table next to the bed. Then he sat on the stool and withdrew a med kit.

Arden sat up on the cot with her wounded shoulder facing him. As much as it hurt and as sore as she was, she perversely didn't want to feel better. Being miserable kept her from breaking.

Father Benedict unwound the soiled wrap, then checked the wound with deft movements. He pulled out the cleaning alcohol, dabbing at her raw skin. "It's not infected."

Arden made a noise of assent. It was fortunate that her shoulder wouldn't fester. But she couldn't find the will to be thankful at the moment.

"I'm going to use some quick-seal on this. It will hold the skin together enough so that I can use a thinner bandage."

Arden nodded. A smaller bandage would allow for better flexibility. It was as if he were aware that fighting was inevitable for her. If he knew that her actions might kill them all, maybe he wouldn't be so helpful.

She kept her face turned away so he couldn't read her guilt.

"Speak, my child," he urged. "Let it out, or it will spread like poison."

Arden hesitated, her mouth falling open in surprise. Then she figured, *Why not?* He held Dade's confidence. Anything she shared, he couldn't prove. By the time he could use the information, it would be too late.

"I'm in love with Dade." Arden let the words settle in her gut as she said them aloud. She'd known she loved him, even though she had long denied it to herself. It was too soon to have those kinds of feelings. But apparently that didn't matter.

Sad that she'd never admitted as much to Dade.

Father Benedict didn't react. If anything, he seemed supportive. "You haven't told him?"

"It's not that simple."

"I've found that all choices can be simple." He smoothed his hand down the rewrapped shoulder, making sure the bandage was tight. "It's living with the consequences of those decisions that makes life difficult."

"How do you know if you can live with the consequences?"

"Ah, a question for the ages," he said, his eyes twinkling.

Arden frowned, causing Father Benedict to chuckle.

"If you don't speak with him, will you live with regret?" he asked.

Probably, yet she didn't say that. The situation she found herself in wasn't one she felt was fixable. They were from different worlds. She had known forever that divide couldn't be crossed. Even if she had let herself begin to foolishly hope.

Father Benedict sat back now, finished with his doctoring. He began putting the med kit back together. "What is it you want, my child?"

She thought through all the possible scenarios. Discarding the unlikely ones. Knowing that any good outcome would cost too much. "I don't know."

Father Benedict patted her hand. "Then it seems to me you should spend your time here figuring that out."

"It doesn't matter. My life was set before it began."

"Only those who are willing to fight to change their circumstances will be successful." He turned away with a hacking cough. His slight frame bowed forward and shook. It wouldn't be long now until he was bedridden.

The silence that followed wasn't awkward, just full.

Father Benedict rose and walked to the door. "I shall let you consider your path. If you leave before I speak with you again, blessings to you."

"And to you, Father."

When the door shut, Arden lay back on the scratchy pillow. She ignored the meal he'd brought her, thinking over what Father Benedict had said. She knew he was right. And yet, what could she do about it? Dade had sounded resolute when they'd spoken.

Still, she loved him. The thought struck her hard. She could see the truth with a clarity that she hadn't been able to before, as if the blinders had been removed and the world suddenly looked different.

Close on the heels of that realization, she also accepted that she'd commit to being with him no matter the sacrifice. She had to let her family go in order to create a life of her choosing. It sucked, but Arden knew she couldn't save Niall or her parents. They'd made their decisions and would face the consequences. She could no longer carry the burden of that. The decision twisted her up inside, but it felt like the only way she could truly live.

Her datapad blipped with an incoming message. She almost didn't look at it but then figured she couldn't ignore her life forever.

Niall had somehow managed to break her firewall. *Are you coming home?* he asked. In his pings, he always seemed lucid. She knew better than to trust that.

Her fingers hovered over the keyboard until she typed: *Eventually.*

There was a pause. She fingered the side of the datapad, about to turn it off, when Niall's next ping finally appeared.

*It's time to stop crying about Colin and return home.* Niall had always lacked empathy, and this time it cut her deeply.

She would never stop mourning.

*Tomorrow. Mandatory,* he typed. *Blackout is a go.*

Arden closed her eyes and squeezed them hard. Then she let out her breath, forcing herself to relax before she typed: *We'll be slaughtered.*

He replied: *We can't lose this window. They're grieving as well. And they'll be too focused on the wedding to anticipate our move.*

Her hands shook as she typed. *Wedding?*

He responded: *The Croix heir is marrying his fiancée in the morning. It's all over the visicast.*

What? That couldn't be true. Her stomach cramped.

Arden's first reaction was to deny. To insist the information was a lie. Then her rational brain kicked in. She shut down the ziptext program and pulled up the current visicast stream.

A picture of Dade and that girl took up the screen. Their bodies were entwined. The girl smiled up at Dade, looking radiant. Arden couldn't hear the newscast because it was muted, but the ticker feed ran the latest wedding gossip as well as a countdown to the nuptials.

Arden felt faint.

This was what he was hiding when he looked so guilty and sad? Why hadn't he told her? Why didn't he ask her for help?

Arden could have kicked her own ass.

She'd chosen wrong. She knew that now. She should have chosen Dade and not continued with Lasair. Maybe then she'd have Dade, and perhaps even Colin would still be alive. She needed to choose him now. There was no way she was going to let this farce happen. Not if she could stop it first.

And stop it she would.

# Chapter Twenty-Four

Everything was going according to plan until it wasn't.

Dade needed to die. It was the only way to get out of a marriage he didn't want and to sever ties with his family. He couldn't simply leave. His father would never let him go, especially now that Rylick was dead. He didn't have many options left, and time was slipping away too quickly for him to come up with a less drastic plan. Dying would be the only way to gain his independence.

Thankfully, he had friends willing to help. Number one being his fiancée-turned-reluctant-witness-to-his-death.

"This is not a good idea," Clarissa said. She had dressed for the scene in an outfit she could move fast in: purple synth-leather pants and an oversized white sweater that hit her midthigh, the fabric woven with repelling phase-fire fiber. It shimmered with a pearlescent sheen as she moved. Gold-colored metal panels had been threaded through the weave, creating the appearance of scales and adding yet another layer of protection.

"It'll work," Dade said, trying to reassure himself as much as her.

Clarissa made sure her guards were some distance back before she grabbed Dade by the elbow, dragging him into a quiet space between buildings. Clarissa's breath misted in the cool early-evening air as she leaned in to speak. "Maybe I need to break it down for you: this idea is ridiculous."

"What else would you suggest?"

She shrugged.

"Exactly." If there were another way, he'd take it. It wasn't like he relished living the life of a fugitive. It was simply the better option.

They'd chosen one of the high-end shopping strips that Clarissa favored for their plan. Dade had accompanied her there from time to time, so this outing wasn't unusual. And more important, as long as he was with Clarissa and her guards, his father had let him out of the Tower.

His hands were weighed down with her bags while pap-drones buzzed around to get a picture of them on the eve of their wedding. Dade couldn't see them, but he knew they were using long lenses to capture any juicy tidbit for their vid-rags.

"I don't get why the Ghost needs to kill you," she said. "What's the point of that? It could just be a random mugging. That would work too."

He didn't want to go over it again. "I almost got caught, and I know my father suspects me. Now that Rylick is dead, he's not let me out of his sight. It's limiting the Ghost's activities to the point that I haven't been on a run in weeks. Plus, there's no other way to get out of our marriage."

"The marriage thing," Clarissa made a frustrated sound and an equally frustrated face, "we could make it work, you know. We're an amazing team."

"We are," he agreed. "But I'd have to give up everything else, including the Ghost. What would I have to live for?"

She pressed her lips together and shrugged.

"If I'm dead, they won't suspect me. It's the perfect plan."

"Your life wouldn't be over if you married me. We could figure something out."

He felt bad at the hurt in her voice. Of course it wasn't her. He wasn't in love with her, but he certainly loved her. He could trust her with his life, and the last thing Dade wanted was to insult her. He tried to steer the conversation back to what concerned him the most. He knew that eventually she'd realize that this plan wasn't a slight to her and she would forgive him. "People need the Ghost. It's not just about the drugs or saving one person at a time. It's a movement. It's bigger than me."

"If the Ghost is so important, let someone else do it," she said. "Come back to the Sky Towers, we'll get married, and we'll work from the inside. It's as good a plan as any, and it makes more sense."

"It's already happening. I can't stop it." While Dade didn't like the idea of exposing the Ghost to public scrutiny, it made the identity real. To get things done, he knew the Ghost had to be more than a myth. He had to be seen as a champion of the people.

They fell into a tense silence. Dade fidgeted, his gaze drifting over the crowded streets as he checked face after face.

"Don't act like you're waiting for him," Clarissa warned.

He looked back at Clarissa in time to see her roll her eyes. "I'm not."

"That's exactly what you were doing." She let out a long sigh, her red lips puckering. "You know better than that."

And he did. He hated that she was right, so he forced himself to show some contrition. He transferred all the shopping bags to one arm, and then reached out to take her hand. If this was the last time he would see Clarissa, he didn't want to end their friendship with a fight. "I'm sorry."

He meant that for more than just the arguing. He meant for everything: for putting her in that position, for the fact that he wasn't choosing her, and that he'd miss her.

She understood, her face going soft. Then she gave him an impish grin. "Relax, you're only going to die."

Dade snickered.

"Come on, then," she said, tugging on his hand. "Let's get this over with."

They left their alcove. Clarissa wound her arm through his, leaning into him as they crossed the plaza via the skyway to the other side of the concourse. She chatted the whole time, keeping up a one-sided conversation with laughter in her voice, as if she didn't have a care in the world. As if things were normal.

Dade walked beside her, trying to engage and look carefree as well, but too much tension was coiled inside. Feeling the gaze and whispers of shoppers as they walked past, he realized he was too famous to hide without a mask. It left him feeling exposed and vulnerable, raw in a way he couldn't express. He looked forward to a life of anonymity.

Clarissa leaned in to reassure him, her mouth brushing his cheek like a lover. "It's almost over."

Dade kissed the top of her head. He hadn't yet allowed himself to acknowledge that these were the last few minutes he'd ever spend with her. His heart twisted as he thought the same of Saben. Clarissa and Saben always had his back. He never imagined the possibility that he'd have to give up either of them.

"I hope this girl's worth it," she said.

"She is." But he knew he wasn't doing this for Arden. He was doing this for himself. He was willing to sacrifice anything for his freedom.

Saben stepped from the shadows dressed as the Ghost. He boldly stood in the open long enough to attract attention. He didn't resemble Dade in any way. Saben was much larger and his skin darker. They'd had to get a bit creative to make the switch look passable. It wouldn't fool anyone who'd met Dade as the Ghost, but all they needed to do was to trick the city-grid cams and gossip-vids. It helped that there hadn't been a clear picture of the Ghost yet. Dade felt they'd be able to get away with it. Afterward, any difference in size would hopefully confuse the situation more.

Dade's hand slipped from Clarissa's, and the bags in his other hand dropped.

Their plan was simple: The Ghost was a shadow vigilante his father wanted to take out. Dade would confront him, then chase him when he ran. They wouldn't have to speak, which was a bonus, because Dade wasn't sure how good an actor he was. Especially when he knew cameras were on him. He'd die—a fake death, of course—and that would allow him to get away from his family. Then Dade could assume the mantle of the Ghost full-time.

Dade froze at the exact moment he needed to move. His mind screamed questions at him: Was he really going to give up everything? He could stop this, right now.

"Dade," Clarissa said, letting out a breathy sigh, "go."

He gave Clarissa a blinding smile of thanks, adding a silent good-bye. Then he jumped into action, running after Saben. Saben was fast, as Dade had known he would be, melting into the shadows for a few seconds before bursting onto the crowded streets. Dade struggled to keep up. Not because he wasn't capable, but he'd never run full throttle through a crowd before. They weren't as accommodating as he'd thought they'd be. The crowd pushed back, bumping shoulders and sending elbows to his stomach. They shouted encouragement for the Ghost, making sure to keep Saben's exit cleared. Some spat at Dade and called out crass suggestions of what he could do to himself as they crowded in front of him, creating a barrier. The tide of them pulled, keeping Dade from making forward progress.

He'd never be able to manage a clean shot at Saben here. He needed to control the phaser. His intention wasn't to hurt Saben. And vice versa. Though in the end, Saben had to make it look as if Dade took a kill shot.

Saben must have had the same thought. He jumped onto a railing and swung his way up to Level Six, then leapt to his feet and continued to run.

Dade grunted as he hit the same railing. It creaked and groaned, coming loose from the wall as he climbed his way onto it. He tucked his legs, using them to launch himself up, grabbing hold of the upper deck and pulling himself onto the next Level.

Unfortunately, there was a large construction project on Level Six that hadn't been considered when they'd devised this plan. The walkways were torn to pieces with temporary paths made of metal disks. He followed Saben through the maze. They ran beneath and through the scaffolding that had been placed against the building, jumping over the larger holes and sliding across construction equipment.

Dade pulled out his phaser and shot. The ground beneath him shifted as he pulled the trigger, causing his phase-fire to go off course. He dropped low to correct his center of gravity just as Saben shot over his head. They traded volley shots, some coming close, others going wide. Dade felt the heat as they passed by, instinctively ducking away from the burn.

Saben had put some distance between them. He moved through the construction with graceful movements in spite of his muscular bulk. His size didn't hinder him at all. Dade envied him. Though he worked out with Saben every day and could keep up, he had no practical experience scrambling over objects or being in a real phase-fight.

They were running too much, shooting too wide. Dade was supposed to "catch" a blast and die. He kept waiting for the right moment, but it never seemed to happen. It was too crazy here. They were close enough together for the shot to look viable, but the rigging was too complicated, and the beams they stood on were too precarious for Dade to safely fake his death. He'd likely kill himself for real.

It had become performance art, and he wasn't an actor. Yet he had to make it look good for the cameras. That was stressful enough. Add to that the plan wasn't working. He was attracting too much attention from the crowd. They hated him, which was good in a way, but hindered him from completing his goal. Eventually they'd attract even more attention of the sort they didn't want.

Saben stopped, his path forward blocked by a gaping hole in the skyway. On the other side was a large pileup of construction equipment, making it impossible for him to jump across even if the distance had been shorter.

Dade slowed, unsure whether to confront Saben or back off. He didn't think that Saben could make that big a leap, and it wasn't like he could very well turn around and come back at Dade. Though Dade wondered if that was exactly what Saben was going to do. He shifted back a few steps, scanning the area. It was the wrong place to have the final duel. He couldn't fake his death here. There was no place where he could make the death look real.

Saben tucked his phaser into the back of his pants and took a running leap toward the hole in the skyway. There was a protracted moment as he flew, feet moving, hands reaching forward, suspended over the space, before he slapped against the bulk on the other side, barely making it across. His hand scrabbled on the concrete bricks, fingers digging and clawing to climb up the other side.

Staring in disbelief, Dade stood at the edge of the wide, empty space that stretched between them, taking a gulp of air as he looked down at the crowd gathered on the skyway below. Faces peered up at him with slack jaws and wide eyes. And then the pointing began. They definitely recognized them. So that part of the plan had worked.

He shot off another few rounds, knowing they'd land nowhere near Saben, who was now past the construction debris. Dade again assessed the vast gulf between where he stood and where he needed to be. Now that Saben had done the impossible, Dade had to follow. They wouldn't get another opportunity at this. He groaned, while gathering his courage to mirror Saben's insanity. His palms became slick with sweat, making it difficult to handle his phaser. The leap wasn't going to get any easier the more he freaked over it.

Dade let out a long, frustrated breath and tucked his phaser at his waist. Then he backtracked a distance to get a running start and hurled himself through the air. As he flew, he became convinced he wouldn't make it. The distance seemed too long, and his jump felt too short. He regretted the leap the second he left the platform, wishing that there'd been more momentum behind it.

He barely touched the far side. Dade let out a sound halfway between a scream and a grunt as his fingers caught and held. He must have broken a bone or two. He fell into the space between the worst pain he'd ever felt and encroaching numbness. His fingers scraped as he slid, rubbing flesh from his hands. His skin was raw and bleeding, and his hands wouldn't respond when he mentally told them to move. He fought against the shaking. Didn't want to give in to the numb feeling that would cause him to lose everything. He forced himself to hold on.

Dade dug in harder, desperation making him strong. He would not die like this. Not when he was so close to freedom. This was not how his life was meant to end.

Below him, people screamed. He heard their cries, though he forced himself not to give them his full attention. Neither would he look down. *Forget about them,* he told himself. Yet the noise rattled him, threatening to break his concentration.

Dade was too low to pull himself up with sheer will. He'd have to propel his body upward a few inches to catch a toehold. The slickness of the sweat and blood on his hands didn't help with the traction as he clung. His shoulders burned and his muscles ached as he swung his feet in an effort to create momentum. When he gained enough speed, he let go, swinging upward a few inches. He caught on, gripping deep.

When he finally crested onto the other side, sweat dripped from his brow and his limbs were numb and shaky. Phase-fire whizzed by his cheek, the flare of the blast hot and bright, sending him sprawling onto the ground. He pulled his phaser from his waist and returned fire. His aim was unsteady, and the shot flew wild. His fingers had difficulty squeezing the trigger. The agonizing pain of moving the misplaced bones shocked his system.

He pushed forward on his hands and knees, then got to his feet and began to chase Saben once again, though his heart wasn't in it. Certainly his body was past the ability to fight. He was tired and aching and wished to be finished. To get to an area where they could follow through with their plan and end this charade.

Ahead, Saben ran into another blocked walkway, where a building had crumbled, its side spilling onto the street. Saben didn't pause. He jumped onto a beam that projected out of the debris and stretched across the open sky across to the opposite skyway. It had been secured in place by several stabilizing cables.

As he ran, he shot one of the cables, detaching it from its mooring. As it swung out, he launched himself onto it, using it as a pendulum to swing across the expanse. He was graceful when he did it, holding his phaser in one hand and returning fire to Dade, his other arm and a leg wrapped around the cable to keep him steady.

Dade stumbled to a halt, letting out a staggering breath. No way. Perhaps they should have been clearer about the death-defying feats this chase would entail.

He made his way out onto the beam much slower than Saben had, perfectly aware of how crazy this was. Then he let that thought go and simply ran, pushing his body forward with as much momentum as he could, while his feet slid along the slick surface of the metal, unable to gain traction. He began to wobble too far to the right and threw his hands out to balance himself.

Saben chose that moment to shoot at him.

Dade ducked to avoid the blast, but that shifted his weight even more. His foot slid off the edge, his body falling after it. He moved his weight, centering his balance on the other foot in an attempt to stay on the beam. It left him swaying as he looked over the vast darkness of the static cloud below.

Slowly he brought his dangling foot onto the beam, leaning back into his other side while readjusting his weight. His heart hammered, fighting his instinct to lie down and hug whatever surface would keep him from falling. Sickness rolled his gut and burned through his chest, leaving him hollowed out and shaky.

He knew that Saben wasn't trying to kill him. He was sure it was an accident. But really, that was too close for comfort.

The beam shifted beneath Dade's feet, unsteady, the final cable stressed. He crouched low and grabbed on to the edge. Dade needed to get off this beam as soon as possible before it gave way, and he needed the last cable to get across the expanse. He looked back at the crowd of construction workers calling out to him. The beam shifted again, a bigger tremble this time. Dade surged forward, shooting at the remaining cable as he ran. It detached, spinning into the air as Dade launched himself and caught it. He felt the beam give way beneath him and fall into the dark static depths below.

His feet landed on the skyway, and in the next moment he was blown to the ground as the walkway beneath him gave way to phase-fire. Dade shifted to avoid the debris, stumbling to his feet. He tripped forward to run, disoriented as to which direction he should head.

In the distance, he saw Saben drop and roll behind a metal sign to avoid being hit with a sudden volley of incoming blasts. Phase-fire littered the area, tearing up the walls of the buildings and anything else in its path. The shots came in from all sides, blocking where Saben had holed up. He peeked out, looking for an escape while returning fire.

Dade couldn't identify who was shooting at them or from where. The phase-fire seemed to be everywhere at once. The blasts along with the growing pile of debris made it impossible to distinguish any sort of a pattern, cutting off Dade's ability to see much beyond where he was currently crouched.

There was nowhere for Saben to gain cover going forward. He slipped out and sprinted back toward Dade. Another volley of fire hit the street behind him as he ran. Though Saben was too quick to get caught.

Dade looked at the space between the buildings behind them and knew that Saben was headed there. He tried to head there as well, but phase-fire cut him off, sending him sliding behind several parked hovercars to take a better tactical position. His adrenaline kicked in. This he could do. Real danger had been the missing piece in his chase with Saben. For some reason, when his life was on the line, he didn't stop to think, and helping Saben was high on his priority list.

He leaned out and shot, clearing a path for Saben, who switched directions and ran to where Dade sheltered. Dade could see them now, govies closing in on their position. They were being boxed in by swarms of them, too many to have been called in via the emergency comm system. They were geared up and ready for a fight.

Somehow Dade and Saben had wandered into a trap. It must have been logical, to the govies at least, that if the Ghost was prevented from stealing VitD, he'd make a public appearance eventually. It frustrated Dade that he'd been so shortsighted.

Saben slid in next to Dade. Covered in sweat, he gulped huge pockets of air, coughing them back out. He yelled over the sound of exploding phase-fire, "Who's shooting at us?"

Dade shot off three more rounds, pulling back as the hovercars were blasted, shaking against their backs. They'd taken a lot of damage and wouldn't last much longer. Dade could hear the ping-ping-ping as the hot beam melted the metal on the other side. "Govies."

Saben made a rude comment.

Dade grunted in agreement.

The govies had to know that it was Dade who crouched behind the hovercar, and yet they still continued to shoot. There were no thunks of sleeping gas as the spheres hit the ground, no flash grenades. The govies weren't trying to capture the Ghost. They were trying to execute him, and anyone who happened to be around him would get killed as well.

"Were you trying to kill me with your crazy acrobatic stunts?" Dade asked while leaning out to return fire.

Saben gave a short, amused laugh. "I had to make it look good."

"I almost died a dozen times."

"I thought that was the point."

Dade pulled back to yell at him. "Not real dying."

Saben grinned while leaning around the hovercar to pick off the govies who'd started to crawl closer. "I taught you well enough, you were never in danger."

That was a matter of opinion. Dade glared at him before returning his attention to the fight. The tension that had coiled in Dade's body now focused him, making his shots precise.

The hovercar was taking too much damage, though, melting in on itself. They needed to move.

Saben gestured to the building across from where they hid. It was mangled, the windows blown out and the doors blasted through. "We have company."

Looking up, Dade realized that a person inside the building was waving at them. He did a double take when he saw it was Clarissa. She had her phaser out, shooting at the govies from the depths of the building's carnage.

"Go," Saben shouted, already moving.

Dade followed, knowing Clarissa would cover their backs. He ran in a low crouch, following Saben. They crashed through the open door of the building, rolling across what was once a luxurious lobby while taking fire. Things exploded around them: glass from the front doors, floor tiles, chunks of concrete. Dade could barely see. He kept one arm crooked up over his face, his nose tucked into the bend of his elbow as he hacked and ran. Tears streamed from his eyes as they flushed out the smoke and dirt so that he could see.

As soon as they were close enough, Clarissa also turned and ran, leading them into the blackness beyond.

Shooting and running, Saben and Dade followed, jumping over anything in their path and fully trusting her to get them out of there.

Hitting the doors open to an industrial stairwell, she slid to a stop on the landing. She signaled for Saben to take the stairs up, while pulling Dade in the other direction. "We have to separate. You can't be caught together."

Saben nodded once, already moving up the stairs, which he took two at a time.

"No," Dade shouted, but neither responded. He watched Saben get farther away from him with every second.

Clarissa pulled on him with a surprisingly strong grip, getting him to move. He ran beside her, going double time down the stairwell.

"You can't be caught with me either," he said. The repercussions at this point would be just as bad for her. He regretted putting both Saben and Clarissa in this situation.

"I'm not going to leave you."

Dade cursed and muttered under his breath. They didn't have time to argue.

Three Levels down, they checked the exit to the skyway. He peered out the door, phaser at the ready. But everything looked ordinary. People were walking along, going about their everyday life, seemingly oblivious to the chaos several Levels above. There were no incoming blasts. He checked above, looking for snipers. Deciding it was clear, he nodded at Clarissa before tucking his phaser away and exiting the building.

Dade brushed his hair out of his face, pushing his way into the crowd. He felt Clarissa behind him, knew she followed close. They couldn't run. The point was to blend in. They moved faster than normal, though, as quickly as the crowd allowed them.

A single shot sizzled through the air. He heard it a second too late, realizing when it was close enough that he could feel the pulsing energy as it spread through his body that he couldn't avoid it. Dade felt the burning in his chest as it thunked into the center of his vest. It burned white-hot, sending out searing agony and pain. The vest's fibers felt like they were melting into his skin.

"Dade," Clarissa screamed.

He was going to die. The reality of the moment slammed into him. He hadn't meant for this to happen.

Another shot hit him dead center again, sending him off balance. Dade careened over the side of the walkway, going limp and numb as his pain receptors shut down.

He fell, felt the sky rush around him, the static cloud enveloping him like a thick blanket. Dade closed his eyes and let himself be taken.

The Levels rushed past.

Then everything went black as he passed out.

# Chapter Twenty-Five

Arden watched her datapad in horror. Her lungs burned—she couldn't draw a full breath. She shook while tears streamed down her face, wondering whether somehow this was all a bad dream, whether she was really witnessing Dade's last moments.

Normally she didn't waste time on visicasts, never bothering to look at the news unless Lasair was involved somehow. But the chatter she heard as she'd made her way through Undercity had her finding a dark corner so she could figure out what the commotion was about: buildings burning, shooting in the streets, and the Upper Levels at war. What she hadn't expected was the devastation that greeted her.

She enabled the volume to hear the commentators' reaction to the coverage, wanting to know every possible bit of information she might have missed. Her mind was a blur. Perhaps if she could work out what had happened to start this mess, there would be a way to make it better, to rescue him.

Each vid-angle became more painful than the last.

She needed a moment to process, but the events didn't slow. Thankfully, she was alone, because she couldn't have concealed her emotions, the utter devastation she felt. How could she explain to anyone from Lasair why she was crying over a Solizen? She would never be able to answer with the truth.

Her eyes continued to track the situation playing itself out on live visicast. Every moment of the fight captured, displayed for the whole city to see. At first Dade had been in a phase-fight with the Ghost. That hadn't bothered her. She didn't know who was playing the part of the Ghost or for what purpose, and she really didn't care as long as Dade was safe. Perhaps it was a plan of some sort. She trusted that Dade knew what he was doing. At the start, it had been entertaining to watch all the stunts they'd pulled off. She'd been impressed with Dade's skill, and a little hot for him, truth be told.

It was no longer amusing.

When the govies had shown up and Dade had switched sides to fight alongside the Ghost, the tone of the commentary shifted. Now it was speculative, with Dade on the wrong side of the discussion. They were all but calling him a traitor.

"We've got positive confirmation that the first shooter is Dade Croix, son of Hernim Croix and heir of Croix Industries. We don't know who the Ghost is at this time," the woman said. The commentators' images were at the bottom corner of the screen so that both visicasters could be seen while also covering the live feed.

"It appears they're working together now. Weren't they just shooting at each other?" the male visicaster asked.

"They were, Hal." The woman's mouth puckered as she watched the feed along with the rest of the city.

Hal leaned forward, practically salivating. "A bit of gossip landed the Croix heir in hot water just this morning."

"What's that?"

"A series of photos posted on a gossip site show the young Croix heir buying Shine in the slums on Level One. Sources said the pictures were taken three weeks ago. Along with this, it makes me wonder what Dade Croix has gotten himself involved in."

The woman loudly inhaled through her scrunched lips. The surprise seemed insincere. It was a calculated move. They'd probably sat on this piece of news in order to release it at the right time. Perhaps they'd even known the govies had planned to confront Dade. The city loved to watch a Solizen fall.

Arden did too. She couldn't deny it. This was different, though. This was Dade. It made her spitting angry that they dared to say such awful things about him, especially when he was fighting for his life.

Grudgingly she admitted that they had a point about questioning his allegiance. It was foolhardy for him to have publicly aligned himself with the Ghost. Maybe Dade hadn't thought of the repercussions of the actions in the seconds he'd had. Perhaps he wanted to help a friend, which was completely in character with the man she loved. She smiled softly in spite of the ache in her chest and the tears on her face.

The visicaster continued to speculate. "Does Dade Croix have a drug habit? Perhaps the Ghost is not a humanitarian, but rather a drug dealer? Are we seeing the aftermath of a drug deal gone wrong? Perhaps Dade Croix is the connection the Ghost uses to break and enter the drug facilities."

Bright sun, Dade would be held accountable for this even if he made it out alive. That kind of suspicion didn't go away. It grew like a cancer. She wanted to punch both visicasters in the face. This was a very dangerous path for people to start speculating on, and they were heralding the charge.

"It seems a logical conclusion," the woman agreed. "If that's the case, the Croix heir has an almost unlimited drug supply."

Arden didn't want to hear any more, but she couldn't force herself to silence the stream. Their comments made her sick, but it was important to know the totality of the consequences Dade would face. The fallout would be more troubling than the visicasters suggested. They were effectively painting a target on Dade. If the city believed that the Ghost was in the drug business and not just being a do-gooder, then he'd become a bigger target in her world than he already was. Lasair wanted him now, but that was because he affected them specifically. If it was perceived that he cut into the drug profits of the whole city, he'd be hunted by other gangs as well for encroaching on their territory.

There was also social perception to consider. It would open the doors to stricter laws, and then maybe a civil war. She could see the spin now: a rich Solizen keeping life-saving VitD from the people, while flooding the streets with Shine.

Maybe Niall was right. Perhaps civil war would happen with or without the Lasair prodding things along. There would be a fight eventually, and people would die either way. He might also be correct in his assumption that cutting off the beast at the head was the best way to move forward.

Dade and whoever was playing the Ghost made a run for it into the blown-out building. She knew that building had several exits. The govies couldn't cover them all. It looked like they would have a chance of escape if they chose wisely. Unfortunately, they didn't know some of the hidden passages that would take them to Level One nor the bolt-hole into Undercity. If she had been there, halfway across the city, she could have used the bolt-hole to rescue them.

Arden tried to convince herself that they'd be okay. Dade was resourceful. He'd proven to her that he was smart and capable of taking care of himself. She wanted to believe in happy endings, even if the logical side of her brain didn't agree.

She watched with the rest of the city as the battle ceased for the moment, practically holding her breath the whole time. She felt the burn from lack of air and the ache of the unknown. Her head felt light too. Being on this side of things—watching and not doing—was the purest form of torture she'd ever experienced.

The visicasters continued chatting. Recapping the last ten minutes. Speculating and discussing the situation with supposed experts. It was complete rubbish. They had no clue what was happening, but they needed to fill airtime.

The picture was set on a repeated loop, showing the last part of the chase that had ended in the phase-fight. Then the picture switched to show a full shot of the visicasters looking directly into the camera.

Arden held her breath.

"We've gotten a preliminary report that the Ghost has been shot." Hal delivered the announcement in a somber tone. "Once again, we believe that the Ghost—the menace who is believed to have stolen our precious VitD resources—has been killed. There's no confirmation at this time, but we will bring you more information whenever we get it."

Arden's stomach twisted. Had Dade stayed with whoever had played the Ghost? Had he been shot as well?

The woman broke in. "The city is blocking our view of the live feed in an effort to secure the crime scene. Just as soon as we have the live shot back, we'll take you there for the most immediate details."

"Wait a second," Hal said, interrupting her. "We've just gotten word that there is movement on Level Two."

The camera went wide with another live shot. The streets were crowded, as they usually were at that time of day. The shot focused on a door to that same building as before. It caught Dade emerging and the girl, Clarissa, following. They quickly merged into the crowd, keeping their heads down as they pushed themselves through the commuters.

Arden clenched her jaw, sending pain streaking through her face. Resentment rolled through her, making her seethe. Of course Clarissa was there, fighting by his side, because Arden couldn't. And that, she realized too late, was so many levels of wrong. She should have never relinquished her spot to fight beside him.

"Is that Clarissa Hemstock, Dade Croix's fiancée?" the woman visicaster asked.

"I believe so," Hal agreed.

The woman looked flabbergasted. "What is going on?"

Hal shook his head, equally dumbfounded.

Arden's gaze stayed on the video feed, taking in as much as the camera angle allowed. Dade and Clarissa weren't moving fast enough, and they didn't realize they'd been spotted. She panicked. Her heart thundered in her ears, and her already twisting stomach threatened to rebel. Why were the govies focused on him and not on the Ghost? Dade was a Solizen. They could pick him up at home without a problem. He posed no threat, unless the govies were declaring war on the noble class. Arden had a sick, sick feeling that was only confirmed when the blast hit Dade.

His mouth made an O, and his eyes opened wide in surprise. The cameras caught every nuance.

Arden felt it as if she'd taken the blast herself.

Clarissa looked up, realizing they were under attack. She glanced at Dade. Arden knew there was nothing Clarissa could do. If she had been in the same situation, she would have calculated that there'd be no way to help him and that she should save herself at that point. Clarissa must have realized the same thing. She moved to the right, running fast, and the camera lost her as it stayed focused on Dade.

Arden wanted to scream. Instead, she choked as tears streamed from her eyes, and she hiccuped in a sob. The horror of watching nearly undid her. Dade could not die. In no scenario had she ever fathomed that happening. He had to be wearing protective gear. He'd run. He'd hide. He'd be *alive*.

Even the visicasters were buzzing with this development. They talked over each other, making it difficult to understand what was happening.

Chaos erupted around Dade. Hundreds of people screaming, running away from him like a starburst.

She tried to memorize his features, the slide of his brow, his strong, confident nose. Because she knew the outcome. Even though she had yet to see what happened next, she *knew*. Her heart lodged in her throat as the hand that held the datapad shook uncontrollably. She felt sick and utterly devastated, not wanting to calculate his odds of survival, yet unable to stop herself. Her heart thumped loudly in her ears. The darkness of despair pressed against her mind.

Another blast hit Dade. This time it pushed him off his feet and over the side of the skyway. He fell, his arms flung wide, simply surrendering, no fight left in his body. She watched his body as it was swallowed up by the static, so thickly gray that it took the view of his last moments of life away from her.

Arden pressed her fist against her mouth to block the desperate sounds leaking from it. Tears left her eyes, unchecked now. She gasped in half breaths, half sobs. Never quite able to fully inhale. Her heart broke. She could feel the ghost of it in her chest, a blinding pain that twisted into knots. She'd never touch his sun-warmed skin again. Never kiss his lips or smell his skin.

This could not happen. She refused to accept it. Why hadn't he told her about his plans? She would have helped him.

Arden understood the need to escape. They were together in that. Now that he was gone, she didn't want to live by herself. He was her sun-star. She couldn't survive in the darkness without him. There was nothing left for her here. Not anymore.

That was when she realized that the best way to honor him was to hit those bastards where it counted, even if it meant her death. She'd pay them back for taking Dade from her. He was the only good thing in her life.

The tears fell faster now. Her breath morphing into gasping sobs. She gazed at the datapad, watching the last few moments of his life replayed over and over again. Through the tears and heartbreak, she managed a sad smile. They'd be together soon. He'd kept his promise. He'd sworn that he would not marry Clarissa. And Arden would not waste that sacrifice. If they couldn't be together in life, they'd be together in death.

Her datapad vibrated in her hands. It was enough to startle her out of her stupor. She blinked a moment, orienting herself. Then swiped the tablet to pull up her pings.

Niall's summons rang with authority: *Project Blackout initiated. Check in immediately.*

Her decision became clear, the opportunity like kismet—being called to duty felt right. Her path made sense now. She'd right this wrong for Dade and herself. Fix the mess of the world before she left it, even the score if she could.

Dade must be avenged. It was a fitting sacrifice to honor him. Her decision was made before she could fully recognize it. Retribution must be dealt to his family and to the govies. Everyone must pay. It didn't matter if they were manipulating Lasair to attack, as Dade had warned. They would all die today.

Her life was forfeit with the attempt, and that was okay. She accepted it. She'd eventually join Dade in the ever after, regardless. First, she had work to do. They killed him, as much as if they'd used their hands. The govies were in the Solizen pockets. If the govies acted against Dade, then his family knew and had something to do with it. The govies and the Croix family would regret that.

# Chapter Twenty-Six

Arden slapped a charge stick to the end of her blast-phaser. It wasn't like the small phasers that she normally carried. This phaser was three feet long, and she'd wear it strapped over her shoulder. This one meant business. Once she made sure it was in working order, she began to strip it apart to clean each piece. Arden lined up the components beside her along with the smaller weapons and knives she needed to sharpen.

They'd gathered in a staging area, an abandoned gym in an older part of the city conveniently located in the center of three bolt-holes they'd use to infiltrate Above for this mission. It was a larger group than they'd ever assembled in one place. There were at least a hundred members of several gangs coexisting together. Normally they wouldn't even consider it, as it was far too dangerous to congregate in a group so large, let alone to act as a unit. The other gangs and Lasair didn't necessarily get along. But that didn't matter anymore because they'd come together for a greater purpose. They were going to show the Solizen that they may have locked up Undercity, but the people were rising up to demand freedom. And, yes, there was also a more selfish motive: at the end of the day, it opened up the doors for someone else to rule the city. Then it would be each gang for itself.

Moving a group this size took a massive amount of coordination. Thankfully, that task didn't fall to her. Niall hadn't protested when she'd glared and said that she was there to fight, not to play babysitter. He'd left her alone after that. Then she'd volunteered for the most dangerous job, to infiltrate with the first group, the sweeping team. They'd secure the location for the rest of the gang to come in after.

She surreptitiously studied the faces of those around her. She didn't recognize many of them. Arden had good recall and had met most of their gang, except for some of the runners or newer members. Which meant that Niall had recruited.

They were clearly trained. The way they put together and inspected their weapons with military precision spoke of experience. These guys seemed shady, as most pay-for-play mercenaries were. Without any ties or affiliation, they couldn't be trusted.

Some of them were from rival gangs. Those faces she recognized. They huddled in groups, giving a wide berth to the rest of the room. Lasair didn't work well with others. Who knew what sorts of deals Niall had brokered behind the gang's backs, a frightening revelation because every deal had a bite.

Arden figured she wouldn't be around to see it implode, so she pushed that concern from her mind.

As she continued to clean and go over her equipment, she watched them. It was important to identify those who might stab her in the back if given a chance—all of them probably. Her gaze wandered while her hands remained busy at her task.

Tension was like static in the air. It felt like a crackling energy. The jovial bickering that usually amped them into action was lacking. The mood was somber and angry. The tide had changed. Undercity had joined together to create mutiny. It wasn't for Arden to say whether that was good or not. She honestly didn't know, nor did she care. She couldn't consider a future she probably wouldn't see.

For a moment, she allowed herself to feel the pain creep past the wall she'd constructed around it. It splintered her soul, harsh with jagged edges that cut deep. Arden couldn't help but suck in a breath, cut again by the fact that both Colin and Dade—even Niall—were gone, lost to this insanity they'd created. She was alone. Everyone she loved and trusted had left her, either from this world or into the drugs and revenge that fed their life.

She felt tears prick the back of her eyes, and blinked them away. Not here. She could not be vulnerable today. Today was for strength and revenge. It was the only way. Arden concentrated on her task. Closing her eyes, finding her center, and then letting out a long, slow exhale.

She timed her breaths with the movement of her rag across the surface of the metal. It was a task she enjoyed. A centering, so that when she was in the thick of it, she felt as if she had some control. Her breathing slowed, making her focus on just this moment and not on what was to come. Making sure she was free of any negative thinking, taking pride in making her work as efficient as possible. Her skill and attention to detail would keep her alive long enough to get the job done. She wanted retribution, and she couldn't rely on anyone else to give it to her.

Someone stepped into her peripheral vision. Waiting to be acknowledged. Arden glanced up enough to see skintight black pants. She knew who it was before she looked up into Mariah's face.

Mariah didn't appear to be much better than Arden felt. Her expression was pinched, her skin pulled taut around her eyes. Her hair was tied back, and she wore no makeup. She seemed tired, as if she hadn't been sleeping well.

"Can I talk to you?" she asked.

Arden didn't want to talk, but she found herself nodding. They hadn't spoken since the rescue, partly because Mariah had been recovering, and partly because Arden still felt guilty for not stopping her capture. Arden found herself avoiding direct eye contact with Mariah even now.

Mariah took a seat next to her. She didn't say anything for long enough that Arden finished cleaning the phaser she held, before looking up at her, questioningly. That seemed to be Mariah's cue to speak. She rubbed her palms on the knees of her pants, flexing her fingers before she began. "I know you're avoiding me."

"I'm not," Arden automatically denied.

Mariah blew a breath while slapping her hands onto her legs and rubbing them. She glanced away. "Right."

Arden began to reassemble her phaser, not needing to watch her hands work the movements they'd been long trained to do blindfolded. The conversation would stall if Mariah wasn't going to speak, because Arden certainly didn't know what to say.

She stared off, her attention snagged by her brother. Niall was practically a moving corpse. He watched the other gangs with bloodshot, glassy eyes. Bones protruded from his paper-thin skin, leached of color, with heavy dark circles lining his eyes. His lank, greasy hair had been messily tied. She could see the telltale faint red bruising under his nose.

He was going to get himself killed today, either by the fight or a rival gang. He was too weak to lead. Everyone knew it.

Coming to terms with the realization that she'd lose yet another family member to death cut her to the quick. Stole what remained of her sanity. Pain and guilt once again assaulted her. Hot like flash fire, appearing all of a sudden, burning up her chest and lungs. She swallowed, desperate to stop it. Seeking that cool blank space that would let her breathe.

Kimber stood close to Niall, practically glued to his side. Her sketchiness had only grown in the last few weeks. It made Arden suspicious. Kimber would sneak looks at the other gang members, giving them covert signals that spoke volumes. She was planning something.

And Niall was too high to see it.

Not her problem, Arden reminded herself. None of this would matter in a few hours.

"Okay, I get it, you're upset with me," Mariah said, breaking into Arden's rolling thoughts.

Arden startled, her hands falling still, and she pulled herself back to the conversation. She knew she sounded surprised when she asked, "What are you talking about?"

Mariah licked her lips, hesitating.

"You can't say something like that and then not back it up." Arden put the phaser on the bench next to her, and then turned to face Mariah. "Explain to me why I'm angry with you."

Mariah gave a half shrug. "I know you spent a lot of time trying to find me." She paused. "And that I'm expendable. Not like Colin."

"Colin's death has nothing to do with you." Her words brought her even more pain. She hadn't suppressed any of her pain over Dade yet, and now Colin was in the forefront of her mind. The last thing Arden wanted to do was dwell on the fact that he wasn't beside her, as he should be.

"Right," Mariah agreed much too quickly. "I mean, I know that you have other things on your mind."

"I do," Arden said. She wanted Mariah to get to the point and then to be gone. Her presence reminded her of everything she'd lost, rubbing salt into the wound. She wanted to stay numb. It was impossible to do that when someone asked questions that pricked her brain and emotions. "What is it you want?"

"Thank you for rescuing me," Mariah said quietly. She looked down into her lap, twisting her hands together.

"It was a group effort." Arden didn't need credit. Didn't want it. Credit came with heaps of self-recrimination. And she had enough of that to fuel her through the day.

"But you traded in favors. That has to mean something."

That made her think of Dade, and damn it, she didn't want to. Arden picked up a soft cloth and the phaser once more, starting the cleaning process all over again. She focused on each vigorous swipe of the rag.

Mariah nibbled her bottom lip. "Why are you here?"

"What do you mean?"

"You know this is a suicide mission. You've been vocal about it. We're not going to survive this."

Arden snorted and kept polishing her phaser. "I could ask you the same thing."

Mariah swallowed. "I owe the gang."

"No, you don't," Arden said. She stopped to give Mariah her full attention. "It wasn't the gang who saved you. If you don't want to be here, you shouldn't."

Maybe Arden could save one person, save Mariah. Hadn't she tried that before, though?

"I can't leave." Mariah looked over to where Uri worked, cleaning and assembling his own weapons. Then she looked back at Arden. "You know how it is, you risk everything because someone else is more important to you than your own life."

Before, Arden would have agreed automatically, even though she didn't really know, had never really understood. Now she did. And the knife in her chest twisted. A little panting sob, which she immediately coughed over, broke through. Sacrifice was toxic.

# CHAPTER TWENTY-SEVEN

The explosion knocked Arden on her ass. She couldn't see anything beyond the debris littering the air. The once-pristine silver-and-white-walled refinery was now stained with smoke from the bombs they'd planted, light from the phase-fire cutting through the murkiness. She got off the ground, shooting as she ran through a hollowed-out area into the next room and hiding behind a now-mangled machine.

She coughed behind the body mask covering her face. Grit stung her eyes, making them water. She blinked rapidly, trying to clear them.

Mariah slid up next to her from the opposite direction. Her back also pressed against the broken machine. Mariah had ditched her mask at some point, her face stained with ash. Finger widths of soot had been rubbed clean, pushed from around her eyes, where she'd dug out the grime to see. "We can't go back that way. There're too many of them."

Arden nodded, looking back the way she'd come. Knowing that direction was cut off. They could only move forward, which was what the mercenaries they were fighting wanted. They'd blocked them in, goading them onto a predetermined path to face whatever waited for them at the end.

Blackout had been screwed since the beginning. Which was exactly as Arden had foreseen. Lasair had expected resistance, not a trained private army. The rival fighters knew what they were doing. Their plan and implementation were shaping up to be far superior to Lasair's.

"Did you get the charges set?" Mariah asked.

"Almost. This is the last batch I have for Level Seven." Arden dug into her bag to extract a bundle of explosives. "How about you?"

Mariah nodded. "South corner is done."

"Cover me."

Mariah nodded, switching positions with Arden. She leaned over the bulk of the machine to shoot at the closest group of mercenaries.

Arden swung her phaser onto her back so she could concentrate on attaching the trip wires to the explosives. Her hands shook, and her movements were slow and awkward because of her still-healing shoulder. She wasn't wearing a bandage, only a thin layer of quick-seal. It pulled when she moved, tingeing everything she did with pain.

The constant ache reminded her of Dade and Colin. Focused her on the reasons she was doing this. Kept her moving forward even though they were greatly outnumbered.

A hit came close, striking the front of the machine, spraying debris. Mariah pulled back. "Hurry up."

Arden wiped at the sweat that had collected under her face mask. She did not want to ditch it quite yet, as it afforded her some protection from the elements and would help her breathe if the mercenaries used smoke. She connected the last few wires and then used putty to attach the explosives to the wall. "Done." She checked her watch before setting the charges to detonate. "Three minutes."

The initial bomb they'd detonated had taken out most of the processing factory on Levels Five and Six of the refinery. The plan was to work their way up so that they could escape into the University District on Level Eight. If they couldn't manage to get off Level Seven before the detonations, they would be effectively trapped.

She hoped the others on their side were faring better.

Mariah leaned over the edge once more to check their route. She shot off a few rounds before pulling back. "The hole they made for us is getting crowded."

"No way out but through," Arden said pragmatically. She leaned out the other side, shooting the whole time. Then pulled a concussion grenade, unpinned it, and chucked it in the direction they needed to move.

Both girls took cover.

The blast shook the area. Then they were on their feet immediately, standing up, shooting, and running. The phase-fire came hard and fast in their direction, but they didn't change their course.

Arden fought hard. Using no caution. Death was a certainty. She'd die here or later, so it didn't matter how she used her body or the chances she took. It made her ruthless, bordering on a near-frenzied obsession. Having nothing to live for lent a certain crazed strength to her fighting.

Another blast knocked them behind a crumpled mess of what was once furniture—a desk of some sort, and maybe a twisted bookshelf. Drywall rained on them. Arden shot in several directions before they both stood up again, gaining traction before sliding forward.

The next room was one of the largest by far. Probably a former warehouse. Though now it was hard to tell, as it had been completely destroyed. What it did provide was lots of spots to hide behind.

Both girls saw Uri at the same time. Mariah pointed and moved even as Arden made to follow her. He was crouched behind a hunk of smoking metal, pinned in by several mercenaries. The girls took out the most immediate threats before sliding in beside him.

"Go back," Uri said. He pulled off his mask, gulping for breath. Sweat dripped from the side of his brow down onto his neck.

"Can't." Arden pressed her back up against the shelving. "The charges are set in that direction. The only way out is up."

"They're forcing us that way."

"I know," she agreed.

But it didn't matter. She'd never planned to leave the refinery alive in the first place. Destruction was the only way. Her hope was that the charges she'd left behind would take out the majority of the mercenaries so that she could continue to fight till the end.

"We've lost a quarter of our men," Uri said, disgusted. "They're jamming our comm signals. Half the group broke off, and I lost contact with them fifteen minutes ago."

Arden grunted. Turning over, she leaned out from behind the smoldering mess to take out several mercenaries.

Across the room, she saw Niall. Kimber fought beside him. They were pinned down in much the same position that Arden, Uri, and Mariah found themselves. Only worse, since their backs were to a wall, with no option for escape. It would be impossible for Arden and the others to fight their way across the room to join them and help.

"Kimber and Niall are taking heavy fire," Mariah said from the other side of Uri, thinking along the same lines.

"We don't have enough time," Uri said. "It's up to Niall to save his own ass. He's resourceful, he'll figure it out."

Cold, but necessary. Uri was probably right.

Arden let it go, focusing on their current situation.

She leaned out once more, exchanging heavy fire with a group closing in on them.

Pain stole her breath.

For a second, she had no idea what happened. Then searing agony flooded her senses. Arden fell back, aware enough to get behind the barrier. Her mind swam on overload. She grabbed at her side, pushing the scorched fabric apart to inspect the wound. Blood seeped through a hole in her bodysuit, flowing over her fingers.

This was bad.

She couldn't tell if the phase-fire had hit anything vital. It felt like it. Though feeling the burn was probably a good thing. It meant she was alive. Arden put pressure on the wound as much as she could even though her strength was running out fast.

"Mariah, check her," Uri ordered.

Mariah was in front of her then. Looming over, so that she was all Arden could see. Mariah's hands felt as if they were everywhere, pressing and tormenting. "The phaser hit her between the armored plates. She's losing a lot of blood."

Arden gasped little hiccups of air while pushing against her side, her fingers pressed against her bodysuit. "Can't breathe," she said, using her other hand to push at the mask that covered her face.

Mariah helped ease it off. But that didn't let Arden breathe any deeper.

"Can she walk by herself?" Uri asked.

"I don't think so," Mariah said. "If I can't get the bleeding stopped, I don't think she has long."

"Cauterize it," Uri said.

Mariah set to work ripping fabric and shifting the armored plates of the bodysuit so that she could get to Arden's skin. She set her phaser against Arden's exposed side. "Three . . . two . . . one."

Arden screamed.

She felt everything. The searing fire kept getting worse, swallowing her up. She might have passed out briefly. There was no way to tell. The misery was crushing. Blackness crept at the edges of her consciousness. She fought to stay alert. It was interesting how in the end, though she sought death, she still pushed away from it.

"It's done." Mariah wiped her hand against Arden's face. Her touch was reassuring. "Breathe. That should hold till we can get you medical attention. Don't rip the wound open again."

As if Arden would be taking on the rest of the mercenaries by herself, or even be able to move at all. Arden nodded dumbly. She could barely understand what Mariah was saying. Agreeing would only get her out of Arden's face.

"We're moving now," Uri said. "Mariah, you first. I'll follow with Arden."

Mariah appeared undecided about following the order.

Uri barreled on. "There." He pointed to a hallway. "That's where we're heading. Get there. Then figure a way out of this hellhole."

Mariah nodded.

A series of shots ran over the top of them. Mariah ducked, and Uri fell over Arden, using his body as a shield. A large chunk of detritus dislodged, flying into Mariah's face. It hit her in the temple, causing a gush of blood.

"Mariah," Uri screamed, reaching up to pull her close to him. He fingered the wound.

Arden hiccupped and muttered. She knew what was happening around her. Yet had a difficult time processing the information. She tried to get to her hands and knees, but only flopped sideways, causing her side to burn brighter.

"I'm fine." Mariah pushed Uri's hand away. Half her face was now covered with blood. It dripped off her chin. "I think that was our cue to leave."

"Go." He pushed her into motion.

Mariah ran hard, under the smattering of cover fire that Uri provided.

Arden turned onto her back, staring up. She tried to regain her ability to breathe. Her body couldn't quit now. She still had too much to do. It needed to last another hour at least, and then she could rest.

That was when she knew death had found her.

He was an apparition. An angel come to lead her into the next world. He was streaked with soot. His hair pulled up, displaying his sun-star. He moved forward through the muck like an avenging angel, shooting mercenaries with deadly precision.

Arden smiled, happy beyond measure. He'd come to lead her into the next beyond. She knew that skin, knew the tattoo, wanted to place her lips there, to kiss and taste.

That snapped her back.

It was him.

He was real.

How was he alive? Or was this a trick of her mind? She couldn't process much of her surroundings. Everything seemed funneled through a small hole. It was hard to believe, especially since she'd seen him shot, then watched him fall into the abyss.

It didn't make any sense.

Uri looked over his shoulder. Then did a double take seeing Dade. He turned, falling backward into the barricade so that he faced Dade and Arden. He raised his phaser, focusing it on the center of Dade's chest. It was like the same nightmare all over again.

Dade raised his phaser as well, his finger tightened on the trigger.

"Stop," Arden screamed. She flopped forward, managing to push herself between the two men. It wasn't graceful, her body jerking. She hoped she could be heard over the explosions before they managed to fry each other.

Dade's eyes grew wide with horror. "Are you insane?"

Maybe? She knew only that she could not watch him die a second time.

Pain kicked in the second after her panic fled. She screamed out, falling the rest of the way to the ground. The blood from her wound oozed profusely now, pulled open again by her movement. Maybe she did have a death wish. At that moment, she didn't care. Her breath rattled in her chest as she struggled to make her vision clear. Grasping at the light so she wouldn't faint.

The move had worked to keep them from killing each other, at least.

"What the hell, Arden?" Uri yelled.

Everyone was screaming while the shots around them kept coming, the noise and the chaos too much for Arden. She focused on the one thing that mattered.

Dade.

He leaned over her. His hands running all over her skin, her face, her arms, and checking her exposed side.

"Is it really you?" she asked.

He nodded. Focused more on checking her wounds than on answering her.

"How?" It seemed like such an important question. Even in the midst of the current hell they were in, she needed to make sense of the senseless, come to terms with the possibility that she might be losing her mind.

"That's a story for later. We need to go."

"But you were dead."

He shook his head. "No, I'd never leave you. I promised, didn't I?" His brow was pulled in a worried line as he propped her up.

# CHAPTER TWENTY-EIGHT

Dade was glad he'd been to the joint refinery before. At the time, he'd seen it as his biggest defeat. Now he saw it as a blessing. It gave him a plan and a path of escape. Looking at how bad off Arden was, he whispered his thanks to the sun.

"Can you stand?" he asked.

"No," Arden slurred, her words followed by audible pants.

He had to lean close to hear her, his ear almost pressed to her mouth. But he also wanted to be close enough to make sure she wasn't aspirating. The factory exploded around them, and he didn't care. Arden remained his focus. Getting her out of this mess alive became priority number one.

She was fragile, a word he'd not associated with Arden before, because whenever he'd been around her, all he ever noticed was her core strength. That had been tested now. She appeared vulnerable and near death, her pain palpable. Her face leached color, white as a death shroud. She watched him with eyes half-open and haunted. Sweat soaked her skin, mixed with soot and blood, sticking her hair to her face.

His hands protested because of his broken fingers, but he reached forward anyway, taking her wrist to check her pulse. He'd taped and wrapped his fingers, making it difficult for him to count the beats. Her heart rate was slow but steady. That gave him some hope, though she didn't seem to feel the pressure he exerted. Her fingers lay limp when he squeezed.

The boy next to her glared at Dade as he checked Arden, letting them silently know that he'd rather shoot them both than help. But as long as the boy continued to pick off the encroaching mercenaries, Dade was fine with the glares.

He moved away from her wrist to check her side. The fabric of her suit had been cut open. Blood seeped through it. He reached forward to separate the fabric so he could get a closer look at the wound. It looked as if someone had managed to get the bleeding stopped at one point, but now it sluggishly leaked again.

Her hands came up to push him off, but they never connected with him. Arden's eyes rolled, and she made a pained sound.

It was clear she wouldn't be able to stand on her own. Not only that, he also wasn't sure that she'd stay conscious. Dade left the wound for now. Scenarios played through his head on how he could manage to get them out of there, but first and foremost he had to get her to her feet.

Sliding an arm behind her back, he moved through his own pain to pull her up. He worked as efficiently as he could, feeling every stretch of movement. She didn't help him in any way, her body's deadweight and the pull of her working against his efforts. When he managed to get her standing, she stumbled forward into him. He wrapped his arms around her middle, trying to keep from touching her wound.

Arden leaned heavily into his side. She made small noises that reminded him of someone being tortured, interspersed with whine-filled breaths. She opened her eyes, blinking first at him and then her surroundings. Her brow screwed up tight.

"Uri," she said to the mean-looking boy who maintained his position.

The boy looked at her. Dade was surprised he'd heard her, considering her voice was paper-thin. Then Uri snarled, his feeling of betrayal evident with his lip curled and his eyes narrowed. "I'm helping you only because I owe you for Mariah. After this, we're even. Finished. You have three seconds to get out of my face, or I'll shoot you myself."

Pain bloomed on Arden's face, this time clearly emotional, not physical. She nodded at Uri. Then she lurched forward, half tumbling, into Uri so that she could brush a kiss on his cheek. "I understand. I'll miss you."

Dade had kept a grip on her, and now he pulled her back, frightened by the naked hatred apparent in Uri's eyes.

"We're enemies now." Uri gave Arden a penetrating look. "Don't come back. If I see you, I'll shoot you on sight."

Arden let out a long exhale, sinking back into Dade's side. "I understand."

"This can't be forgiven."

She offered Uri a sad, defeated smile. "I know. It's okay."

Uri seemed wrecked by her acknowledgment and forgiveness, like he'd been slapped. Then his face went hard, and he turned his back to them. He shot a few more times at the mercenaries, clearing a path before he leapt over the barricade.

Dade needed to get Arden to safety as well. With Uri gone, there was no one keeping the mercenaries from tearing into them. The task of dragging her across the room seemed impossible. Yet all he could do was move forward. He'd ignore anything that could distract his attention, even Arden's gurgles of discomfort.

He tightened his arm around her middle, and then began to half pull, half carry her while shooting at anything that moved. He cleared a path like Uri had done, knowing that their escape wouldn't be as quick. When they got into the open, he pressed his phaser to her temple as he dragged her backward.

She let out a high-pitched mew, choking back a sob. "It hurts."

"I know," he said into her hair, just above her ear. "This is going to be uncomfortable."

Arden tried to help him, seemed to understand this game he played. She scooted her boots along the tile, in an attempt to gain momentum and lessen his burden as he carried the weight of them both through the room. She wasn't able to keep herself up, though, and her weight shifted, making it painstaking to maintain his hold.

He pulled her tighter whenever he felt her slipping. It lent to the appearance of a struggle, but he hated her cries of agony. Then Arden passed out. He was extremely thankful for that, though it made his progress slower. As much as he had tried to block out her cries of pain, they twisted him up inside.

If he could get them up two floors, there was a forgotten trash shoot that had a steel plate bolted over it. It looked like part of the reinforced walls. But he knew that the sheet only looked like it was secured. Neither he nor Saben had resealed it when they'd left. It was the only bit of luck he'd had recently.

He kept the phaser pressed to her head as he dragged her. He hoped that whoever saw them, from whichever side, would think that she was his captive and not shoot. The mercenaries because Arden was obviously Lasair from the way she was dressed, so they'd assume Dade was working with them. And Lasair because they wouldn't hurt one of their own.

The plan worked for the most part. Occasionally he traded shots with a mercenary, taking the individual out when he could manage a clear shot. And he hadn't seen anyone from Lasair, which was worrisome. The bulk of the fight seemed to be moving up the facility, with Dade and Arden following behind.

They moved slower than he wished. Arden hadn't woken. He couldn't stop to check her, so he kept going, clearing a stairwell and dragging her up with him. His entire body protested. His muscles were pushed to the limit. He knew he was tiring and didn't know how much stamina he had left.

An explosion rocked several floors below. The building swayed, the floor unstable. Dade managed to maintain his footing, but he fell heavily against a wall, Arden's body on top of him. He panted and sweated as he righted them. There'd be more detonations to come. Knowing what little time they had before the entire place imploded spurred him on. Let him gather what few resources he had left and push through the pain.

He exited onto a restricted floor and was halfway down the corridor when a girl stepped in front of them. Her phaser was up, pointed dead center of Arden's chest. This girl wasn't a mercenary. She wore the same running suit that Arden sported, though hers was still pristine, with her hood pulled back as if she didn't care who saw her face.

"Stay back," Dade said to her as he jostled Arden in his arms, tightening his grip. He kept his phaser pointed at Arden's head.

"Like you're going to shoot her." The girl rolled her eyes. "Do it, then. That's something I'd like to see."

Dade blinked. The hand on his phaser hesitated. Wasn't this girl part of Arden's gang? She *wanted* him to shoot?

Arden opened her eyes on a gasping sob. She wheezed, "Kimber."

Kimber grinned, raising her phaser higher. Her finger tightened on the trigger, her stance determined. "So glad you'll be awake for this."

She was really going to shoot them. This girl was crazy, and they had nowhere to hide. If he had to shoot her to get to the end of the hall, he would. Though he worried that Arden would never forgive him.

A shot rang out.

Dade jolted, frozen for a moment before realizing that it was Arden who'd shot. The phaser shook in her hand as she sent blast after blast the other girl's way.

Kimber ducked. She slunk to the end of the corridor, seeking cover.

Dade arced his phaser, following the path Kimber took, his shots joining Arden's. He didn't have anywhere to go except to head for the door at the center of the hall. There was nothing to hide behind, and they had no more than this one chance. He had to make it before one or both of them got shot. He moved quickly, pulling Arden along while shooting, filling the hallway with enough blasts to keep Kimber from returning fire.

He dragged Arden into the room, shooting out the hand scanner at the entrance before setting her down inside to barricade the door. The thin heat shield wouldn't hold out against repeated fire blasts, but maybe it would last long enough for them to get out of the building or for that Kimber girl to be taken out by someone else.

Arden groaned. Her body was slumped half against the wall, mostly falling onto the floor. She'd curled into a fetal position, protecting her injured side.

He put his hand to her face, feeling her cold skin. If she had a head injury, he didn't want her to sleep. "Stay awake." He shook her as gently as possible but allowed no argument to his request. "Arden, open your eyes. I want to see them."

She blinked, unfocused, as if not knowing where she was. Then her gaze settled on him, and she gave a soft smile, exhaling in happiness. "Hi."

Dade grinned. He was ecstatic that she was alive. It seemed unreal. When he'd gotten to the refinery, he'd thought she'd been lost to him. He leaned down to press a quick kiss on her mouth. He couldn't help himself and needed to taste her even for a second, to settle the terror inside him. "We're getting out of this mess, love. But I need you to stay awake. Can you do that?"

Arden nodded her head as she closed her eyes. "Thank you for coming for me."

He pressed another kiss on her lips. "Always."

# Chapter Twenty-Nine

Arden held on to Dade tightly, grateful he didn't let her fall. He carried her more than she moved on her own. She struggled to remain conscious, her breath leaving her in a hitching wheeze. It would be that much harder for him to maneuver the streets if she passed out again.

He pulled her into the shadows. Pressing her up against a wall, he made sure she was propped so that she wouldn't slide down. Then he slotted his body in front of hers to act as a brace. He pulled aside her suit to check her wound.

"How bad?" Dade asked, his voice slightly winded and grim.

Her lips wouldn't move to answer. She opened her mouth, but instead of speaking, she hitched another breath or two. Her torso was covered in blood. It was all she could see as he moved the fabric, baring her side: lots of tacky red. It soaked everything, making her cold and sticky. She focused on the warmth of his fingers as he pulled apart the material rather than on how much it hurt, closing her eyes against the sting. A shiver wracked her body, pulling her muscles. The bodysuit was made to regulate her core temp, but perhaps her body temperature had dropped too fast.

She knew she needed help desperately.

Dade poked at the wound, testing its depth.

Arden hissed. She wanted to knock his hand to the side but didn't have the strength or coordination. Instead, she gritted her teeth.

"It looks like the phaser went through the fleshy part of your side." He pressed against it. "It's bleeding heavier—" His voice broke. Then he cleared it. "I'm going to wrap it until we can get you medical attention."

Arden licked her lips and nodded, her head resting on the wall behind her, her eyes shut. Who they'd see for med help, she had no idea. They couldn't go to either family, nor could they walk into a med center.

They were truly on their own.

She had to let Dade worry about the details. It hurt too much to think.

"Don't ever put yourself in front of a phaser again," Dade said. Anger seeped into his voice. It cut through her, focusing her wandering thoughts.

She swallowed several times before managing, "Okay."

"Do you hear me?" he asked again.

Arden nodded, her head wobbling. It felt too light, like she might float away.

Dade pulled off his tunic and undershirt. He didn't seem to react as the bitter chill hit his skin, though she could see goosebumps pebble up along his chest and torso. He focused intently as he ripped his undershirt into strips, his movements hampered by his taped fingers. Folding a square, he pulled apart her suit to place it on her wound. Then he wrapped the rest of the material around her waist.

She tried to help by moving off the wall, slipping a little.

He was alive. Arden still couldn't believe it. It was enough to catch her heart for a moment, before she was able to calm it again. He stood in front of her even as she replayed seeing him fall off the side of the building. There was no way he could have survived on his own. She needed explanations—now.

It hurt to speak. Her throat was raw, and her mouth felt four sizes too big, her lips and face swollen. It took her several swallows to manage a few words. "I thought you were dead."

His gaze flicked to hers, briefly. "I'm not."

That didn't answer her questions. Didn't explain how he came to be standing in front of her. "How . . . What . . . ?" Arden cleared her throat and licked her lips while she searched for the question she wanted answered. "How are you alive?"

His fingers stilled against her side. He leaned forward to brush a soft kiss on her forehead and then an equally soft one on her lips. It was a faint approximation of the kiss she craved. She didn't have the strength to press for more.

He looked down to continue his binding. "I was caught in a net."

Arden blinked. "What?"

"A group—I have no idea who they are—saved me. They put out a net in anticipation of my fall, I guess. It was some kind of synth-fiber retractable thing."

Arden frowned both at what he said and the fact that she had such a difficult time expressing her fear. He acted like his rescue had been of no consequence. That people saved Solizen all the time. But nothing was free. Everyone wanted something. Arden's internal monitor was going haywire with concern. "Why would they do that?"

"You know why, because they want a favor." He didn't look too upset by that announcement.

And there it was. She narrowed her eyes. "What favor?"

"They didn't say." He sighed, looking up. "Listen, I wasn't too concerned at that particular moment. I was happy they saved me and patched me up enough so that I could get to you."

Arden didn't know what to say. Even if she did, she wasn't sure she could make the words work. Exhaustion took over now that her adrenaline was gone. Her eyes drooped. The only thing keeping her awake was the pain that pulsated through her body.

Dade seemed to understand her need for answers, though, because he said, "Hopefully whatever they ask for won't go against my code of ethics. But honestly, they can force me to do whatever they want even if I didn't owe them. They were powerful and well weaponized."

Arden wheezed and coughed, wanting to protest his statement. Frustrated that he was in this position and she couldn't even stand up on her own, let alone help him figure a way to fix it.

Dade continued to frown. His focus never left her side as he fussed with wrapping her wound. "They said they'd find me. Pretty sure they inserted a tracker in me while I was passed out."

Arden whined. If he was tagged with a tracker, they needed to address that soon. This mysterious group would collect sometime, but it was better to meet on Arden and Dade's terms instead of being surprised and ambushed.

"I know." Dade tied off the material. Then he cupped her chin and pulled up her head so that their gazes connected. "We'll worry about that later." He nodded to her side. "This should hold till we get somewhere safer."

Arden gave him a faint smile, knowing that it probably looked more like a grimace than reassuring agreement.

He pulled back on his tunic. "It's you and me now."

She knew what he meant. They'd both made their choices. There was no going back. Surprisingly, with her life currently spun out of control, Arden was happy.

He gave her another kiss, harder this time. His breath tickled against her mouth with the promise of something deeper. She felt safe, knowing that everything would work out. Maybe it would take a bit of effort and some bloodshed, but they'd get there.

Dade pulled away, rubbing his nose against hers.

"You and me," she agreed. "Forever." She realized what this commitment would cost her, and she was willing to pay the price.

# Acknowledgments

It's a blessing to be surrounded by many incredible people. I'm thankful to each and every one of you.

I wouldn't be writing this without the hard work of my agent, Carlie Webber. She is smart, honest, and nothing short of amazing. I'm thankful and appreciative of all the time she dedicates to making my dreams come true. Thank you for taking this journey with me and always having my back.

I would like to send a big hug to my editor, Adrienne Procaccini, who saw the potential in my story and gave me the tools to make it into something infinitely better than I could have dreamed. Thank you for believing in me and Dade and Arden. The three of us will be forever grateful. And to all of the Skyscape team who have been wonderful, making each step of this process a joy.

To Amara Holstein who whip-cracked this book, thank you for your kind words and thoughtful insights. You made this book shine.

Hugs and kisses for my husband, Steven, the man behind the curtain. My life couldn't run without you. Thank you for pitching in when I sometimes forget to cook dinner, or never batting an eye when I'm still in my pajamas when you get home. Your sacrifices made this happen. I'm so lucky to be married to my best friend.

I want to thank my kids, Seth and Rebekah, who take seriously their job of making sure I don't become old, from keeping watch of my clothes and hairstyles to making sure that I know the current slang. It's so much easier to write YA fiction with you in my corner.

Thank you to my mom, Beckie, who is the first person to read every word I write. I know the common advice is, "Don't show your mom your work, she'll just say it's amazing." Well, those people haven't met my mom. She has zero problems telling me, "It's not there yet, keep working." She is my toughest critic and the one whom I can't live without. Moms know what they're talking about. I always listen to my mom, even when I don't like what she has to say.

To my cheerleader, Anissa Maxwell, thank you for being honest, thoughtful, and constant. I'm so lucky to have you as a friend. I'm glad we're on this writing journey together.

Finally, to all my other family and friends who have read drafts of my work or listened to me moan about the hardships of publishing, thank you for believing in me. Your support means a great deal.

# About the Author

Heather Hansen was born in California, the oldest of five children. She always knew she wanted to be a writer, and she wrote her first book, a murder mystery in the style of Agatha Christie, in seventh grade. Unfortunately, she never could figure out who the murderer was, so the book went on for hundreds of pages, introducing new characters only to kill them off in the most gruesome ways her twelve-year-old imagination could invent. Her teacher was equally impressed and horrified.

Heather has a degree in English from California State University Fullerton and has traveled the world with her husband, a retired Marine. Her favorite place they've lived is Okinawa, Japan, where she had her choice of ramen, Japanese curry, and sushi every day. Along with their two teens and three dogs, they now live in Las Vegas, where she spends her time writing all day and eating Nutella with a spoon. *The Breaking Light* is her first novel.